PRINCE OF BLAZE AND EMBERS

EMBERVEIL EMPIRE

BOOK ONE

ZANDER WOLFE

COPYRIGHT

Sign up to the Reader's Group
www.ZanderWolfe.com

For Liv Zander.

*For the inspiration that made this book
and world possible.*

BOOKS BY ZANDER WOLFE

Allovan

The Shimmermere Sea

Calcaedus

Raven's Bane

Great Skymirror Lake

Emberveil

The Faewood

Brakenstone Ridge Mountains

The Harrowhorn Mountains

Salazan River

Bramblebash

Sun Sea Isles

The Emerald Crest Isles

The South Cape Sea

100 Miles

CINDERYN

Passage from the Tomb of the Elements. Chapter 3, verse 3.

Unquenchable fires raged deep within the Cinderyn. Their lust for power knew no bounds, and their tempers flared with the might of the gods themselves. Flames burned in their veins. It heated their blood and made them the legends they were born to be. Savage lust throbbed from deep within as they scoured the lands for their next prey.

Beware the wielders of fire, for they were born of scorn, hatred, and overpowering domination over all beneath them. The Cinderyn were as old as time, as feared as the grandest volcanoes, and as deadly as the plague.

Of all the elementals of Allovan, the Cinderyn had always retained ultimate control, for no other could match their thirst for power and destruction.

Yet, there was hope.

One day, their raging fire would be extinguished. Their hatred would be tamed, and their wrath would fade into the endless sea. It was the prophecy. Once the great one returned to the skies, the balance of our world would return, and peace would be the law of the land once again.

-Written by the Prophet Dantris Oireillus. 676 of the Ember Age.

CHAPTER 1

The bloody, terrifying roar of the dragon in the sky made my whole body shudder. Terror gripped me, mixed with the wild envy of such a free, magnificent, yet deadly beast. On the sandy shores of my small prison of a town, my feet urged me forward, captivated by the wondrous dragon as its shadow enveloped me, breaking the sun's golden rays. The chains around my ankles clattered as my step halted mid-stride, though.

"Ash! Are you seriously just standing there?" Bella grabbed my wrist with surprising strength, her blue eyes wide—not with terror, but with that exasperated spark she always got when things went sideways. Her long blond hair whipped wildly in the sea wind, and despite the smoke and screaming, she huffed, "Unless you've got a plan to flirt with the dragon, we should move."

Those that were smart in my small seaside town ran. They ran for their fucking lives because who in their right mind would stand on the beach looking up at a monster that could sear all your flesh right off your bones? Me, I guessed.

"Right," I muttered. "We need to get the hell off the beach, now!"

Bella released me, and I grabbed her hand, our fingers interlocked, pulling her behind me up the long sandy shores of where Bramblebash met the crashing waves of the clear blue South Cape Sea.

Bramblebash clung to the crescent curve of the Allovan coast like a seashell forgotten by time—its cottages cobbled from pale driftstone, roofed in faded white tile, and always dusted in sea salt. The scent of fresh honeybread wafted from the bakery on the main square, mixing with the tang of iron and smoke from Garris' forge where horseshoes and hinges never stopped clanging. Fishing nets hung like ghosts on wooden posts, and wind chimes made of coral bones danced in the breeze. Even as the dragon's roar echoed from the cliffs, the familiar sounds of gulls and waves made it all feel impossibly real.

As more riders on dragons darted down beneath the clouds, I couldn't help but watch their splendor over my shoulder, pulling my best and only friend behind me. I couldn't tear my gaze away from them. Their majesty, their magnificence, their utter ability to be free of the world tore hard at my core.

I wanted nothing more than to be like that, able to leave any place at any time, but the chains that cut into my ankles brought me back to reality.

"They're wearing crimson and gold." Bella huffed behind me, clutching her small leather bag, sending a new worry deep into me. I swallowed hard, causing the fear to sink deep into my stomach like molten iron. "They're riders of Emberveil and the queen."

"Emberveil? What are they doing this far south?" My words were nearly cut short by a tugging at my ankles that caused me to plummet face-first into the sand.

"Slow down, you wretch," Garris panted behind me, his fat fingers tight around the other end of the chain that yanked my shackles out from under me.

The rider on the largest of the dragons' back, high in the dim cloudy sky, whipped the reins as the dragon's enormous wings flapped, sounding like massive ship's sails biting and cracking in the sea winds. Its long tail slithered behind, and its huge, horned heads broke through the gray clouds as it hurtled through the air.

Bramblebash was just ahead—a measly sea town of a few hundred people—and only a couple of miles wide. Its white buildings resembled teeth poking out from a bottom jaw. It wasn't much, but it was all I ever knew since being sold there when I was five. The snowy caps of mighty mountains cradled the sky far beyond my town, always tempting me, taunting me to escape the awful life I had.

"Wait for me." Garris trudged through the sand, holding both our chains, and holding us back as more dragon riders zipped below the clouds.

"Those aren't Emberveil riders." Bella's voice resonated with worry.

The new dragons and riders wore capes and armor with the silver and black colors of the rebels against the empire… "Storm-scales," I muttered, fully feeling the dread of what was churning in the sky above my small piece of the world—war.

A dragon's roar filled the air all around me. I clapped my hands over my ears, and Bella did the same—trying desperately to dull the ear-piercing roar that caused my head to splinter. The vibrations from the beast's painful screech shook my chest, my nerves, and even as deep as my bones. My entire body vibrated under the violent erupting roar of the monster above.

I looked up just in time to see the dragon and its rider plum-meting to the ground, a massive spear sticking out from the gray dragon's bloody chest. The rider yanked with all his might back on the reins, but they hurtled down at frightening speed, right at us!

Garris, with his sweaty, fat fingers, pulled hard, using Bella and my weight to pull himself up the beach. My fingers dug into the wet sand, fighting not to fall back from his hefty body weight, which outweighed both of us girls combined.

I mustered all the strength I had to pull Bella forward, and by default, my master's miserable ass up the beach. The rider and dragon tumbled at breakneck speed toward us, blood gushing upward behind the roaring beast.

"Wait!" I shouted, throwing both hands up into the air, praying to Odiun as I dragged Bella and Garris far enough away. The dragon let out one last ear-piercing roar from all the wind still in its lungs. The rider yelled out one last desperate attempt to get the dragon to pull back up into the sky. The dragon and rider collided into the ground so hard that the tremor rocked all three of us to the ground.

The dragon's brown, scaly body twisted and broke under the impact. Its wings snapped like huge branches and angled awkwardly over its motionless, immense body. The jagged, bloody bones in its neck protruded through its thick skin, and the wild sparkle in its devilish eyes faded.

The rider died instantly, being pinned under its weight. His head was spun all the way around, with his chin parallel to the back of his spine. Blood gushed out from under his helmet and out of his nostrils and mouth.

I was left staring straight into his eyes—blood-red, forever wide, a twisted look of agony etched across his face. We were mere feet from the violent fall of the dragon and rider, and Bella and Garris were both left fraught in terror from the narrow escape with our lives.

"Get up!" I yelled, yanking the chains at my ankles to get Garris moving, his mouth fully agape and his eyes fixed upon the horror before us. "We've got to go, now!"

Garris stumbled up to his feet, and we finally got moving again, back up the sandy banks to Bramblebash, filled with frightful screams below the dragon battle in the sky.

Dragons dove at one another, sweeping across the sky like

divine beasts or demons. Their huge, violently sharp teeth flashed, their enormous wings flapping, sending the dragons hurtling through the sky at breakneck speeds. Dozens of them, all wishing to end the battle quickly.

Bella and I ran for our lives back toward town, pulling our panting master behind.

"What are they doing all the way down here?" Bella asked, running beside me, squeezing my hand tight. "The Emberveil riders almost never come this far south!"

"The question is, what are the Stormscales doing fighting them down here?" I was unable to hold the excitement in my voice back. The exhilaration of dragons this close to me, and nearly dying, had my heart pounding so hard I felt the vibrations in my ribs. "The rebellion does everything it can to plan out its attacks; why here? Why right now?"

"It's the queen," Bella gulped. "She'll send her army to the underworld itself to kill every last one of them."

I'd seen the recent posters in town from Emberveil. Hefty rewards for leads on where the Stormscales were hiding. The war had grown in recent years, and tales of their dragon battles rung in even our tiny corner of the world.

"But here? In Bramblebash? This far away from her kingdom? She must be getting even more ruthless than they say..." My words were cut short by another roar that entered the sky like booming, legendary thunder.

It was so thunderous and commanding, it made every other dragon in the sky pivot, instinctively moving away from the approaching beast.

As the new dragon emerged from the thick, dark clouds my jaw dropped and my fingers spread wide. My eyes widened at the sight of the beast, and the hairs on the back of my neck tightened, sending goose pimples all the way down the backs of my arms.

It was him...

"By the beard of Odiun," Garris muttered. "It's him... By all that is holy..."

As the dragon and its rider tore through the sky above, my feet froze to the sand and sweat trickled down my arms.

It was him... I'd heard of that black dragon from all the tales. It's unmistakable...

"The Blaze Prince." The words escaped my lips without restraint. The tales of his ruthlessness and conquests were known by every being in all of Allovan, and there he was, sweeping through the skies of Bramblebash, looking like he was born on the back of that horrible, murderous dragon.

"He's as terrifying as they say," Bella murmured, unintentionally holding her breath.

"It's time to move," Garris shouted, suddenly ahead of us as we froze. He yanked on the chains at our ankles.

"One more minute!" Rebellion thickened my voice. I couldn't tear my gaze off such a legendary rider. My heart thumped so hard I felt the blood rushing through the arteries in my neck.

"Ashlyn, you're gonna feel my whip again for your sharp tongue, make no mistake!"

"Good!" I fought back. "I hope you do, you miserable excuse for a man! And it's Ash!"

"We should do as he says," Bella said in a hushed voice, terror gripping her throat.

Her voice shook the last breath of bewilderment from my mind. I needed to get her to safety. This wasn't about my fascination with dragons anymore. Her life was in danger!

And as if fate heard my thoughts, the great ebony dragon unleashed an unimaginable ghastly plume of devastating dragonfire upon one of the Stormscale dragons, incinerating it in a heartbeat. I couldn't get my feet under me fast enough.

We rushed back toward town, the shanty beach community of single-story buildings of wood, strong enough to survive hurricanes, but definitely not dragonfire. My feet dragged through the slick sand, both sets of our ankle shackles clattering as we ran up the hill to Bramblebash, the tropical trees surrounding it whipping in the stormy winds, invigorated by the dragon wings beating in the cloudy sky.

That fuck Garris hadn't run more than six feet in his miserable life, I bet, except for when the dinner bell rang. He'd whip me for sure for talking back, but still, as I ran, my gaze was absolutely stuck onto the infamous black dragon that terrorized the sky—Krakos—the one and only. Sharp ebony scales, huge wings that cut the air like a razor through sheets of papyrus—its eyes as animalistic and demonic as the tales say—an unnatural shade of red that reminded me of somewhere between a spring rose and deep, spilled blood.

The Blaze Prince led the awful, murderous beast through the sky like nothing I'd ever seen. I dreamed of riding my own dragon, pairing with one for life, but not with that thing in the sky! I never wanted to be anywhere near it, not after hearing all the tales of its primal, ruthless, insatiable destruction...

As Krakos' fire eviscerated another dragon and its rider from the sky, it became quickly apparent, and my words couldn't be any better than Bella's...

"We need to get the fuck outta here!" She squeezed my hand tighter as we ran. She'd always been faster than me, with those long legs of hers... ones I'd honestly always been jealous of. "We've got to get to shelter, now! I don't want to die out here, not like this!"

Her words gripped me, haunting me instantly. I realized, as I watched the Blaze Prince ravage the Stormscales above, that all those I cared about in my tiny little corner of the world were in the exact same predicament we were...

I ran as fast as my bare feet could carry me, finally hitting cobblestones in our town. The forge was up ahead, only two hundred yards up and around the bend by the circular town square. Unlike the cobblestone roads that led to the square, nearly all of the houses of my town were perfect kindling for dragonfire. That made me all too keenly aware of the danger of the battle erupting in the ominous sky above.

We ran ahead of Garris, panting like a dog, but suddenly found ourselves stuck. He'd keeled over, hunched with his hands on his fat thighs; beads of sweat pouring down his wrinkled, bald brow.

"Hurry!" My gaze drifted back to the sky battle, just in time to see one of the most terrifying sights of my nineteen years in this world...

"The Blaze Prince," Bella yanked hard on her own chains, trying to pull Garris out of his exasperated stupor. "He's coming!"

Krakos was in pursuit of the largest of the rebel dragons, a mighty green drake with aqua-marine spikes fanning all the way down its back. Murder was deep in the mighty Krakos' eyes. The pursuing dragon was over twice as large as the one it hunted. The Blaze Prince was ducked low on his dragon's back. He wore a dual-horned helm, a blood-red cape whipping hard in the wind behind him, matte-black armor covering every inch of his huge body, and a trident of flames blazing in his hand, eager to find its way into the rider he chased.

My fingers covered my mouth as I felt the gasp escape from between my lips. Every fiber of my being was stuck in awe and terror, tugging futilely to get Garris to his feet. Wretched flames and smoke built in Krakos' maw, and the light of dragonfire glowed in between the black scales of the beast's chest.

The chains in Bella's hands slacked as we all glared up at the chase in dread.

Garris perked up; the words, "Great Odiun," escaped his vile mouth.

The fire built within Krakos, growling like pressurized magma before a great volcano eruption, ready to unleash upon its foe as the two dragons and their riders rode straight at us.

We only had seconds. In moments they'd be on top of us, and

I didn't even have a knife to protect us, not that that would do a damned thing, but shit... I had nothing!

I'm not ready to die yet! And I'm sure as the Infernal Depths not going to let them hurt Bella, or any of the children here. They've done nothing to enter the queen's war, and I'm not going to let them die for nothing!

My fists clenched impossibly tight, and my breath hastened as my chest heaved.

I can't let them destroy my home. I can't let them destroy the only thing that offers a shred of comfort in this piss-infested, chain-rattling life of mine. I can't let them take the only things I truly love in this world.

And as the flames poured out of Krakos' maw, exploding into the green drake and its rider, I felt something stir inside of me. It was so deep it felt buried, like an egg inside I never knew about that was hatching, breaking free of its hard exterior shell.

The unworldly hot dragonfire incinerated the Stormscale dragon but kept pouring out, and it was still heading straight at us.

The colossal dragon flew down toward the city as the smell of the smoldering green dragon and rider filled my nostrils with its unbearable stench—like hot iron and burnt flesh.

The flames were so enormous, they were going to blow down onto us and all of Bramblebash. So many lives were going to be ended forever...

Something shifted inside me. It wasn't fear—not exactly. It was deeper than that. Like a thread being pulled in my chest, tight and hot, like it might snap. Krakos's roar cracked the sky, but what rattled me wasn't the dragon. It was the pulse rising in my ribs—steady, ancient, wrong and right all at once.

My legs kept moving, dragging Bella behind me, but my skin prickled like the wind was whispering secrets against it. The ocean surged louder behind us, crashing like it wanted me to turn around.

There was something in me.

Not mine.

But also… mine.

I could feel it humming beneath my breastbone, like water boiling just under the surface. My throat closed, and for a second, I thought I might scream—or burst into flame.

I swallowed it down.

Not now.

Not yet.

But it was there. Awake.

A light surged inside me, welling from deep within, like lightning electrifying my soul, filling a well that I didn't even know was dry. And as the light escaped me, pouring out of my mouth and eyes, sizzling out of my fingertips, Krakos' deathly eyes widened beyond his evil flames.

The golden light erupted from me like an unstoppable hurricane. Violent winds ripped out of me with a fury I'd never felt. I got angry, oh by the gods, I got angry! My teeth gritted, grinding as I glared up at the horned Blaze Prince and his genocidal dragon. I felt like I could move a mountain, change the tides, summon the moon!

And as the golden orb of light exploded out from me, the dragonfire collided with it, erupting in an explosion that rocked the ground beneath my bare feet. I felt the impact in my chest, stomach, and knees, buckling me down to a knee. The weight of the dragonfire was crushing me like an ant under a boot heel, but I was holding it at bay, keeping us from its unbearable weight.

Krakos roared like nothing I'd ever heard—like the Infernal Depths tore a hole in the earth, letting out every demon imaginable—his flames evaporating into the air. His roar was of sheer frustration, rage, and discontent.

My hands would have covered my ears from such a hellish roar, but they were all that was keeping us alive as the magic poured out from my hands to the gigantic golden orb that repelled his devouring, fiery breath.

Though the battling destructive dragonfire and shielding, dazzling golden magic, something grabbed my gaze like a magnet. Through the eye slits in the horned helm of the Blaze Prince, his deadly gaze locked with mine. I was stuck, glued to them like cold water to hard ice.

Krakos roared again, ending his furious flames. I dropped to my knees, severing the addictive gaze of the evil prince as the dragonfire receded.

My golden light faded too, evaporating like mist under the bright afternoon sun.

The Stormscales took their chance, unleashing a devastating, coordinated attack upon the Blaze Prince, sending him and his huge dragon scurrying into evasive maneuvers as it rolled and dove away from the rebel dragonfires.

As the dragon battle moved back out over the South Cape Sea, I heard Bella and Garris both gasp in unison. I looked at both of them as their eyes went wide, peering in shock at the side of my neck.

"Ash..." Bella muttered, "your neck... it's... glowing..."

"Huh?"

Bella dug her hand into her bag, fumbling for something, and pulled her small mirror free with shaking fingers.

I grasped it immediately, angling it toward my neck, and what I saw made my stomach drop. I felt both eyebrows raise, and a wind gusted through, blowing my long hair off my neck and behind my back, revealing to me what the two were awing over.

Upon my neck was a mark I'd never seen before, glowing in brilliant gold, in the shape of a curving crescent moon, streaks cast through it like rolling waves.

In the reflection, my free hand shot to cover my mouth. My jaw dropped, and my mind raced to figure out what the hell was going on with my body. I took a staggering step backward, nearly toppling over as my knees wobbled. As the light glowed on my neck, I forgot all about the danger we were in, running my quivering fingers from my mouth to the golden light. And as my fingers glided over the light, a terrible pain shot through my mind like a pickaxe entering my ear, and a voice I'd never heard before spoke to me.

The voice was grim, hollow, commanding.

Its words took me, cutting through my defenses like a hot iron pike through a bar of velvety soap. The words were hallowed in my mind—deep like bedrock in an ancient cave.

"It is time. You must free me. You've awoken to your true self, and so you must awaken me…"

CHAPTER 2

*T*he strength in my body fizzled away to nothing, and my whole body felt like it was bearing the weight of a giant moose on my back. A daze took my mind as the events whirled like a cyclone in my head.

Magic. I had just used magic. Me.

I tried to force myself to wake up from the dream, but the smell of burnt flesh still filled my nostrils. This was no dream. My hands were trembling, not from pain—but from something else. Something alive. My heart thundered like it wanted out of my chest, and the air around me shimmered with the echo of whatever I'd just done.

Magic.

I had used magic.

The word hit me like a slap—wild, impossible, illegal.

I looked down at my hands, half-expecting them to be glowing or scorched or changed somehow. But they were still mine. Dirt-streaked. Callused from years of scrubbing floors and hauling buckets. But they didn't feel like mine anymore.

They felt… powerful.

A spark lit in the hollow of my chest. Not warmth. Not safety. But something sharp and addictive.

I had power.

Me.

A slave.

I didn't know whether to run from it or fall to my knees in worship.

When we entered the forge, I got the overwhelming feeling my life would never be the same.

Sure, the smoke from the bellows smelled the same; the sounds of hammers hitting hot iron rang in my ears dully. This was my home—and I hated it.

So, a new life didn't really seem all that bad. And as Garris led us into the back room immediately, all eyes from the other slaves were on Bella and me. Even after a dragon attack—a fucking dragon attack! They still forced us to work nonstop, pounding, polishing, riveting, fitting, organizing, sweeping, mopping. As if dragons didn't just set roads ablaze and fry innocent people in the alleys between. As if I didn't just use magic.

Garris took us into the dark room, shutting the wooden door behind him.

We knew how this went now. I just dearly hoped he only whipped me and not Bella. She didn't do anything wrong. I was the one who talked back, and this time I didn't care. I could take the pain. I had done it before, and I would do it again. What's different this time is that I couldn't get that voice out of my head.

Awaken me...

Was that real? No, Ash, you idiot. There wasn't a voice in your head, and if there was, then you had bigger problems than the whip.

But that voice. It sounded like no voice I'd ever heard. It sounded as ancient as a mountain, as hollow as a deep, sacred cave. I didn't think I'd ever forget that voice—if I lived through that day.

"You little bitch," Garris seethed in rage, hissing through his yellow teeth as he pulled down the whip from the wall, uncoiling it with a sinister flick of his wrist.

Bella didn't say a word. She was smart that way. Arguing always made it worse. Always.

I turned and faced the wall, torchlight flickering on both sides of me, casting a matte glow on the rock wall before my face. I slid both sleeves off my shoulders and down to my elbows, revealing my bare back to him. I heard him laugh in spite. He was going to enjoy this. He always did.

"Would've gotten her back quicker if you hadn't disobeyed me." I heard him take thick gulps of wine from a mug beside him. "Wouldn't have been in that trouble in the first place. Next time, you'll do as I say. I'll teach you the hard way not to give me lip."

"She saved us!" Bella shouted. I spun to face her. I shushed her, but her fists were balled at her sides, and she'd got that mean glower I knew all too well. That's the face I got when I knew arguing with her wouldn't do any good. "That dragon would've killed your miserable ass if she hadn't done that back there. She saved you! You're only still breathing because of her."

Over my shoulder, I saw the confusion in his beady eyes. "That's another reason why you deserve this!"

The whip flew through the air with a thick uncoiling sound. It struck my back like lightning—searing heat shooting up and down my body like venom. The pain overtook me, but I clenched my jaw. I wouldn't let him have the pleasure of my cries. Not this time.

"Magic. You had magic, and you hid it from me? Who do you think you are?" Hate filled every speck of his words. "You think you're special? You wanted to hide that? Not tell me? There's nothing special about you, you brat. You're a rotten, worthless, meaningless little tart who's never gonna amount to more than the shite on the heel of my boots!"

He slithered the whip on the floor back toward him as the

warm blood dripped down the cool skin of my bare back. My lips quivered as I pressed my forehead to the wall.

You can get through this. You've been here before. The pain is temporary. It's only temporary...

The latch to the door behind him suddenly clacked, and the door opened inward, pouring sunlight onto me and my exposed back, the shiny scars and fresh blood surely glistening in the light.

A pair of Garris' men entered. They both worked in the forge, sometimes staring at me a little too long once they were too drunk to think to wipe the ale's froth from their hideous mouths. They were perfect for Garris; dim, dull, the smell like a raccoon that had been stuck in an outhouse and couldn't outsmart a pigeon. But they were strong, and once they got you by the wrists, there was no use in trying to escape.

"The whole town's in a frenzy," one said, waving his arms over his head, sweat pouring down his brow.

"She attacked the Blaze Prince." The other swallowed hard, his eyes stricken with panic. "He's gonna kill us all. We're all gonna die..."

"The bitch used magic against him!" the first said. "He'll burn this whole place to the ground because of her!"

I wanted to yell out that I hadn't. I wanted to refute their accusations, but I couldn't find the words. I didn't use magic! But I did, didn't I? I fucking did. Shit...

I had used magic. Magic. But I had to try to save the town. I had to try to save Bella.

"Magic wielders are forbidden in Allovan; any that use magic outside of the queen's command are either turned or killed. It's the unwritten law," the second man said what we all already knew. "We gotta get rid of her. They might think you've, we've, been hiding her, and that magic, from the queen!"

"Wait a damned minute," Garris said; fuming. "She belongs to me. I'm not sending her anywhere for free!"

"Sell her to the crown," one of the men said. "The Blaze Queen would surely pay for her."

"You moron," the second said, shoving the first's shoulder. "The queen doesn't pay. She just takes."

"She's not going nowhere." Garris slammed the whip on the table beside him and took another wet gulp of wine. "That wasn't magic. That was some kind of… trick! Look at her. She's as frail as a mouse. I need her here. We've got deadlines."

The men looked at one another, unsure. They shook their heads; one itched his arm.

Garris took one long, menacing glare at me. Beads of sweat poured off his brow like a deluge rolling down a canvas tent. His dark eyes were unwavering as I saw the hate brimming deep. The side of his face twitched, and he snarled. Taking a long gulp of wine, he finished the glass.

"You're always more damned trouble than you're worth. Maybe I will gladly take some coin for your worthless hide. Should've never bought you in the first place. Should've stuck with my gut and bought girls that are at least something to look at."

"Because going with that gut has always worked out so well for you. So devilishly fit and handsome you are, master." I couldn't fight the words as they erupted from my mouth. "Sell me, you rotten oaf!"

Instead of picking the whip back up, he hastened and grabbed the club by the door. It was sturdy and thick, not something I wanted anywhere near me. The only other time he picked that up, I hadn't woken up for a whole day.

"Garris, no." Bella used her soft, soothing voice. "If the crown wants her, they're going to want her in good shape. If that was magic, then they'll pay you plenty of royals for her, but they'll want her fresh. It's not every day someone uses magic to save a whole city."

Did I? Did I use magic? It sounded so insane. And that thing on my neck. What the hell was that?

My fingers glided up my neck, feeling for anything there, but there was nothing.

He suddenly hurled the club all the way across the room, tumbling end over end through the air, slamming into the rock wall beside me. It startled the shit out of me, but I swallowed my nerves, barely flinching.

Garris was as awful as anyone I knew, but he was strong as an ox, even if dim as one too. Always best to let him get his wicked energy out on his own.

The two men shuffled out of the room behind me. They knew Garris well enough to know talking with him in that state was like trying to reason with a wild boar.

"My life is gonna be so much better when your worthless little hide is gone. Let the crown buy you. Let the Blaze Queen torture you to death for all I care!" He rushed out of the room, leaving Bella and me in the quiet.

She rushed to me and wrapped her arms around my neck. I stood breathless. My fingers slid down the wall to my pockets. My heart pounded. My entire world was changing so fast. I did want to leave the rotten city. I did want a life I could never dream of. But I couldn't leave Bella. She was my only friend, and as she squeezed me, I knew she felt the same way.

She released me and stood back. "What the hell are we going to do, Ash? We are really in a predicament this time. I don't know how we're going to survive this one. Where did that come from?" Her hands flung out wide, shaking as if demanding answers I didn't have. "Why didn't you tell me you could use magic? That was amazing! Like, the most incredible thing I'd ever seen. We would've been dead if it wasn't for that gold that shot out of you!"

"I—I didn't know. You know I didn't know. I would've told you if I'd known. I couldn't keep a secret like that from you."

"Well, I believe you." She scratched my bare shoulder with her nails. "I still can't believe it. You of all people, and here, of all places!" Her hands dropped, and her shoulders slumped. "How are we going to get out of this mess?"

"I think I'm going to the capital… they're going to take me away to Emberveil."

Bella wanted to refute, but bit her lip instead. Her glacier-blue eyes and kind smile reminded me of a fresh fear.

I can't leave her. I'll never see her again if they take me. She's the only person who cares about me in this rotten world. My stomach dropped, and an emptiness consumed me. I'm going to be alone. I'm going to be all alone again…

"I'm worried, Ash. I'm scared what's going to happen to you if they take you. Everything I hear about the Blaze Queen terrifies me. This civil war has driven her mad. And her dragon makes the prince's look like a puppy. I saw her once, did I tell you? I saw the queen riding Brigodon, Lord of the Dragons. She was far away, flying over the mountains, but it still brought tears to my eyes. It was the most terrifying thing I'd ever seen… If you go to Emberveil, I'm worried you'll never return, and I'll never see you again…"

Again, she wrapped me in her arms, and I embraced her back.

"We've got until tomorrow to think of something," she said, rubbing her tears away behind me.

But she won't. She can't. She's a slave. She's a slave just like me. I spun and sighed into her neck. It's going to be up to me. I've got to get myself out of this mess somehow.

I want a new life. I had always dreamed of one, but being taken to the capital wasn't exactly what I had in mind. Escape may be my only option. But I'd need to get out of these fucking shackles. There's no way I could run with these on. They'd find me in no time. There's got to be a way.

I heard Garris staggering back long before he barreled back into the room, shoving the door in with his fist as it slammed into the rock wall.

Bella didn't back away as he strode toward us, wild rage in his eyes, and strong spirits stinking from his breath.

"Garris," Bella muttered as he easily shoved her aside, sending her falling onto her side.

My pulse sped and my heartbeat thumped like a drum as I gritted my teeth. "Don't touch her, you rotten bastard!" My throat scratched and vibrated as the words rushed out, inches from his disgusting face.

He was so overwhelming in strength and anger when he entered that I didn't notice the new shackles on his hands until he dropped to a knee, placing the second pair above the old ones. He bound them and locked them so tight it took my breath away.

He rose with a groan, glaring at me like I was less than human. "You're not going anywhere until I figure out what to do with ya." Spit from his lips hit my cheek. "If this war doesn't kill us all, and if the queen doesn't kill you, then I'd take pleasure in making that rebellious glint in your eyes fade. I'd enjoy wiping that smirk off your face, once and for all..."

I wanted to scream. I wanted to hit him so hard his head spun backward, if for nothing else, for the way he knocked Bella to the floor. But I held it in. Sometimes the best way to fight back was to save it for another day. I knew that look in his eyes, the savage, bitter predator that was begging to get let out.

So, I said nothing, bowed my head, and he eventually staggered back out of the room.

Bella held out her hands, and I helped her up. She brushed the soot off her clothes and bent down to try to alleviate the tightness of my fresh shackles.

If they took me to the capital, I was dead. If they caught me trying to escape, I was dead. My mind raced to figure out a solution where it didn't end up with dying, but they all escaped me.

The only thing that soothed me was having a friend like her in this wretched world.

Everything else was just misery.

CHAPTER 3

*H*ours later, Bella and I were hard at work. The smoky forge bustled all around us. Embers launched into the air from hammers hitting hot iron. The sharp clanging sounds would normally annoy eardrums, but they'd turned somewhat soothing over the last few years. Nothing was enough to erase the thought of my impending fate. It never left my mind.

Escape. That's all I could think about.

As the oil from the cloth in my hand soaked into my skin, I wondered—could I use that same magic I had used on the beach against the dragons—again?

Bella and I both polished armor, a job we shared frequently, because our small hands fit into crevasses the men couldn't reach. We both sat with our backs to the wall, watching the others, paying special attention to Garris' men. I evaded more gashes and scars on my back that time, which shocked me because of my serious lack of restraint in talking back today. I took it as a small victory, but I didn't expect many more like it anytime soon.

The forge smelled the same—char and sweat and scorched steel—but everything felt off-kilter, like the world had tilted slightly and no one else noticed. My hands moved automatically over the armor, polishing grooves I'd scrubbed a thousand times, but inside I was coiled tight. The spark I'd felt on the beach still flickered somewhere deep in my chest, alive and terrifying. I kept expecting the metal to heat beneath my touch, for someone to smell the change in me, for the world to crack open again. But no one looked twice. Around me, life in the forge trudged on, routine and cruel. And yet I couldn't shake the feeling that I didn't belong to it anymore.

"Where do you think he is?" Bella whispered, continuing to wipe the gauntlet in her hands. "He's been gone a long time…"

"I don't know." I had been curious about where Garris was too. Usually he'd be plopped down, smoking his pipe and drinking wine by the barrel. He always liked to watch his property to make sure they weren't slacking.

"Supper's soon, and then off to the bunkhouse." The tone in Bella's voice was laced with unmistakable worry. "The sun will be up before we know it." Her bottom lip quivered. "I'm scared. I'm scared of never seeing you again… What if they come for you tomorrow? What if that's the last time we… see each other?" Tears streaked down her soft cheeks, parting the soot smudged on them like a stream through dirt.

I patted her back, pressing reassurance through her. But she didn't buy it. I could tell by the look in her wet eyes she knew what was coming.

"I have a plan," I said, even though I didn't. I glared down at the shackles on my ankles, and I felt their constant, aching bite. "I'm going to try to use it again. Tonight. I don't know how, but I'm going to use it, take these chains off, and get out of here before they know anything's up."

"You're going to use it? How?" Before she could get another

breath in, she said the words I knew I was going to have to argue with. "I'm coming with you."

I shook my head hard.

"No. Too dangerous."

"It's not up for debate." Her voice grew harsh; forceful. "Where will we go? They're going to send scouts out. Hunters too."

"I was thinking the Faewood Forest, or go deep in the Harrowhorn Mountains, or hide out in one of the Emerald Crest Isles."

Bella sighed, continuing to polish the gauntlet as she pressed harder into the strokes of the oiled cloth. "How? Even if you could use that magic again, and that golden symbol glowed on your neck again, how would we get there? And what? Are we going to hide forever?"

"Yes. That's the plan."

"You stopped the Blaze Prince's dragon, and it could've died after that for all we know. You think they're going to just let us go hide in the woods or the mountains?"

Honestly, I didn't have an answer to that question. Everyone in Allovan knew the Blaze Queen, Mortriana Vissex, would never let that kind of incident go. She'd hunt me to the ends of the world to get my magic for her own, or kill me to squash any chance of further rebellion in the war.

"That's the plan," was all I could come up with.

We both sighed simultaneously, as if rehearsed. But the truth is we had just spent all our waking time together.

There was commotion outside the forge; men running and shouting. All within continued working, but every ear perked up. They all knew something was happening as Garris' men poured out of the forge into the square. Many gazes drifted to me, as they all knew about what I had done at the dragon battle earlier.

Garris entered. He'd changed clothes. He was wearing his

nice, unstained white shirt and his knee-high leather boots, freshly shined. Shit. He's got company.

Behind him another man entered. And I thought Garris had a mean look to him. The man who entered behind my master was a tall man with thinning gray hair, age spots on his brow and temples. He was missing a nose, presumably from the flat bandage that covered it, and one pale eye stared off at the side of the room.

Garris pointed at me immediately as they walked over. Sweat soaked my palms, sliding between the folds of my hands. Bella dug her nails into my arm subconsciously. I blinked hard at the ground, knowing there was nothing I could do.

Not a single slave stopped their work, but all watched nervously. We may not have been a family in the forge, but we cared for each other. We were all stuck in the same rotten life. And as the two men walked toward me, and the tall man licked his dry lips, I got the sinking suspicion my life was about to get a whole lot more rotten.

As Garris waved the old man closer, that strange thrum stirred again in my chest—like lightning curling beneath my skin, desperate to lash out. I could feel the heat rising in my palms, the spark of something unshaped and wild. But then I glanced past the man's hunched shoulders to the others in the forge, busy stacking scrap metal and hammering new stuff. What if I lost control? What if whatever lived inside me burst free and lit the forge sky-high? I could end them all—Bella, the others, even myself—in one fiery heartbeat. The risk wrapped around my throat like a chain, tighter than any Garris ever forced on me. I blinked hard and buried the feeling deep. No. Not here. Not with lives that weren't mine to gamble.

"Get up," Garris pointed at the door to the back room again.

I considered telling him to shove it up his ass, but reason calmed me. This wasn't the time. Not yet. I needed to play it cool until we were in the bunkhouse. I couldn't use magic in front of everyone like this, if I was even able to use it again in the first place. Be patient…

I stood and walked over to the back room, unlatching it and opening the door. Bella followed me.

"Not you," Garris put a hand up between us.

"Please, Garris…" Bella's voice was as sweet as she could muster.

Garris looked at the tall man with no nose, giving the kindest glance and curtsy she could. The tall man nodded. Garris removed his hand, and Bella followed me into the room—two torches and scant candlelight gave the room a flickering, ominous glow. The room had never treated me well; ever. Every time I thought about the room, I got shivers…

"Over there, in the middle," Garris said, shutting the door behind him once both men were inside. It was only them, and us.

The door sealed, hiding away any light from the other side.

"Now… strip." Garris folded his arms over his round stomach. He had that proud tone in his voice I detested. I hated how he had power over me, but in the end—he always got what he wanted—no matter how hard I fought.

The other man with the dead eye glared hard at my body. I swallowed hard in disgust. He was old enough to be my grandfather, or great-grandfather. Not that I ever knew either of my parents, but that man had to be in his seventies; eighties even.

"You heard me," Garris said harshly, but with a slight excitement in his voice. "Clothes off. All of 'em. Now!"

I knew what this meant… the fucker was trying to sell me. He was trying to sell me before the queen's people had their chance to buy me.

The greedy prick was trying to make some extra royals; probably expecting a measly bounty from the crown, so he was taking a chance at a bigger price. God, I hated him…

I didn't want to, but I had to do it countless times before. I slid my sleeves off my shoulders and down my bare arms. Bella did the same. I brushed my hair from my back over the front of my chest, before I let my shirt fall all the way down to my ankles. Bella and I both undid our belts and slid our pants down next, underwear and all. A chill bit my skin.

There we stood, naked as the day we were born. My hair did its best to hide my breasts and nipples, which I could feel hardening from the chill. I folded both hands over my crotch. Bella did the same.

Garris then folded his hands behind his back, taking slow strides to my side, and then behind me—directly behind me. "This is the one." He took my hips in both his greasy, fat hands, squeezing. I wanted to spin and rake his face with my nails, but forced restraint. "She doesn't look like much. Skinny, freckled, weak, sharp-tongued with dull brown eyes and that matted thick hair... but... I saw it as sure as I've seen anything in my life. There was the mark on her neck. The one you described."

The tall man nodded, pleased. A smile rose at the corner of his wrinkled mouth.

"But, for what she lacks in beauty, she's a hard worker. And... she's a virgin, if that's your thing. Which increases the price."

He knew I wasn't a virgin. He was the one who sold me off for nights with those men. Garris took his coins and drank them down his gullet for me spreading my legs for the three of them. I never had any pleasure with sex. Forced, kicking and biting my way into their beds, but they always got their way. Always. No matter how hard I fought.

With one last squeeze of my naked hips, he let go, walking to my side, sliding his slick finger up my arm, over my shoulder, and to the side of my neck. He brushed my hair back as it fell onto my back, exposing half my chest and my bare breast.

I felt so vulnerable I wanted to scream. But I didn't.

"Interested?" Garris asked. "The other is for sale too, if the price is right."

"I don't need the other..." the old, tall man said with a croaked voice. "Just the one. If you're absolutely certain she has the golden rune on her neck. I'm a sort of... collector. When I heard of the sighting, I had to come see... You are certain she is the Gold-Marked?"

"Without a doubt." Garris gave me a mean wink as he flicked my hair back over my chest. He leaned in and whispered in my ear, "Good fucking riddance."

I turned my head quickly and whispered back, "You'll get yours, you miserable prick." I spat right into his ear.

He recoiled and pulled a kerchief from his pocket, wiping my spit out. The twitch in his eye showed he wanted to strike me down. Kill me even. But he didn't.

He laughed and returned to the tall man's side. "I'm sure you'll teach her some manners. Manners I've failed to teach. So, do we have a deal? You can take her now if you wish. I'll draw up the papers."

The tall man nodded, a wicked smile curving on his lips. He rubbed his frail, age-spot-covered hands.

Then, we heard it—the distinct flapping of wide wings out in the courtyard. Similar to ship sails, but thicker, and much, much higher. By the gods... is it happening again? Another battle? Those dragons could turn the whole town to ruin.

There were dozens of screams from beyond the door; outside the forge. I recognized the screams, as they were the same kind I heard when the dragon battle erupted earlier in the day—full of panic, dread, and terrible fear. As the shouts and screams grew, a new sound emerged from back out in town. It was the now familiar sound of a mighty dragon's roar filling every nook and cranny of the town. It came from just outside the forge.

Having lived in Bramblebash most of my life, I'd never heard people scream like that. It was a new kind of terror that pierced my ears and sent shivers down my back.

Garris went to the door, his slimy fingers trembling as he unlatched it, peeking through its narrow opening. The old man stepped back into the room's dark corner. I heard the murmurs from within the forge hush, and all hammering and grinding ceased to a heart-stopping crawl.

Garris released the door latch and staggered back into the room, walking right up to my side. The linen of his shirt scraped against the side of my bare arm. I was so terrified of what was outside the door, and within the forge, that I forgot I was completely naked still. I was doing my best to hide behind my arms, covering my breasts, and my hands, covering my groin.

A dark-hooded man entered the room. He had to duck his head to get under the doorframe, and the distinct smell of drag-onfire poured into the room with him. It was the musty, thick smell of ancient bellowing brimstone mixed with a sulfuric metal scent. And as the man entered the room, towering over all of us with his muscular build, all air rushed from my lungs at the sight of him...

The Blaze Prince... he's here...

I'd never been so terrified in all my life...

Terror gripped me, freezing me in place. My feet sucked into the floorboards, my fingers cocked, spread wide before my chest. Air caught in my throat as my body forced an inhale, but my pounding heart caused my breathing to flutter. He was... enormous...

He towered over all of us, including Garris, who had slithered like a cold-blooded snake behind me. The prince had a mask of black metal covering his face, probably to hide his grotesque, hideous Cinderyn face. The fire elemental children of Allovan were surely deformed by the fire magics they wielded, and the Blaze Prince had a reputation for being the most fearsome, deadly dragon rider in all the lands. That was, except for the bloodthirsty mother of his—the Blaze Queen herself.

Bella gripped my hand, pulling our bodies together. I immediately felt her body trembling, hard goose pimples scratching against each other.

"It's him," she muttered through shaky breaths. "He's come… he's come for you…"

Me? Oh, fuck… he did, didn't he… he came to kill me for what I did… I'm going to die right here, right now, for a magic I didn't even know I had… Shit…

$\mathcal{M}$y nerves broke—fleeing down through the floorboards and dissipating into the air from my nervous panting. As he approached, I felt the hot air escaping my nostrils and my mouth left agape.

He's... he's huge.

I didn't think I'd ever felt so small in all my life.

He towered over me. Fucking towered over me.

I'd never seen such a man in all my life. As vulnerable as a doe left to be ravaged by a starving wolf.

He was clad in black armor; finer in design than anything ever produced in our little forge. His ebony mask was sculpted to sharp angles, representing the likeness of a savage wolf. The angles of his dark armor carved around his muscular body like water flowing over dense boulders. The way his armor moved as he strode toward me impressed me in every way. And as he finally stopped before me, glaring down at me behind the ebony mask... I saw eyes that stopped me in my tracks on the beach.

Blue as the sky, deep as the vastest ocean, and as exciting as it must feel to glide through the air on the back of a monstrous dragon—I got lost in those breathtaking eyes. They pulled me in so deep a shiver shot up my core, setting me ablaze from the inside.

"Blue eyes," Bella whispered low. "He's got blue eyes. Cinderyn have red fiery eyes. Right?"

I was so lost in them I didn't react. They pierced so deep into me it took me a full breath to notice my mouth hung open.

"Name..." he muttered, his voice hollow and deep, but far younger than I expected him to sound.

I couldn't find the words as I stood there shivering, completely naked from head to toe, bare as the day I was born, and just as vulnerable. I couldn't remember my name! How embarrassing...

As his eyes locked hard onto mine, my cheeks flushed and my ears heated.

"Ashlyn Mist," Garris forced the words out of his own cowardly throat.

"Ash," I said, mustering all the courage I had. But I hated my real name so much it almost became instinct to correct it.

"Ash Mist?" The Blaze Prince put his hand on the hilt of his enormous sword at his hip, twisting it behind him. The leather of it squealed, and his armor clacked as he twisted.

I was so overtaken by the fear that gripped the room, I felt a deep urge in my core. Something primal, something that caused my body to heat and throb. The raw power that emanated from him was unlike anything I'd ever felt. Garris recoiled like a worm in staggering sunlight. I was awestruck.

Then, he did the unexpected. He reached out for me, straight for my throat. My entire body tensed so tight I thought all the moisture might get squeezed right out of me. I wanted to cry. I wanted to scream. But I didn't, and his gauntleted hand turned just before it reached my neck; instead, he ran his fingers through my hair. He pulled it up just high enough that I felt a chill air hit my nipple directly, causing it to stiffen; just what I didn't want. I didn't want him thinking I liked any of this.

"A Mist, huh? An orphan?" He pulled his hand back, but not before tossing my hair back behind my shoulder, leaving my chest bare.

The round room felt like it was closing in on me as my entire world spun.

"No parents," Garris said. "Found on the beach to the north after a battle when she was a child. I purchased her fourteen years ago. Good worker, small hands for tight jobs, virgin too..."

The prince glowered at me suddenly behind that devilish mask. He may have sounded young, perhaps in his early twenties, close to my age of nineteen, but those deep sapphire eyes gazed at me with a wisdom I'd never seen in a man. He was like a god. Sculpted like one, as tall as one, and as terrifying as Gigas—Lord of the Underworld.

He leaned in so close I could feel the cold metal of his mask on my nose. His glare was so deep into mine I forgot where I was, but I remembered one thing, and it sent a shiver all the way down my back.

This is the Blaze Prince, son of the infamous Blaze Queen. He's killed more men than anyone alive. He and his dragon have killed thousands probably in his war.

"She's a virgin, eh?" he said with a slight uptick in his tone. His hot breath hit my lips, and I wanted to melt and wash away like the tides.

"Yes, Blaze Prince," Garris sniveled. "She ain't much to look at, but what's between her legs is unspoiled by any man."

The Prince snorted unexpectedly. I turned my head to the side, forcing my eyes shut hard. I wanted to be anywhere else, anywhere else in the world but there.

"You're the one who used that magic on the beach." The prince sidestepped, the sharp nose of his helmet skimming past my ear. My shoulder was just at the point between his two massive pecs. Garris lumbered back at the prince's swift movement. Bella squeezed my hand tight.

"Answer your prince!" Garris shouted with shaky breath.

"I—I don't know what happened." I didn't know what I was supposed to do. Tell the truth? Lie to hopefully get out of it, and he might leave me be? Maybe he wouldn't kill me for what I did? "I..."

"I know what I saw," the prince said with a rough-edged tone. "You cast that spell, and I saw the symbol glow on the side of your neck. It was you. I remember your hair, your eyes, and the blinding light of your spell. It was you. You're the Gold-Marked. It's you."

Gold-Marked? I'd never heard that term, and I certainly didn't want to be whatever the hell that meant.

"I've been searching for you. The queen has been searching for you, probably for longer than you've even been alive. And here you are. Standing before me now. You're the one who is so dangerous to her? You're just a girl..." He scratched his chin.

My breath caught as his other hand flashed, sending the dark metal of his gauntlet flickering in torchlight. From his other side a sleek black dagger shot toward my neck, its razor-sharp edge feeling like ice against the soft spot where the golden rune glowed earlier in the day.

He muttered behind his mask. I couldn't tell exactly what he said, but at the end of his rant, I heard the words, "I could end this all right here, right now, and it would be done..."

"Please, sir, no!" Bella suddenly cried out. "She didn't do anything on purpose. She didn't mean to make you get attacked by those other dragon riders. That was all an accident!"

His gaze never left my neck as the blade glided along my soft skin, causing my entire body to tense. I was so afraid I wanted to jump out of my skin. Bella's words didn't faze him even a pinch. Cold sweat wetted my skin, causing a great shiver down from my neck to my toes.

"No," he muttered again, pulling the dagger from the side of my neck and sheathing it as quickly as he sent it flying from his hip.

Garris finally let out a deep exhale, as he'd been holding his breath as well. "So, you want to buy her?"

Buy her? He's going to sell me to that bastard mass-murderer? I knew with every ounce of life in my body that the prince was going to kill me if I went with him. I couldn't let that happen. I'd got to run...

But get real, Ash, how in the fuck could you run away from the dragon-riding prince of Emberveil? I'm so fucked...

"Who is that man?" The Blaze Prince's voice deepened, and he sent an icy glower at the man in the room's corner—hiding in the shadow as best he could.

Garris' lips seemed glued together as he struggled to find words behind his lying mouth.

"He was gonna sell me to him, because of whatever it is you all think I am..."

The prince's intense glare shifted slowly to Garris, who sulked back toward the back wall. The Blaze Prince, in his hulking and very intimidating armor, squared his massive shoulders off against my cowering master. "You were doing what?"

"Forgive me, my prince," Garris sniveled to the prince but side-eyed me as meanly as he ever had.

"Did you not know this girl was to be handed over to the crown, to my mother, the queen? Magic is forbidden by those not under her employ. You knew that... you know that!"

Garris swallowed hard, and I could feel his nervousness as he wiped his sweaty palms on his thighs.

"D—don't mind him," Garris said after clearing his throat. "A misunderstanding. Ashlyn was always going to the queen! I just wanted to get an idea of her worth before I bartered for payment."

"Liar!" I shouted, spinning to face the awful man. Heat rose in my core, and my skin crawled; like ants scurrying up my arms. I wanted to smack him. I wanted to smack him even more than when he lashed me with that nasty whip and snarled through his yellow teeth. "You were going to sell me to that man so you could get a higher price!"

"Ash…" Bella whispered. "Careful…"

I was so steamed that I hadn't noticed that the lumbering mountain of a man was standing right next to me, fuming at my master. I felt as insignificant as I ever had in my life. The raw power within the prince fumed like a geyser. He had magic. He was beyond wealthy, and he had killed men with his own bare hands. As completely terrified as I was, I had to admit to myself that part of me liked being beside him. He was as dangerous as the devil, but at that moment, he made me feel like someone had my back. Someone was supporting me against the man who'd beaten me more times than I could count—and I liked it.

"You would sell the Gold-Marked to someone else, for… profit?" The prince was roaring with rage. I could hear it building deep in his powerful chest.

"So?" Garris forced the words out. He sounded more like his cocky, arrogant self, and I was loving it. "What was the crown gonna pay? Five hundred royals? She used magic! She should be worth five thousand!"

"You worm…" As the Blaze Prince said that, he raised his arm, and I could immediately feel the heat emanating from it. His hand, covered in layers of black steel, glowed. His fingertips burned with a fiery golden orange light, and as he clenched it into a fist, flames erupted from its top and bottom.

Bella and I inched backward as the walls of the round rock room were bathed in the bright, intense light from his hand.

As the fiery flames poured out from his hand, burning into long lines toward the ground and ceiling, I saw there was something within the flames. And when the flames and light died down, and Garris looked like he wanted to shrivel up into nothing, a marvelous staff appeared in the prince's hand.

Its top was a marvelously sculpted bird's head. Its eyes shimmering rubies, its sharp beak was a white-crusted jewel, and its fiery red feathers spread sharply in two fans for its wings. The staff was gold from tip to bottom, with streams of red gemstone like lava snaking down it.

The staff's ruby eyes sparkled as he held it up before Garris, and I was so entranced by the spectacle of it—hell, I'd never seen magic before that day—I didn't notice the elderly man with the age spots slip out the door until it closed behind him.

"I'll give you a good deal," Garris whimpered.

"A good deal, eh?" The prince's words seemed laced with blazing fire.

I stood there, still completely nude, covering my body the best I could while the Blaze Prince pointed the tip of his red-bird staff directly at Garris, hovering only inches from his face. Garris poured sweat, and his gaze was fixated upon the staff's glowing ruby eyes.

"Two thousand royals," Garris' voice trembled. He was a bastard, but he coveted money more than anything, so he was sure as hell going to try to get the best deal he could.

"Two thousand, eh?" The prince sounded deep in thought, letting a moment slip by as his staff's tip was held like a statue at Garris.

I was so caught up in the conversation I didn't really grasp that the infamous, murderous Blaze Prince was trying to buy me. To take me with him to Odiun knows where, and probably be tortured to death.

Garris licked his lips at the thought of the payment, but his smirk dropped to a sickly frown.

Flames roared down his staff from his handhold on it to the fire-bird's tip, casting a bright light onto Garris' face. "How about ten, instead?"

"Ten?" Garris' jaw dropped nearly to his chest, and his slick brow furrowed. "You are joking..."

The Blaze Prince didn't respond, but instead lowered his staff and took lumbering steps toward Garris, who cowered back against the wall of the cave. His lips quivered, and the expression on his face showed he was in an absolute struggle between bitter anger and overwhelming fear.

"You're lucky I don't have my dragon burn your entire operation to the fucking ground."

Garris swallowed hard. The Blaze Prince hunched his back and lowered his wolf mask to look squarely into my master's eyes.

"For trying to sell the Gold-Marked before our queen would give you a fair price for such a young girl? Yes, you're lucky I don't incinerate your whole forge, take her, and send your other slaves unshackled, running for their freedom."

Garris's anger overtook his shaking cowardice. "One thousand...?"

"Five," the prince spat back quickly. He then pulled back, turned his head, and whistled loudly. The ringing whistle filled the air with a perfect tune, followed by the ear-piercing roar of the fearsome dragon just outside the forge. I'd never heard anything roar like that before. The roar filled the room, vibrating off the walls, sending dust and tools falling to the stone floor. I'd heard dragons far, far away, up in the sky, but nothing like that. Yet, as small as I felt at the sound of the beast, the thought of riding on the back of one sent a curve to the side of my lips. It didn't only sound like death and destruction to me; it sounded like—freedom.

The prince pulled a single coin from his pocket and held it out. A five royal coin.

What a slap in the face to Garris. I'd never seen him sulk like this before. I absolutely loved it.

"Take the coin. Trust me, Garris Bardenal, originally of Coppertown, son to two aristocrats, and who's got two children out drifting in the world. If you want to keep your little life just the way it is… take the coin."

The prince's words were as hard as iron, as cold as a wintry blizzard, and made the adrenaline rush through my veins as if I'd just been chased by a tiger. I'd never heard anyone talk like that to him, and I loved every bit of every second of it.

The prince was so powerful I couldn't believe my eyes. Butterflies erupted in my stomach. I've never felt the presence of a man so utterly powerful… to belittle and humiliate Garris like that. It was about more than coin; it was about power.

As I was filled with complete elation—hugging Bella, partly out of the excitement of my master's shame, and partly just to keep fucking warm—a new fear gripped me as the coin exchanged hands… I was about to have a new master. Possibly the most feared man in all of Allovan just bought me.

Shit… My life was about to get a whole hell of a lot worse…

CHAPTER 5

"Get your clothes back on." The prince's words were forceful behind his dark wolf mask. "Sign the paper." The way he shifted his tone from forceful with me to sinister at Garris made my skin crawl.

This had to be the most dangerous man in the whole world, and he was about to take me with him.

I blinked hard, rubbing the back of my neck.

My world reeled and spun violently. As I pulled up my clothes, letting them settle loosely on the angular bones that jutted across my body, I heard Garris scribble his name on the parchment the prince had ready.

"Undo the shackles." As soon as the prince finished saying it, I heard the clacking of keys as Garris pulled them from his pocket.

I was going to be free from this wretched man!

My mouth fell open, and a warm tingling took over every inch of my skin.

But then another troubling thought entered my mind as I felt Bella's fingertips skirt across my arm. She stood beside me, pulling her clothes up as well, her lips quivering and her eyes welling with tears.

I couldn't leave without her. I didn't know why that thought raced through my mind as our eyes locked. Fuck. I knew why—because she was my best friend. Hell, my only friend in this rotten world, and for all I knew, I was about to be taken to the worst place in all of Allovan. But something tugged at my heart, forcing my lips to part. The words left my lips before any real thought pushed them out.

"My friend is coming with me."

The feeling of the room shifted before the key could slide into the keyhole at my ankles. Like all the air was sucked from the room, leaving us all breathless.

Garris' mouth flattened hard, and the prince let out a deep growl, his gorgeous sapphire eyes glowering hard at me. But I didn't shrink. I didn't relent.

"She's coming with us. She's a hard worker, young, and I'm not leaving without her."

Bella covered her mouth with her trembling hand as tears dripped down her cheeks and onto her collar.

"Absolutely not." Garris' words brought back the power-hungry, hellish brute he was. It was as if the prince wasn't in the room, and it was just the master and his two prisoners again. "That bitch stays here. Right where she belongs."

"You—you wish for your friend to come to the capital?" There was a hint of confusion littered with curiosity in the prince's voice. He sounded human for the first time and not a blood-thirsty monster. "You may resent that choice once you see what waits there."

"I don't care." Bella's hands dropped down to her sides. "I want to go."

"You wretch!" Garris lunged forward much faster than a man his size should, his palm opened and ready to strike her face. He rushed past me quicker than I realized, his shoulder knocking me over nearly to the floor. I fell to a knee, and as I looked up, I saw the most powerful thing I think I'd ever seen, and that includes seeing dragons roam the sky.

What I saw sent a hot rush through me—my breath hitched, my legs weakened, and desire bloomed low in my belly.

For as swift as that bastard Garris was, the Blaze Prince was far faster. In his dark gauntlet, the prince caught Garris' wrist, squeezing so tightly Garris' face twisted in pain. The prince stood between Bella and Garris, and the heat radiating from the powerful prince made my throat catch. Heat rose from my chest to my ears, and my vision tunneled only onto him.

"I'm taking her, too." The prince's words were cold enough to freeze the Infernal Depths. "Five hundred. And don't even think of trying to barter with me... weak man..."

I swear, I thought Garris was either going to have an aneurysm there or just explode from his frustrating position. But for all his faults, he was smart enough to know he was overpowered, outclassed, and in way over his head against the prince of the Emberveil Empire.

"Fine," Garris said through clenched teeth. "Take both the bitches far away from my sight. More trouble than they're fucking worth."

The prince released his wrist, and Garris pulled his arm back, rubbing it. The keys jingled as they hung from his fingers. He bent down with a groan and slid the key into my shackles. With a click, the metal lock released, and I felt the cool air hit the open wounds underneath. He undid Bella's next.

I wanted to kick him. I wanted to kick him so badly, right in the fucking temple, but I somehow restrained myself. All the beatings that bastard laid onto me, all the times he touched my sides or my ass —all I wanted to do was shove my knee right into his fat nose. But instead, I came up with something less violent, and more... lasting.

"Someday..." The word was laced with pure hate as it left my lips. "Someday... I'm going to repay you for all your... nastiness...

one thousand-fold. Mark my words. You're going to get yours, and I'm going to watch you squeal like the little piggy you are."

Garris was about to bark back. The hate in his eyes was unmistakable. But instead, he found a gauntlet holding up five hundred royal coins his way.

"Take it and sign."

"Fine," Garris said, seething. Bella wrapped both of her arms around me so tightly, it squeezed a wide smile across my face.

"I don't know if it's the right thing to do, but I couldn't leave you here with him," I said, squeezing back.

"I know. Thanks, Ash. Whatever comes next, at least we'll be together, and far, far away from here."

"Come," the prince said after Garris scribbled again on the piece of paper, the contract that held our 'freedom'.

Freedom. What a strange word to use for this scenario. From one slaver to the other, but I had a feeling this was going to be so much more adventurous, even if it led to my end.

I may not be in chains, but the prince has a different sort of ownership over me. The way he treats me... there's a darkness in him... but it's different from Garris. He doesn't seem... cruel. He's more... distraught and dark. But he's worlds more handsome. I hope there's something to that. I feel deep down that this is better. Or at least, I desperately hope it is.

I'd rather live a little than not at all.

I didn't want to die, but I wasn't living any kind of life anyway.

We left the cold iron chains on the stone floor of the back room of the forge, Garris falling back into a chair, sulking, shoving the gold royals into his pockets. Before we left the room, I made triple sure to turn my head and stick out my tongue at the prick.

Bella rushed beside me out of the forge. We locked arms, and my core heated like a furnace. Following the dark prince, with his cape flowing behind his massive shoulders, its cape tails glided along the floor like ribbons cut to the exact length to not discolor at its tips.

In some strange way, there was a feeling of safety that enveloped me like a warm bath after being out in an ice storm with frozen fingers. Even though I knew he was evil, even though I knew his reputation, even though I dreaded where we might be going and what horrible things might await—it was exhilarating. All of it.

And then there were the dragons…

Going out into the last bit of daylight, as soon as we stepped foot outside the forge, it was all that filled my vision.

Massive. Terrifying. Enchanting. Dangerous.

Krakos was waiting just outside the forge, filling the entire square. The endless South Cape Sea whipped with crashing waves beyond the dark dragon. The hills that surrounded Bramblebash rose high, making the tiny town feel as if it was the whole world. After all, it was for me. I didn't remember anything else but this shit town.

Beyond Krakos, another dragon waited. It was stone-gray with black stripes down its back and the webbing on its wings. It was smaller than Krakos, but almost every dragon was—even half the black dragon's size was impressive. And the dragon that waited behind Krakos was slimmer, with pale white eyes like clouds, and small crimson horns all the way up the sides of its snout and up to the two huge curling ones. Its rider leaped down from the saddle as we approached.

My chest tightened, and Bella squeezed my arm hard. I gulped.

Once we were out in the courtyard of Bramblebash, there were so many gazes upon us from all their hiding holes; I thought it was a weird way for the town to say goodbye. I'd known them, and they'd known me my whole life. But as a low slave, the only respect ever given was between all us slaves. I wouldn't miss a single one of the others and their high noses and disdainful glares.

"I'll miss the children," Bella whispered into my ear. "That's all."

"We'll come back to see them again," I lied.

I had no illusion we would ever be back, even with the threat I promised to Garris.

The prince spun, his cape tails flowing behind him. Suddenly, unchained and standing before my new master, he seemed like a mountain of a man. He glared down at us, his iceberg-blue eyes shimmering like perfect waters behind his black metal mask.

The smoldering smell of dragonfire burned my nostrils. It was an ancient kind of burning, like brimstone and some sort of rock being scorched by unnatural, god-like heat. The man behind the prince joined him at his side. He was shorter, but not by much. He wore dazzling copper-colored armor with accents of black at its tips, and his helmet framed his handsome face perfectly. His tan skin glistened in the fading sunlight to the west, shimmering on his carved nose and perfect lips. His auburn hair gusted at his brow as the winds picked up.

"Oh my," Bella gasped. "He's gorgeous."

"Don't get ahead of yourself. We don't know these men. They could be worse than Garris. Keep it together. Stay close to each other."

"My prince," the rider in copper armor said. His professional demeanor changed immediately as he eyed us, and he raised an eyebrow. "So, this is the Gold-Marked? And why are there two of them?"

"I—I did it just to spite that bastard. Less toys for him."

Toys? I was no fucking toy…

"We ride then?" The rider in copper turned to the side, revealing the dragon behind him, snorting with plumes of thick smoke erupting from its huge nostrils.

"We ride." The prince glared down at me with an icy gaze. "You're coming with us whether you want to or…"

My feet couldn't move quickly enough. As I ran toward the monstrous dragon, thinking only of all the dreams I'd had of the freedom that came with riding such a magical creation, my legs caught. I was so eager to get up onto the dragon's back that I stumbled over my own two feet. I caught myself with my hands on the sandy cobblestones, and I instantly felt the heat of embarrassment flush my cheeks.

The rider in copper chuckled, but the prince never took his stoic gaze off me. I got to my feet and brushed my knees off. "Tripped on a rock…" I said, trying to play it off cool.

"Come." The prince's voice was commanding as he spun and walked toward his great dragon. I slowed my breath and walked deliberately beside him. The rider in copper waved for Bella to join him, and she walked shyly, with her hands before her and her chin tucked to her chest.

Even if I wanted to run, or escape from the wicked prince, the dragon was too enticing. Also, the enormous sword at the prince's side was surely swift enough to catch me. Not to mention the hidden magical staff he made appear only minutes ago. That made me think about my own magic. I would have looked at my hands were I able to take my eyes off Krakos. It was the single most magnificent and horrifying creature I'd ever seen, and I couldn't wait to get up on that saddle and into the air! I wanted to feel that air rush through my hair and smell the smoke from its mouth!

"Up." The prince pointed up at the saddle as the dark dragon unfolded its wing before me, like a set of stairs being laid out before a princess.

You're no princess. You're still a slave. He's taking you to the queen because you used magic against him, I had to remind myself. You may be about to ride a dragon, but you're a prisoner.

"Go on," the prince said. Before I walked up the huge wing, I looked to see Bella getting up onto the other dragon, with the rider in copper getting into the saddle behind her. I quickly looked at the huge prince next to me in the most wicked, extravagant, expensive armor I'd ever seen, and realized he was going to be sitting behind me.

My knees buckled, and my stomach tightened. That mountain of a man was taking me for a ride, and the thought of him touching any part of me made my ears hot and cheeks flush.

I walked up the wing, feeling the sturdy scales under my fingernails, scraping as I climbed. My leg went over the saddle, and its leather squealed under my pant leg. I cupped the horn of the saddle in both hands, subconsciously bumping up and down with excitement. Thrill ran so feverishly through me that I didn't even notice the prince run up the wing, throwing one leg over the saddle directly behind me.

His inner, strong thighs cupped my hips. I swallowed hard. Both our legs were spread as we sat upon Krakos' back. His warmth poured into me, still chilly from standing naked for so long. His raw power made me feel like a child again and strangely, like I was safe.

The prince's arm suddenly slid under my arm and wrapped around my stomach. He pulled me into him. I nearly lost all my breath as he pulled me completely against him—his chest, his stomach, and his legs. We were so close that I felt we were nearly one.

My lips parted, and I moaned without meaning to. He whistled. It pierced the air, echoing all around the walls of my tiny beach town. Or former tiny beach town—my smirk turned to a wide, toothy grin.

Krakos rose to its hind legs, and even more so, I was shoved back into the prince. But he didn't move. He didn't move a fucking muscle. There was so much muscle behind me, squeezing me into him. I'd never been so hot; I swear. I didn't care how bad he was or how mean. I shifted in the saddle, driving my ass into his groin, and he squeezed me harder with his arm. His breath heated my neck.

"Ready?" His low voice growled.

"Abso-fucking-lutely."

With his free hand, he flicked the reins, and Krakos' wings flapped. The air whooshed under them, sending sand flying in all directions. One flap, then another, and then another, and before I knew it, we were hovering in the air, twenty feet above the ground.

Many came out of their homes and shops to witness the great dragons take us. But not Garris. That little weasel couldn't even stand the sight of me or the prince who'd bought me for five measly royals.

My hands grasped the saddle's horn as hard as I could. The thrill erupted through me as Krakos took to the sky.

I couldn't contain my excitement anymore. After all those years of watching dragon riders split the sky, and I was finally up there myself. And all of a sudden the world looked so, so small. I screamed as he lifted us up into the air.

It was the freest I'd ever felt.

I didn't care where we were going.

I didn't care what was going to happen to me.

All I cared about was that moment.

And I never, ever wanted it to end.

CHAPTER 6

*T*he winds bit hard at my face. Brimstone filled my nostrils and stained my hair, which whipped violently at my shoulders. The first glimpse of moonlight beamed directly ahead as the town of Bramblebash turned into a speck on the horizon behind.

I'd never felt so... free.

Everywhere was at my fingertips, and the lands of Allovan made my breath catch in my throat. It was so vast. So wonderfully, beautifully, breathtakingly vast. Snow-capped mountains, rich rivers that snaked through plains and forests, all beneath my feet, and beneath the dragon that carried me through the sky.

Everything about it made me feel the most alive I'd ever felt.

The prince behind me sat stoically, like a deep-rooted tree. And as the tight grip of his arm went from holding me around the top of my waist, just under my breasts, dropping to the bottom of my stomach, I felt a rush of excitement throughout my entire body. The way he pulled me into him made me feel enchantingly vulnerable. I licked my lips subconsciously, not wanting him to see. I belonged to him now, and as much as I hated it, I had to admit to myself that being owned by a powerful prince was a tall step up from the miserable prick back down there in the forge.

No more mopping in the summer heat, scrubbing dishes for endless hours, being on my knees polishing hard-to-reach armor sets, and no more greasy-fingered men running their fingers through my hair. God, I hated that more than I hated those squeaky rodents that came out at night and skittered across my pillowcase. Ugh, disgusting vile men they were!

I wanted to ask where we were going, where he was taking me, but I didn't want the moment to end. I didn't want to think about landing somewhere, or being taken to the infamous castle of Raven's Bane, erected upon the monumental mountain—Calcaedus, the grandest peak of all Allovan, standing one hundred times taller than any other mountain peak on the continent. I'd only seen it in my dreams, but I imagined it to be the most inspiring, and at the same time—intimidating sight in all the world.

The Blaze Prince cocked the reins to the side suddenly, causing Krakos' right wing to drop, and we tore through the sky at breakneck speeds. The moonlight glowed pale heavenly light as the sun faded under the far western edge of Allovan. Krakos pulled his wings in tight as we dove through the thick, dark clouds. The moist smell of the clouds filled my nostrils, and I felt my stomach in my throat as we dropped, falling at the most thrilling speed I could have ever imagined.

As we dove, my eyes glossed over from the biting winds, and my fingertips dug into the prince. The smell of the crisp air filled my nostrils, mixed with the intoxicating aroma of dragonfire. We burst through pillowy clouds like they belonged to us.

I couldn't help it—a thrilling scream flew from my mouth as I hollered in excitement. My scream barely hit my ears, as the rushing winds drowned out everything. My hands gripped the saddle's horn as tightly as they could, pulling myself into the dragon, as the prince pulled me in tightly to him. His chin inched over my shoulder, and his helmeted face was right next to mine. His brilliant eyes made my neck heat and my toes tingle.

But there was something else that drew every morsel of my attention, something firm pressed into my back, something thick and hard above my belt.

Could it be? He couldn't be... No, I'm certain of it... He's getting hard, pulling me into it.

Oh my god... he's as hard as iron back there.

His eyes didn't show it, and by the way he whipped the dragon's reins, it didn't slow his drive to send Krakos careening through the pillowy, gray clouds.

My legs straddled the saddle, my fingernails scratched at the horn, and I bit the side of my lip. His long black hair tickled the side of my neck, as I felt his raw power. The prince was a born warrior; fearless. Odiun knows how powerful he was, and I was in his arms.

By the gods, I never even saw his face, but I wanted him. I wanted him to take my chin in his fingers, turn my head, remove that devilishly crafted mask, and put his lips onto mine. Fuck, I didn't even know what he looked like, but that rock-hard cock digging into my back was driving me fucking insane.

It had been a year since I last was with a man, and I described that best to Bella as a man convulsing on top of me until he lay in a panting, sweaty mess.

But this man, the prince, this legendary soldier, this powerhouse—I'd never felt so vulnerable, so susceptible, so enthralled. And damn, that cock felt huge...

Descending swiftly through the clouds in the magical moonlight, I felt as if we were drifting toward the top of a mountain just below us. It was the highest peak around, with the rest of the mountain range cresting down on two sides. The dragon's wings spread wide to slow our descent. And all the while, even when Krakos' feet touched the rocky ground, that cock still dug into my back.

Even when the prince released his grip on me, sliding his arm out from around my stomach, I was in no hurry to get down from the saddle, and that oh-so-amazing feeling.

"You can get down now," he grumbled. But I could hear something else in his voice, something animalistic, something barbaric. There was a wild animal inside him, most definitely caused down in his pants, and if he would've asked, I would've done almost anything he asked me to. Krakos nuzzled against the prince as we both got off. The great black dragon groaned as the prince petted its massive head.

Their bond is amazing... if that dragon trusts him... maybe there's something good about him...

What the hell is wrong with you, Ash? You don't even know him. He may be as evil as Gigas, Lord of the Underworld. I had just one time where the sex wasn't paid for, and I was treated like a woman, not a piece of meat...

"Ash!" Bella ran to me, and shaking off the powerful urges filling my body and hips, I leaped down from the huge black dragon. Krakos' neck arched, and he glared at the two of us as we embraced. His devilish, serpentine, dark slits of pupils in his fiery eyes glared at us curiously, and I glared right back.

"You all right?" I asked, releasing our embrace.

She nodded. "Better than alright." She let out a tremendous breath from deep in her lungs. "That was incredible. I'll never forget that as long as I live." She sighed deeply and brushed back the hair that was sweat-stuck to her brow.

Suddenly, I realized the two soldiers had us surrounded. They stood on both sides of Bella and me—towering over—I should say.

"Wh-what are we doing here?" I tried hard to keep from fidgeting with my hands, so I shoved them into my pockets.

The rider in copper seemed to be waiting for the prince to be the one to respond.

"We'll make camp here tonight," the prince pressed both

hands to the sides of his sharp, angled helmet that made him look like a dark wolf god—or demon, rather. As he lifted the helmet up, I had to force my teeth to clench, to avoid my jaw hitting the ground.

As he lifted his helmet off, and his long dark hair folded down to his shoulders like silk drapes, I couldn't tear my gaze off him.

Oh my god. He's fucking gorgeous...

My knees buckled as I remembered his grip around my waist as I almost orgasmed flying on the back of that magnificent dragon.

His face was chiseled like a stone statue. Cleanly shaven, with a firm jaw that could chip marble, and lips that pulled at the strings of mine, the prince was as handsome as any man from any story I'd ever heard. As his blue eyes pierced through me, sending unbelievably powerful waves rushing through me, every desire sparked aflame in me, and I wanted him to touch me again. I craved—hell, begged—for him to touch any part of me again.

Instead, he stood there with a glare frosted with blizzard snow.

"We'll camp here until I decide what to do with you tomorrow." He propped his helmet under his arm, as the rider in copper went to the prince's side.

Bella whispered, "I don't think I'd rather be stuck with any two other men in the world right now..."

I just nodded, my lips finally separated, hot breath squeezing out.

"I hope that feeling ends up being right," I whispered back. "Because we are stuck with them, at least for now..."

The rider in copper went off, striding out onto the mountaintop.

We were in a flat expanse near the very top of the mountain, just above the tree line, which the rider in copper walked down toward.

The prince took down a large bag from his dragon, unbuckling it. I had to fight hard to not completely stare at him as he did so. He took the pack, walked over, and handed it to me, which I took, and it was far heavier-looking than I thought. It nearly pulled me down forward, and the prince's perfect lips curved to a smirk, only just slightly, but enough for me to see some playfulness in there.

As he turned, his fingertips traced the length of my forearm, igniting a current beneath my skin. His devilishly handsome gaze caught mine—so deep and consuming that heat erupted from my core like a volcano breaking open. The soft drag of his fingers sent a rush through me so fierce I swore steam might rise from my very breath. A hint of a smile ghosted across his lips—barely there, yet devastating. I wanted to melt into a puddle at his feet. He was the most dangerously beautiful man I'd ever seen. And when his touch finally fell away, I realized I'd been holding my breath, too spellbound to even gasp.

God help me, he's perfect.

"There are blankets in there. Cover yourselves up. We'll have a fire going shortly."

My feet hit the ground, and my mind whirled in so many directions. The butterflies that fluttered in my stomach darted away. The majesty and thrill of freedom from being upon the dragon's back high in the clouds flushed from me. New thoughts flooded my brain like a dam bursting wide open.

First, the prince had to think about what to do with us? He didn't know? There we were on top of a giant mountain, with no plan? I was sure he was taking us to Raven's Bane Castle, and to the Blaze Queen. If we weren't going there, then where?

Second, and with every passing second, the sensation and curiosity inside me compounded to an anxious thrill, and overwhelming sense of dread. The magic that poured out of me, and was somewhere deep inside, was what caused all this mess. It slumbered so deeply I couldn't feel a thing. I never had any hint that anything was different about me until I saw that dragon coming down from the sky ready to kill everything within reach of its awful flames.

What was it? Where did it come from? And why in the Infernal Depths was it in me?

There was never anything special about me. Hell, that's all I'd pretty much heard since I was born. Even the way people looked at me spoke volumes about how they viewed me. The snarls, the eye rolls, lips curling down. It all spelled that I was lower than low.

I was meant to scrub, not shine.

"What's wrong?" Bella pinched my elbow skin. Her voice was brave, showing no fear of those around the forge listening in anymore. Actually, there wasn't anyone for miles, and I craved that feeling—the feeling of freedom.

I sighed, but she spoke again before I had the chance to.

"At least we're together. We can get through this, as long as we have each other. I know that glowing thing on your neck changed everything. But we can figure it out. We can learn what it was and maybe even how to use it again! There's always hope!"

That's Bella... always looking for the sweet center of the sourest fruit.

"Yeah," was all I managed to say.

"But for now..." She took me in a huge hug, and spun me to stand before her. "Just burn that image into your brain."

Before us were the two dragons, still standing on their tree trunk legs, muscle rippling through them behind their thick scales. Smoke smoldered out of their black nostrils, steaming up and into the crisp mountain winds. The moonlight glistened off their massive bodies and wings like the same light that lit the ocean waves they saw through their barred windows in Bramble-bash. Beyond, the world was cast under a dark veil of night. The clouds cast long shadows that crawled along the world below.

And then there were the stars. Bella came to my side, and we both marveled at the infinite, pinpricked sky with millions of lights beaming in the heavens.

A deep inhale took the night air into my lungs, the thin air making the hairs on my head stiffen. That breathtaking view of the dragons and the world below would stay in my memory forever.

No matter what happened, at least I didn't die with fresh whip marks on my back, buried in a shallow grave or cast out to sea with chains strapped to my ankles, decomposing slowly with my flesh being nibbled away until there was nothing left.

At least I had that moment, and no one could ever take that away from me.

CHAPTER 7

*W*hen I say this was the coolest fucking way I'd ever seen a fire made, I mean... the coolest!

The rider in copper threw the logs in the center of the clearing on the mountaintop. No kindling, no starter, no cotton. Just a pile of broken limbs, wind-worn and battered.

Krakos approached at the command of its rider. It arched its neck, angling its colossal head down at the pile of wood.

"Firas." The prince's voice was firm but had a hint of friendship in it as well.

As the dragon's chest expanded, the inner flames glowed between the flexed scales, casting a golden light all around the mountaintop. Krakos' maw erupted with flames, and the searing dragonfire burst onto the logs, incinerating them in the hellish fire. We were twenty feet away, and both of us had to throw up our arms to shield the heat from our skin.

To my side, I saw the prince and his rider both stand motionless, stoic like statues, their wild hair whipping behind them madly. In the intense light of the dragonfire, the prince looked even more devilishly handsome. The angles of his jaw, his perfectly straight nose, and his strong chin made the blood in my veins rush like a river. My nipples hardened and scratched against the frayed shirt that gusted from the flames.

The fires receded back to Krakos, and the great ebony dragon stared into his work, the fire below reflecting in his savage, primal eyes. The slits in them reminded me of a serpent's, yet much wiser. Krakos seemed fiercely intelligent for such a monstrous beast.

Krakos turned and lay beside the other dragon at the edge of the mountain.

Bella and I both waited for the two men to give instructions. After all, we were the prince's property. Dreams of escape would have to wait. And from there, there was nowhere to run, anyway.

"Go on." The prince pointed to the fire. "Get warm."

"What about you?" I blurted out the words before my stupid brain could catch up with what I should have said, not what I wanted to ask.

"We have things to discuss." The prince grabbed his rider by the arm and led him away to the opposite edge of the mountain, both with their backs turned to us.

Bella and I sat by the fire, and the warmth felt incredible on my hands and shins. I didn't know if the dragons instinctively did it or not, but they seemed perfectly placed to block the fierce mountain winds. Maybe they didn't do it for us, but the fire they created?

We sat side by side with our arms touching, huddling under the blankets the prince had given us.

"What do you think they're gonna end up doing with us?" Bella's gaze was hard upon the burning flames.

"I don't know. I really don't." My certainty of being flown off to Emberveil was fizzling.

"Everything's so different. So fast. I don't know what to think of it." Bella, with her elbows on her thighs, cradled her face in her palms. "Yesterday we were stuck in our lives, dreaming of something like this, but I never, ever, would have imagined we'd be sitting here, right here, right now. I mean, look at that view. I couldn't dream of something so beautiful. And it's all because of you, Ash. I always knew there was something special about you, but I never could have guessed like this."

She thought I was different? I thought I was the most boring, obnoxious girl in existence.

"You did?"

She released her face and tucked her chin onto her shoulder, staring at me. "You never felt anything? Maybe not everyone noticed you, but I sure as shit did."

"What do you mean?"

"By Odiun, you're daft. Why do you think we're so close? You're different, Ash. The way you look at things. Your slyness, your cunning, your imagination. There's no one in Bramblebash even close to you. Even the way you look is so different from everyone else. As soon as I saw you years ago for the first time, I knew there was something different in you. And here you sit now, using magic to protect me from a mad dragon breathing fire. Was I ever right!"

"Can I tell you something?" I didn't know if I should bring it up to her, as it might make it that much more real in my mind, but the voice I heard, I couldn't stop thinking about it. "I—I heard a voice after I used my magic. I would've thought it was myself talking to me, but it was so different than any voice I'd ever heard. It sounded old, manly, and... beastly?"

"Beastly? Something said something in your head? You must have been making it up. But on second thought..." She scratched her chin. "Maybe it was real? If you heard it right after that magic cast through you, maybe someone or something helped you. To save us both? I don't know... what did it say?"

The words were etched like stone in me, as if permanently marked on a gravestone. It said, "It is time. You must free me. You've awoken to your true self, and so, must you awaken me..."

Bella didn't respond. She pulled into herself, recoiling, and rubbed her arms, glaring at the firelight. Krakos groaned as he stretched his enormous wings.

"I know… sounds crazy…" I huffed.

"Nothing sounds crazy anymore…"

So deep in thought, I didn't notice the prince until he entered the corner of my vision. He and the rider in copper both walked over and stood on the other side of the fire. Both sets of their armor shimmered in the golden light, capped with moonlight reflecting off their backs. The prince's cape wafted at his heels, tickling the hard ground.

"Did you figure out what to do with me?" I mustered the words as bravely as I could. I feared what the answer would be, but I figured it was better to know than not.

"We fly in the morning." The prince flapped his cape back with his hands and sat on a log; the other rider did the same.

"Where?" I pressed.

"None of your concern," the prince growled. His gaze never returned to mine.

"I beg to differ." God, I really needed to learn to keep my mouth closed. But years of being whipped for saying the wrong things had the opposite reaction my masters intended. I cared so much less about lashings than they expected. Pain was temporary, wounds healed, but those fragments of freedom stacked up one by one, building the wall that protected me, kept me safe, and kept me sane.

"Watch your tone with your prince." The rider in copper waved his hand out at me.

"It's all right, Hunter," the prince said.

Hunter? That only made me more curious about the prince. What was his name? Where was he born? What was his relationship with the Blaze Queen like? What was the capital like? Where did he learn his magic?

So many questions, and I knew getting answers from him was going to be like running through a field of prickly cacti.

"Let her talk back like that." The prince gave me a nasty scowl. "I like it. It's just going to make all the rest that much easier."

All strength left my body, gushing out beneath me, seeping into the mountain. This was the Blaze Prince, the most murderous man in all of Allovan. He could do a whole hell of a lot worse pain to me than cuts in my back.

"I'll grab some food." Hunter rose and walked over to his dragon, rummaging through one of the leather packs.

That just left the three of us. I got tired of the silence, so I broke it. "How did you start riding your dragon?"

He laughed and shook his head, letting his long black hair drift before his eyes and brow.

"Be careful," Bella whispered.

"When did you know you had magic?" I pressed. "And how did you learn to use it?"

He stopped laughing, rubbing his knuckles.

When he spoke, his voice was dark, sinister, twisted. "Do you have any idea how long I've been looking for you? How long the Blaze Queen has sought the Gold-Marked?"

His question deflated me like squashing a cockroach under a thick boot. I was in so far over my head. I was so curious about the handsome prince; I forgot the stakes.

"I—I've never heard that term, and I never saw that thing on my neck before. I swear. I didn't mean anything by it... I'll never do it again if you don't hurt Bella. I'll try to do whatever you ask."

Hunter returned with food in hand but paused at the current conversation.

"You have no clue how happy this is going to make my step-mother," the prince said. I gasped at the term stepmother. I had always assumed she was his real mother. "You are important to her mission of saving this world, ending the war, and creating a new, bright future."

There was something different in the prince's demeanor then. He wasn't all-knowing, all-powerful, and the top predator. There was the slightest hint of apprehension in his voice and in the tiniest twitch of his eye. He was scared. He was scared of the queen. I knew the look of fear all too well in Bramblebash. It lurked around every corner, waiting for its moment to consume.

"What are you going to do with us?" Bella's fingers dug into his knees as she asked that.

Hunter approached her, his armor glowing an even more brilliant shade of golden copper. He handed her two sticks of dried meat, crackers, and hard white cheese. "For slaves, you two ask an awful lot of questions."

We didn't have a response for that. After all, he was right. We were nothing more than slaves. Always had been, and had no reason to believe we'd be anything different, ever.

"You'll find out tomorrow." Hunter then handed me the same food, and I snatched it eagerly, my stomach rumbling at the smell of the smoked meat. "Just relax and rest." The rider looked deep into my eyes, raising an eyebrow at something he saw. He sighed. "Don't worry. Cade and I aren't going to harm you as long as you do what we say. We'll be back on the dragons tomorrow, and we're going somewhere safe. Trust that."

The prince laughed and cracked his knuckles. "Just don't make me throw you off the side of this cliff tonight. Keep all the questions to yourself. I'm not here to do what you say. It's the opposite. I own you now. And you'll behave."

Cade? The prince's name is Cade? Even when he's threatening my life, I can't help but remember his rock-hard dick stabbing into my back.

My mouth watered. I smacked my lips slightly and touched my inner thigh with my bare fingers.

"Yes, sir." The words slid out of my mouth like I'd do anything if he'd only let me touch him. My mind swirled, and as I stared at his perfect face, I felt Bella's elbow jab me in my ribs. "What? I wasn't being sarcastic this time!"

"You two are going to be a handful," Hunter laughed, shaking his head. "I can already tell."

"Just eat and go to sleep," the prince said, accepting the handful of food from his rider. "We've got a long flight ahead of us tomorrow."

Adrenaline spiked through my core, up my arms and into the follicles of the hairs on my head. We were going to ride the dragons through the sky again. That was the new drug I knew I'd chase the rest of my life, no matter its length. I'd forgo mead, pipe tobacco, even wine for another taste of that freedom!

Not only did logic overcome my urge to attack the prince with my endless list of questions, but my heavy eyelids tugged as well. As the food hit my stomach, a deep fatigue washed over me like a warm, soft blanket after a cold dip in the frigid sea.

I slunk into the front of the log, rested my head against the blanket I had wrapped around me, and fell into a deep, dream-filled slumber.

CHAPTER 8

Upon the dragon's back, the world felt incomparably small compared to how it felt before. I could go anywhere, see anything, become someone new. My old world felt like a nightmare, left in the past to rot. Brisk morning winds tore through my hair. The smell of the soft clouds filled my nostrils, sending the hairs on the back of my neck straight. The saddle's horn between my legs was my anchor to the mighty Krakos, and I'd never let go.

Below, the forests looked oh so different than they did on the ground. The tops of the trees danced in the cool breeze. The sunlight cascaded off the canopy, making it look like a rippling sea of trees. The plains rolled on endlessly, and the mountains and rivers broke up the vast world like a puzzle, perfectly fitted together over the millennia.

And to top it all off, the prince's muscular arm gripped me tightly around my waist, just under my breasts, and his muscly legs cradled me between them. He had his dark metal wolf mask back on, but the way he held me made me feel more like a prize than a possession.

Get that thought out of your head, Ash. He didn't buy you to be his lover. He bought you because of the magic inside of you. That's all he's interested in... I mean, look at him... and look at me...

"You see that down there?" He pointed to a snaking river through an expansive grassland. "Do you know what that is?"

I shook my head.

"That's the Salazan. As beautiful a river as they come. They say that's where the Dydrus swims."

"The Dydrus?" I scratched my cheek with one hand and rested my other on the arm that gripped me tight.

"The Great Water Spirit. A god of the old world."

"An old god? A water spirit?" Amber sunlight glistened on the river below, causing it to look as though it was lit from underneath by a rock bed of pure gold, emanating from the fires of the Infernal Depths. "I've never heard of it."

The prince didn't answer but gave a curious groan behind his mask. Because he didn't answer, I shifted in the saddle, pressing back into him slightly. Every ounce of me wanted to feel him get excited again, even though he never acknowledged the last time. I wanted to feel him again. My dreams were filled with thoughts of him naked, and all I wanted to do was spin in the saddle, press my lips to his, and shove my hand down into his pants. I hadn't had a sex dream like that in a very long time, and the fantasy consumed me. It was driving me insane...

My hand on his arm forced his grip tighter around my rib cage. I dreamed of him putting his strong hand down my pants, sliding between my legs, and using me however he wanted.

"And that," he pointed to a meandering set of hills past the huge snaking Salazan River, "that's the Brakenstone Ridge. And beyond that is..."

"The Faewood," I muttered.

"You know it?"

"I've heard the songs. We sang them often at night after supper. There was even an old painting on one wall of the forge.

I've always dreamed of going there and seeing the creatures the songs talk about."

"Well, I guess dreams can come true," the prince laughed. Krakos let out a roar that echoed for miles. The dragon behind returned the roar.

I guess dreams do come true... I never once in my life believed that saying, but here, now... I'm beginning to see that they can. At least for now. And on the back of this dragon flying through the air... this is enough. I've never felt this alive!

"We're going to the Faewood?" I asked, knowing the question probably wouldn't get an answer from the dark, stoic prince. And I was right.

Twenty minutes later, though, I got my answer, as we flew over the glowing Salazan River, over the Brakenstone Ridge Mountains, and the dragon began its descent—straight for the sprawling forest that seemed to go on endlessly. My heart hammered in my chest, and my palms sweated. One hand on the leather horn, the other on the back of his metal gauntlet.

The moment Krakos angled his wings down, dipped his head, and his long black tail raised behind us, a sadness overtook me. A heaviness settled in my chest, and my vision blurred. I didn't want that moment to end. I wanted to feel the wind gust in my hair, the rustle of my clothes, and the heat between my legs from the dragon's internal furnace.

The feeling of flying made me want the man who took me riding even more. The desire burst in me like the way Krakos blew the fire last night on the mountaintop, exploding the wood in an eruption of mind-whirling heat. I dreamed of the prince taking me on my back, thrusting deep into me, taking me, but... I didn't trust him. I didn't know him. And I sure as shit didn't want him taking me and Bella to a secluded place in the forest to torture me.

I had to figure out how to escape. That was our only real chance. Once we got to the forest and the men were asleep, I'd need to get Bella and me the hell out of there. I knew if we stayed with them long enough, we wouldn't like the end result. Freedom was the dream I truly wished for. And being a slave my entire life was not an option. I'd rather die than be tormented like I was back in Bramblebash. The taste of true freedom was far too sweet. And it was a taste I'd never forget as long as I lived.

The world whirled as we sped through the clouds, feeling their moisture on my cheeks. After we sped through the thick clouds, emerging beneath them, a glum haze overtook me. As Krakos delivered us toward the never-ending forest, gliding over the treetops like the super predator it was, the Faewood seemed as vast as the South Cape Sea itself. The branches flashed below us like the sea's waves too, the dread of landing sinking in deep.

Krakos slowed. His wings spread wide, and the wind caught in their massive sails. Ahead was a break in the treeline. It was a round clearing with a single, ancient tree poking out from the canopy like a tower as old as time itself. The prince pulled back hard on the reins, angling Krakos' neck back from the tug. The mighty dragon tilted back, letting out a chaotic roar, and sent my weight back into the prince.

The pressure built between us as my back fell onto his sturdy chest, and I felt his biceps tense as he pulled me in even tighter. I held on tight to the horn and his arm. Turning my head slightly, a break in his armor at the neck showed, and his enchanting smell caught my nostrils. My hair rippled at his neck as I breathed in deeply, smelling his musk. It was enough to make me reach my lips up and kiss that bare spot of his skin. His raw power was all over me—taming me, owning me, overpowering me.

The two dragons carried us into the clearing, landing below the enormous tree that rose three hundred feet from the ground. Once down, the prince released me, but not before there was movement down in his pants, throbbing into my back again. My mouth dried, and an inaudible moan pushed from my throat between my lips.

I didn't want to get down. I wanted to savor the moment, but as the dragon angled its huge wings down to the ground, I resiliently got up from the saddle and walked down the ebony-scaled wing. The prince remained on the saddle, glaring out into the Faewood.

Bella slid down the other dragon's wing and ran to me.

We stood together, side by side, watching the prince and Hunter scan the ancient forest. Both of them had their hands on the grips of their swords, and from the prince's free hand, his golden staff with the fiery bird's head emerged, wafting with wisps of magical smoke.

He stood and strode down the wing. I fought hard not to stare. But even the way he walked made my brain tingle and my tongue slide along my lips. Krakos and the other dragon sniffed the air, and both seemed calm as they stretched out their wings and stiffened their tails after the flight.

"Come," the prince said, not looking at either of us but motioning with his golden staff west.

We both followed, with Hunter walking behind. We were sandwiched between the two men, two of the most infamous riders in all of Allovan. It filled me simultaneously with a sense of safety and terror. There was no way out of this. Nowhere to run, only an endless forest that appeared as dense as a jungle, coursing with vines and dense brush.

"It's just up ahead." The prince was at the tree line, and we were not only leaving the clearing behind but the two dragons as well. I swallowed hard. But as the prince found a narrow trail that led out of the clearing, giving one last hard look around, he walked into the forest, and we both followed.

The world darkened instantly, and Bella's hand found me, clasping on as if that single grip would save us from anything that came from the dense, deep woods.

"Don't worry." Hunter's words from behind were indeed soothing, but we were two girls without weapons, so if anything came, it would be up to the two soldiers. I had no idea how to call my magic unless an evil dragon started descending on us again. And by the gods, I did not want that again! "We're almost there."

"This is the Faewood," Bella whispered into my ear. "They're not taking us to Raven's Bane Castle, or the queen…"

"We don't know anything yet." I scratched my cheek. "Just because we're not there doesn't mean we are out of danger."

But we both knew the truth. The prince bought and owned us. We were legally his in every sense of the word. I'd been a slave as long as I could remember, and the lack of knowing what the prince was like was the scariest thing of all.

After fifteen minutes of walking along the path, following the prince and his cape that scraped along it, we approached another clearing.

What I saw made my jaw slack. Bella's fingernails dug into my forearm as she gasped.

"It's a house," Bella gasped. "Or… a castle?"

In the middle of the clearing, a two-story building rose from the Faewood floor. Built into a bulbous ancient tree, the building consisted of piled stones, mortared together, embedded into the hollow tree. The tree had died long ago, with withered branches and a cracked base, but the shell of the old tree harbored half the building. The stonework looked hundreds of years old, possibly thousands.

As we approached, the front door opened wide, and an elderly woman walked out. She had curlers in her hair, a lace apron, and a crick in her back from her old age.

The four of us met the woman as the two dragons circled high in the sky.

"These two will be staying with us." The prince took his mask off, holding it at his side under the crook of his arm. The musty smell of his hair bit at my nostrils, and the skin on my arms and legs tingled. "Make them comfortable."

"Will you be staying, my prince?" The old woman's crow's feet deepened at the corners of her eyes as she scanned Bella and me. Even from a couple of feet away, the smell of strong tobacco smoke wafted with her.

"We will be in and out," the prince said. "We have things that need attending, and questions that need answers." He suddenly turned toward me. "This is Rosa. She will tend to you while I am away. Treat her with respect, or you'll have to answer to me. And…" His enchanting eyes narrowed upon me. "…Stay put. Do not wander off into these woods. There's more than what you heard in songs roaming the Faewood. The last thing I need is you getting yourself killed while I'm away. Understand?" He raised a finger between my eyes. "Got it? Stay here!"

Locked in his gaze, seeing past the fiery speech, I was lost. I nodded, dumbfounded by his rugged handsomeness. His firm jaw, his perfect nose, his dark eyebrows, and the long hair that swooshed along the sides of his face. The muscles of his neck and the sharpness of his Adam's apple—I'd never seen anyone so gorgeous in all my life.

"Good." The prince took off his gauntlets. "Rosa, would you show them to their rooms, please?"

"Where—" The question left my mouth before my brain had recovered from his face so close to mine. "Where will you be?"

The prince scoffed, rubbing his nose and turning his back to me. My brow furrowed, and I picked at my fingernails behind my back.

"We will be here and away while we figure some things out," Hunter said, also removing his gauntlets. They walked to the far side of the house, toward the half built into the tree.

"Come, my darlings," the old woman said as she opened the door wide for us. "You must be famished."

CHAPTER 9

With a pop of the lock, the inside of the house in the enchanted forest revealed itself. Rosa ushered us in with a bow and a wave of her hand. The inside of the house was as immaculately clean and furnished as any room I had ever seen.

Smooth wooden floorboards shone under the sunlight that poured through the oval windows. Table skirts lined the two long tables in the main room, both a vibrant green color with golden trim, and a great spindly chandelier hung between the two. Rocking chairs of fine craftsmanship rested before the massive hearth at the room's far end, between two doors that were shut. I wondered what lay behind them.

Rosa slid the skeleton key from the keyhole and tucked it into her pocket, closing the door behind us, which I also noticed had a keyhole and not a lock. I'd grown up with those doors, so I was trained to see if I was free to leave a room or not. In this case, we were stuck.

"I'll prepare supper fer' ya," the old woman said, rushing to the open room adjacent to the main one, a lavish kitchen with two wood-burning stoves and a vast table on their backside. It was topped with a massive slab of black stone with spiderweb-like veins streaming throughout. "Go wash up in those rooms. I've laid out fresh clothes for ya when you're washed up."

I didn't know what to think. Fresh clothes? What in the world was going on in this place? And why was this woman cooking us dinner? She had to be a slave too.

Bella shot a curious gaze at me with a raised eyebrow, and I believed I returned the expression. My clothes were tattered, singed, and smelled deeply of dragon. My arms were tainted with black charcoal-like filth from the dragon's breath blowing back at us, my ankles still bled through the scabs, and my hair was knotting. I couldn't deny that a bath and clean clothes, regardless of our situation, sounded like the most fabulous dream I could pray for.

"Guess we don't have a choice." Bella pulled out the sides of her pant legs; charred and torn. "I'd say let's race, but I may take my time with this one."

"Abso-fucking-lutely I am as well!" We both raced to the rooms. She reached hers first because of those long goddamn legs of hers, and she let out the most thrilling scream I'd ever heard from her in my life, and when I opened my door, I felt myself scream. Not from my mouth though, it was a full-on deep gush from within. As I saw the mattress fitted with clean, fluffy sheets and two white pillows, my stomach shot into my heart. My fists clenched and my hands bobbed at the sides of my head uncontrollably. A huge smile lit my face, and at the first sight of the tub filled with steaming water in the room's corner, I couldn't tear my clothes off fast enough. I didn't even close the damn door behind me. Hell, I was so used to being naked in front of disgusting men, what would I care about an old woman who was cooking me fucking supper?

I would've jumped into the porcelain tub, but a sudden logic appeared out of nowhere, screaming at me to not waste the hot, soapy water, so instead, I slowly slid my toes in first, then my aching ankle, and then my bare leg. It felt like heaven. After a ride on the most ravishing, thrilling dragon in all of Allovan, that bath took my breath away. I slid in like a rainbow gliding into a soft, pillowy cloud.

I let the warm water rise to my ears, held my breath, closed my eyes, and submerged myself. The soap slathered my hair, and my fingernails scratched my scalp, sending waves of ecstasy down to my core, and beyond. All the pain in me evaporated with the steam, and all was right for those breathtaking minutes.

When the water finally cooled, and my limbs went as limp as banana peels, I dried off with the softest towel I'd ever touched, surely soft enough for a queen. I walked to the bed and sat. The cushiony mattress enveloped my legs, and I looked at the clothes Rosa had laid out for me.

There was a velvety blue top with a low-cut collar and sleeves that went to the bottom of the shoulder; the cuffs were a darker shade of blue and purple stitching. The pants were deep gray with pockets at the front and back, and a tan leather belt curled beside them. New undergarments were the first to get on, and as soon as the fresh white cloth hit my clean skin, I moaned hard. The sigh that followed might be like how I sounded while a man kissed my neck, but when the rest of the clothes wrapped around my body, a deep moan came as if I had just done so.

Leaping into the air, I crashed onto the soft mattress, lying on my back as if lying in a grassy field in the springtime, peering up at the passing clouds. But something made my ear twitch. It was like the scraping of claws on wood. My stomach lurched up into my throat, and my fingernails raked the sheets.

I wanted to yell out through the still-open door, but instead, I reached deep within, hoping it wasn't a slimy snake or a putrid skunk, or... one of those little tiny furry things with tails...

I pulled my head over the edge of the bed with all the courage I could muster, and to my absolute astonishment, it was none of those things. But it certainly was much bigger!

"A—A turtle? How the hell did you get in here? You sure as shit weren't here when I…"

The turtle was two feet high from belly to top of its murky green shell. Its legs were like tree stumps, propping up its immense body, and its wrinkled, triangular face angled up at me. Old beyond my age surely, with big yellow eyes streaked with fiery oranges and deep reds. It had blue stripes on both sides of its head, from its beak to inside its shell.

"How in Odiun did you get in here, big guy? I don't think I've ever seen a turtle as big as you in all my life!"

"Turtle?" The animal said the word with such finely articulated clarity out of its beak I nearly wet myself. I shook my head in disbelief at first, but then scampered off the bed, ran to the table at the back of the room, fumbling with nervous fingers for the metal candlestick and holding it between the talking turtle and myself.

"I'm dreaming! I have to be dreaming!"

The turtle slowly moved its legs, pointing toward me. I gulped deeply, my palms sweating against the cold metal.

"You're not dreaming, and if you'd be so kind as to stop calling me by that name, and address me by my proper pedigree: Tortoise, please. Turtles are such… small, simple creatures…"

"You're… you're a talking turtle…? I mean… tortoise?" I shook the candlestick, ready to strike. "Stay away from me! Wake up, Ash, wake up. This is so silly. This is the dumbest dream you've had in forever. Wake up!"

"You are awake," the tortoise said, blinking slowly. He smacked his lips, the wrinkles around his beak deepening. "In fact, you're more awake than you've been in your whole life, I might add."

"What are you talking about? Who are you? What are you? And how did you get in this room?"

The slow-moving tortoise did little to soothe my nerves. I

squeezed the candlestick so tightly I thought I was about to snap the solid metal in half.

"Let's start with introductions. You are Ash, and I am Cornelius. Pleased to finally meet you." The tortoise closed his big eyelids and bowed his head slowly.

"You have a name? And you're talking? Great..." I threw my hands up in the air. "That's it. I've officially lost the roost. I'm insane. It's official!"

"You're far from insane," Cornelius the tortoise said, lifting his head back up to look squarely at me. "You may be the most sane person in all of Allovan. But to be fair, I haven't spoken to a human in what... a dozen years? Strange creatures you are. Not many things walk on hind legs with their arms hanging like ropes."

I set the candlestick down on its base and rubbed my eyes.

This can't be real. This can't be real. It has to be a dream.

"This is very, very real, Ash," the tortoise said with an intense, ethereal gaze in his large yellow eyes filled with golds, oranges and a deep wisdom. "Your power has awakened, and so... I have come to show you your path." His knowing eyes narrowed. "Your life is nothing like what it was before your magic woke. Be prepared, Ash. You are about to change this world... forever..."

There was a knock at the door. I spun. Bella was fully in the doorframe, leaning on one arm, and her eyes were as wide as I'd ever seen them. Her jaw dropped so hard I thought it might burst through the floorboards at her feet.

"I—It can't be real," I muttered, pointing behind me at the tortoise. "It talked to me."

"Ash." Bella finally picked her jaw back up. "I've never seen anything like it! Wow! Absolutely ravishing!"

It took me far too long of a moment, but I finally noticed Bella was staring straight at me, and refusing to look at the tortoise I was pointing to right behind me.

"Don't you see it?" My whole head dropped as I turned back

to the tortoise. My chin collapsed to my chest, and both my eyebrows blasted up in shock. There was… nothing… nothing but wet footprints that were my own. I ran over and kicked through the air where he had been. My leg struck nothing, and I felt like an absolute fool.

"Ash?" Bella raised an eyebrow. "Should I be worried about you?"

"I—I…" My head shook from side to side, trying to figure out what the hell had just happened.

Did I make up that whole thing? I even came up with a name for it.

I laughed so hard I slapped my thighs with a shrill cackle.

"Ash?"

"Yes, Bella… the clothes. They're to die for."

"Are you all right?"

"Oh, I thought I saw something, but I suppose I didn't."

"Girls, supper is ready. Please be present in tha' next ten minutes, or yer food'll get cold, and all my effort will have been fer' cold potatoes."

"I'm absolutely famished." Bella licked her lips. "C'mon. I don't want to wait."

She pulled me by the wrist out the door, and as I looked back to where the tortoise Cornelius had been, I saw the faintest shimmer of rainbow-colored light reflect off where his shell had been. Or where I thought it had been.

CHAPTER 10

The aromas from the table hit my nostrils as Bella pulled me from my room, my gaze hanging over my shoulder to where the tortoise named Cornelius was, and perhaps where I had left my sanity.

Rosa pulled out a chair for me without even a glance. She'd been doing this a long time, and I didn't think I'd ever had a chair pulled out for me in my life. I'd normally think there was a catch, some price to repay or some secret debt owed I wouldn't discover until later, but my gurgling tummy screamed for me not to worry and sit. On the green table skirt were three dishes, all covered with white kitchen towels.

Rosa scooted the chair in under me and then went to remove the napkins. What I saw before me made my taste buds tingle on the sides of my tongue. There was an enormous mound of roast beef slathered in its own brown juices, a heaping bowl of mashed potatoes, and lastly, a crunchy loaf of bread with jars of fresh butter and jam beside it.

"Are we waiting for… them?" Bella fought to take her gaze from the food to the front door, closed shut. I wasn't sure if the door was locked from the inside or not, but even if it was unlocked, the feast before me overtook any dreams of running off into the forest, seeking out true freedom.

"Begin, begin!" Rosa waved her arms overhead. "I didn't work on this all day to have you two sitting waiting for the men. One thing I've learned about powerful men over my lifetime is that you have to expect their work will always take precedence." She leaned in toward me, whispering into my ear, "And to always keep some food warm for them when they do finally show up." She pointed to two plates of food on one wood-burning stove, both covered in napkins. "So dig in, girls! Before it gets cold! You got that dragon stench off'a ya. That's good. Now eat."

The bread crunched in my hands as I tore it. The soft butter slathered like pure bliss upon it before I shoved it into my mouth, letting my eyelids melt and causing another deep moan of ecstasy.

"Where did you learn to cook like this?" I squeezed the words through the mouthful of heavenly, buttery, salty bread.

"Aren't you going to eat with us?" Bella asked between shoveled spoons of whipped potatoes.

"I'll eat later. Too much to do now. You two girls enjoy."

"You think it's poisoned?" Bella whispered to me.

"Definitely poisoned." We both laughed, and I nearly choked on the not-chewed-enough bread. Bella clapped my back.

Five minutes in, after the first round was shoveled down, Rosa returned from the kitchen and laid two carafes of deep red wine on the table with four glasses.

Bella and I exchanged bewildered glances. All the wine I'd ever had I had to steal from my masters, and if they found out, my ankles and back were sure to be left healing for days after.

"Go on," Rosa said, throwing her hands up again and clapping them down onto her flour-covered apron.

"Why are you doing this for us?" I asked, lightly touching the carafe.

"It's my duty."

"We're slaves," Bella responded.

I poured wine for both of us, not wanting to wait until the world changed its mind about all the treats being offered to us. The second the wine hit my lips, I realized that all the other wine I'd had in my life was far inferior to the silky, delightful one that I sucked into my mouth, swishing it around to consume my whole mouth in the taste.

"Slaves," Rosa scoffed under her breath.

Bella and I shared a confusing glance with one another. Why'd she say it like that? It was almost as if she detested the word.

But isn't she a slave? Or is she here of her own free will? Why would anyone choose to be here in this secluded place with such dangerous men?

Rosa walked back to the kitchen without finishing her thought.

"Thank you," I said between shovels of bites.

Another five or ten minutes passed. The meat was as tender as anything I'd ever had, and a smeared piece of bread with jam hit my tongue last, letting the sweetness take me.

After our stomachs were full and our mouths wiped with delicate lace napkins, we both sat back in our chairs, curious about our new situation, and surely the near future.

I gazed around the room. Books by the hundreds lined old wooden shelves built into the round walls. Everything from history to fables to books titled in words from a language I never heard of. Thick curtains hung heavily on both sides of the glass windows. The glass was old enough to stretch over the many years. The glass was thick at the bottom, like slightly melted candles oozing hot wax. A haze hung in the air from the cooking Rosa had done in the kitchen. From my full belly, slowed mind, I felt as if I may be in a dream—being in such a magical, enchanting place.

The footsteps on the other side of the door only gave us a

faint second to realize Prince Cade and Hunter were back. The door swung in with fury, and the two men were deep in the middle of a heated conversation. I looked at him, obviously, but he didn't even glance my way.

Why would he? I mean, look at him—dripping with sexuality, a towering man with all the wealth, power, and rugged good looks deserving of a prince. And then there was me… all I'd been told my life was how worthless, undeserving, and not special I was.

"She's not going to stop," Hunter followed Cade into the room, a flicker of a glance shot our way. "No matter what…"

"I know, I know," Cade shook his head; anger tracing his words.

They were both quickly in the kitchen, picking up both plates. Cade touched Rosa's shoulder ever so gently, and she bowed her head.

"We can't hide here forever." Hunter gave us another glance, seemingly curious about our own expressions by the pursing of his lips and his narrowed eyes. "Even with the old magic in these woods, it won't stop her from finding this place."

"I know. I'll figure it out. I just need time," the prince turned and made his way to the front door.

"We don't have time, Cade. She's going to want answers, now."

Cade groaned. "Not before I get my answers first…"

His head dipped toward his shoulder, and his gaze focused on mine. It was steely and cold.

Even him looking at me a little made me want to melt into the floorboards. He, looking dark and angry, tightened my chest like a ball of yarn squeezed taut. Those eyes, those lips—I couldn't help but want him to walk up to me, take me in those powerful arms of his, and kiss me.

What the fuck is wrong with me? I'm infatuated with a mass-murdering psychopath!

But the more I watched him, the less sure I was I believed my own thoughts. He'd done nothing to show me he was the evil man from the tales.

As they approached the door, both with their plates in their hands, still covered with napkins, the prince stopped. He turned and angled toward us at the table, both frozen in our thoughts.

"Do not leave this place. Do you hear me? Stay put."

I gulped down the last bite of bread and jam in my mouth. He was so firm in his words; all I could think to do was nod. So I did, and that seemed to be enough for him.

He and Hunter left the room, closing the door hard behind them. I felt crushed. For some reason, I thought they'd sit with us, enjoy their food, and I could get to know the real prince. But that didn't seem to be on his 'important—to-do list—get to know his new Gold-Marked slave.'

"What do you think they were talking about?" Bella put both elbows on the table and leaned in toward me.

"We can't hide here forever," I muttered, as much to myself as to her. "They're going to take us somewhere else."

"They said she's not going to stop." Bella pursed her lips and cocked an eyebrow. "Are they talking about you? Or the queen? Or someone else?"

I thought about that for a long moment. "At first, I assumed they were going to take us to the Blaze Queen and Raven's Bane Castle. But now they're talking about us hiding here?"

"Hiding? From what?" Bella said in a hushed breath.

Rosa came and began pulling plates from the table, completely uninterested in our whispers. She even hummed to herself.

"Do you know what's going on?" I asked her, deeply expecting an answer.

"I don't gossip with guests." Her hands wiped the crumbs before me onto my empty plate.

"So we're guests now?" I grabbed my plate, and she tried to

tug it away. Her stony gaze hit mine. "What is going on here? Why are we here?"

Rosa snatched the plate from my vice-like grip with far more strength than I expected from the aged woman.

"You think I made it this far in my life by gossiping and betraying Prince Cade's orders? Think again." She leaned in so close I could smell the tobacco on her breath. The feeling made me feel sick. "You may think you know the world and know what Allovan is like. But you have no idea what is going on behind this war. There are things I hope you never have to see and know. I pray that for you girls. And I pray the prince can figure out what needs to be figured out. Time is not on his side, and for the sake of all of us—I pray he succeeds."

"Succeeds in what?" I asked, pressing my gaze even closer to hers. Our noses nearly touched, and I could feel her deep groan.

Her fingers grabbed me by the chin forcefully, squeezing. "Presumably, figuring out how to keep you alive."

My life? Why would he be trying to save me? I thought he was just taking me to the capital? And it didn't seem like he was trying to do anything except avoid me and be a dick.

"What do you think?" Bella hunched over her elbows, leaning toward me.

"I think we're in way over our heads, and I feel terrible it's all because of me. If only I could use this magic somehow to get us out of here. Get us new lives somewhere else. Somewhere far, far away. But I can't…"

"Don't talk like that." Her hand hit my shoulder. "We'll figure it out. They don't seem… completely awful. Better than Garris at least…"

"We don't know that… yet." I popped my knuckles under the table, staring down at where my plate had been. "This new life has just begun, and I have this terrible feeling something awful is going to happen."

"Why do you say that?"

"Ever since that thing spoke in my head, I just feel like there's something out there, lurking, waiting. Something so powerful and dangerous that it somehow spoke to me from somewhere so distant that they'd have to be a god or something. Or... I'm losing my mind."

I thought about the turtle... or tortoise, rather. My head sank into my hand, and I shook it.

"You're not losing anything," Bella sighed. "We've got each other. That's what matters most. We've been all each other has had since we were kids. We'll get through this. Just hang in there."

My gaze crept over my shoulder back to my room, and where the huge tortoise had been.

Did I make that whole thing up in my head? There's no way that thing was real. I mean, how in the Infernal Depths could that huge thing get in there and then just... vanish?

"Maybe we should get some sleep." Bella yawned, complacent from a soothing meal after such a long trek upon the dragons' backs. "Who knows what tomorrow is going to bring?"

I nodded, and her hand left my shoulder, her fingernails skirting down my arm.

We went to our rooms while Rosa scrubbed dishes, muttering to herself with her back turned to us. Bella and I exchanged brief glances, but with a great yawn, she disappeared behind her door.

I did the same. "You in here?" No response. No tortoise. "You sure you're not in here?" A minute later, still nothing. "That's it. I've officially flown the coop."

CHAPTER 11

*O*cean waves took me.

They covered every inch of my bare skin.

There was salt at the corners of my mouth, and my hair swirled under the violent waves.

The storm intensified, and dark clouds hung ominously, flickering with deep lightning.

I was taken. The sea had her tight grip on me and wouldn't let go. But my eyes were wide, and there was no tension in my body. In the storm, I felt like I was as free as I had been upon the dragon. Nothing could touch me. Nothing could hurt me. I was free.

The world shuddered in golden light like I was buried deep in the sun.

My hands erupted with golden magic, swirling around my forearms like divine bracelets. The magic radiated through me as the waves lapped at my skin. I felt powerful. Powerful enough to explode in radiating light. I was more than a slave. I was a force of nature. I was a weapon. I was a sword wielded by the world itself, ready to strike against those that would harm everything I cared about.

But my dreams were often like that. False. Fleeting. And I always woke up at the end to my miserable life.

That night, however, there was something entirely different about waking.

I shot up in bed, feeling something rustling around my legs. There was someone in the room with me. Someone in the dark. Someone in bed with me, weighing down the soft mattress. My hands clenched into fists, ready to punch, scratch, and claw.

In the dim light, however, as I adjusted in the gloom, a pair of huge yellow eyes were staring straight into mine. They sparkled with dazzling streaks of oranges and reds, and their age calmed me quickly.

"Cornelius? How... how did you get up here?" My breaths were quick, calming slowly from the panic of being awoken by something in my bed.

The tortoise had his tree-trunk legs straddling my thin waist and hips. He was looking down at me with a certain... curiosity... as if thinking of his words carefully.

It did not completely escape me that I might actually be going insane.

Animals don't talk, let alone huge tortoises that can somehow get up onto my bed without me noticing.

"You have much to learn, young one." Cornelius' beak barely moved as he spoke, angling his head down toward me, still flat on my back.

"I think you're right about that. Everything has changed since I did whatever I did on that beach. Do you know anything about Prince Cade? Do you know what he's planning to do with me? I'm worried he's going to take me to his mother, the queen. But he won't tell me anything."

The tortoise's eyes narrowed, and he groaned from deep within. His breath smelled strongly of barnacles and seaweed. It smelled like home to me.

"We don't have much time..." He stepped to the side, turning his long neck, but his foot missed the edge of the bed, and as his huge body tumbled off the side of the bed, I jolted, throwing my arms out to grab his legs and keep him from falling onto the floorboards. My fingers rushed through the air, desperate to help, but they found only air as his body vanished before my eyes, leaving behind only thin wisps of a translucent, rainbow-colored glow. "There's much that I must teach you." His voice was beside me, and I threw my legs under me, sitting on my knees, glaring at him as he stood on the floor beside me.

"You—you disappeared earlier, didn't you? When I tried to show Bella where you were, you were gone, and you made me look like a mad woman."

"I can do many things." He turned slowly and took slow strides toward the side wall. "But I'm not here about me. I am here because of you, Gold-Marked."

"You know about the magic that I used? And the rune that glowed on my neck?"

"Yes, young one. And I hope to teach you to control that magic, for when the time comes, you're going to need to be able to wield it. There are things that will come for you—things far worse than the Blaze Prince."

"Things? What things? And how do you know about this magic? And how did you get off the fucking bed like that?" I stood from the bed; hair strewn all over, barefoot and aching from the long dragon rides.

"The Gold-Marked are rare, and once they are born and revealed to the world, many will seek to control that power you have within you. It seems the prince is taking you to the queen. We cannot let that happen. She is the one who wishes most to use what's in you for her own devices. You cannot go to Emberveil."

"What choice do I have? He bought me. He has dragons. He could do whatever he wants with me. I can't match his strength or speed."

"You have the Spirit in you. The Rune Spirit. When you learn how to control that which stirs deep inside you, you'll be able to defeat ten Blaze Princes. But until then, yes—we are somewhat trapped in our current predicament." Cornelius' beak was nearly flush against the wall. "But we cannot speak here. We need to get out into the forest. Only there can I begin to train you."

"Train me?" I scratched my cheek. "Who... what are you?"

"I'm your guide," Cornelius said with a raised chin and a gleam in his eye.

I thought for a long moment.

So many questions sparked inside me, and my mouth didn't hold back. "What is the Gold-Marked? What am I? What does that mean? And a Rune Spirit? How did I get it? From birth? Or did the dragons do it to me?"

Cornelius just glared back at me, seemingly ignoring all of my ramblings. "All will be revealed. I have come to teach you about what is inside of you. We go to the forest, child."

The woods? The Faewood? But the prince told me not to leave this place. If he catches me, I don't want to guess what he might do to me. I don't ever want those shackles around my ankles, and Odiun knows I've tried my fair share of times to run, but I got caught every single time.

"I don't know if I can..."

"You must," Cornelius barked. "You won't survive without learning how to use your magic. And we need the essence of the forest. I can't teach you within these walls.

"How would we even get out of here? Rosa is surely out there..."

"Just touch my shell. I'll show you."

I didn't know what to do. My fingers fumbled behind my back, and my toe tapped on the ground. I'd tried escaping from my imprisonment before—many times, actually. And each time I was returned to my masters, the lashes deepened, and the shackles tightened. I'd even been sold off for nights to grown men. But this was different.

"Come, Ash Mist. There's so much to learn, and we have no time."

I watched my foot patter and scratched my forearm.

If I got caught, I'd surely get the shackles back, or worse. But if the prince was going to send me to the queen, to be tortured or whatever she'd do to try to get to this magic, then I guess I didn't have any option. Learn to use whatever was inside of me to save what life I had left, or...

Stepping forward, I placed the tips of my fingers on his scratchy shell, which reached halfway up my thigh.

"Ready?"

I nodded.

"Just don't lose contact with me; don't want you becoming part of the wall now..."

A gulp fell down my throat. Become the wall? Are we... walking through it?

"Walk beside me," Cornelius lifted his heavy legs, moving us toward the wall, and as his head slipped into the solid stone, I swallowed hard, closing my eyes, not fully knowing if I was awake or if this was all a crazy dream.

My fingers gripped the dome of his shell as we walked together. After a few strides, the cool winds tickled my cheeks and lashes. My hair flipped over my shoulder, rustling at the bottom of my neck. My eyes opened, and I found Cornelius beside me, gazing out at the encircling trees.

The insects chirped loudly from the dense forest, and the moonlight lit the patchy grass area around the house built into the ancient tree. Before us, though, the forest loomed ominously. I had the strange feeling there was something in there, watching us as we peered into the shadows. Under the thick canopy, little moonlight needled through, leaving a vast expanse of deep shadow.

"Come," Cornelius said, moving with surprising speed, and my fingers left the top of his shell.

I followed and then paused, shaking my head and scratching my brow.

"Hurry." His long neck caused his green head to turn all the way back to look at me. "We have little time, and there's much to learn."

Doubt lingered within my chest. It tugged at me, using logic to pull me back toward the house. Self-preservation held me back from entering the forest, and a battle broke out in my mind. Escape or stay?

Bella was still in there, sleeping on the nicest, softest bed I could've hoped for her, but we were still prisoners. If I went into the forest, and if it wasn't a trap, and if this tortoise wasn't some evil spirit coming to collect my magic for its own, then this might actually help me.

Stay or go with him?

But there was one aspect to all this that pushed me forward, making my legs move under me and compelling me to walk beside the tortoise out of the clearing and into the trees. I had magic. Almost no one had magic in all of Allovan, but I did. And if I could use that, then my life might actually end up being worth a damn.

I was about to be taken to the capital and the Blaze Queen. So, I had no idea how much time I had left. Every day counted. Every hour mattered. And I had to take a chance. The prince firmly warned me not to try to escape, but this wasn't really escape, was it? I was coming back. I just needed to find out what this creature had planned for me. I had to do it for my only shot at living any kind of real life.

So we entered the forest, and shadow accepted us. Leaving everything safe behind and hoping what lay ahead wouldn't kill me as quickly as the queen might.

CHAPTER 12

ool moonlight seeped through the thick foliage overhead, and the sounds of chirping insects and eerie winds filled the Faewood. I'd never been in a forest like that before. Everything in the south around Bramblebash wasn't as dense, as old, or as frightening.

"Here is good." Cornelius cracked his neck and looked up at me. He slowly turned to face me, but I sidestepped a couple of times until we faced each other. We were in a small break in the forest, beside an enormous, fallen moss-covered tree. A gentle stream rolled past the brook behind.

"So you said the Gold-marked were rare and that I have the Rune Spirit. Are there others like me? Or am I the only one, and that's why the prince and Hunter came after me so quickly?"

"There hasn't been one like you since you were born. And the last one who carried your gift passed long before that. He was a good man, full of potential, and still, he failed." There were hints of sorrow in Cornelius' old, wise voice.

"Failed?"

"There's a reason you have the power you have inside of you." The tortoise lifted his head high, to chest level with me. "You

89

need to learn to harness your magic because this world is heading down a dark path. War, power struggles, poverty, slavery, sadness, lack of hope—these are all things caused by the Emberveil Empire, and the gold rune that marked you is the one thing that can stop it and change our world for the better."

"But how did he fail? What happened to the last one who had this?"

Cornelius sighed. "He was tortured and succumbed to his pain. He died after the extraction of his Gilded Radiance."

"Gilded Radiance?" A warm glow filled my chest at the thought of the magic inside me, the rarity of it, and the hopeful power imbued within.

"That's what it's called. It's as old as Allovan itself, older than me even."

There were so many questions flashing through my mind that it was difficult to pick which one to start with.

"How do I not end up like the last one who had it?" was the best I could come up with and seemed like the most pertinent of questions.

"The Gilded Radiance isn't easy to begin using. It takes time—years of training and practice. But years we don't have. The crown made it a law that if one is found, they are to be brought before the court immediately. That isn't an accident; that law was created generations ago. But as our unfortunate luck would have it, your magic flared to life in front of the Blaze Prince of all people. So, what would take years is going to have to happen as quickly as possible."

"Tell me what I need to do." My hands hung at my sides, my fingers spread before turning into fists. "If I need to fight, I'll learn. I'm not going back into chains. And I sure as hell am not going to get tortured and die so easily."

"Excellent." If Cornelius had lips, I was sure he would've licked them then. "Tell me what you felt when you first used the Gilded Radiance. Be specific."

"I saw the dragon and its rider coming at us. I felt we were both going to die, and my life flashed before my eyes, as people say. What I saw reaffirmed that my life had been nothing. I created for others to make them richer or happier. I've even had to pleasure some. That's not a life, and I didn't want to die without experiencing something for me. I felt fear, desperation for something new, and a will to survive in the face of certain death by fire. And then… it just happened. I didn't even know it came from me at first; I thought Odiun had arrived down there in Bramblebash."

"What did using the magic feel like? Where did you feel it?"

"I think everywhere. At first, I guess, it came from down here." I pointed to my sternum. "Then it shot all over like I jumped into the furious, salty sea. My hands, fingertips, scalp, toes—everywhere."

Cornelius nodded as I spoke, blinking slowly as he watched me. "That's usually how it first comes. When you need it most, and there's intense emotion welling up. Usually, it doesn't happen in such a dramatic scenario, but here we are. So, to re-summon your powers, we're going to try to figure out how to trick your body and mind into thinking it needs it so that the connection between you and it grows. It's like a prairie dog poking its head from the dirt, and you with a piece of cheese in your hand. It'll creep closer and closer until it's so close you can pet its head while it trusts you enough to eat out of your hand."

"So how do we do that? Does it have to do with being out here?" I held out my hands wide, marveling at the sparkling moonbeams that slipped through the leaves.

"The Gilded Radiance is the power that grows deep under our feet. Few can sense or wield such power, and you are the only living soul able to command such a destructive and god-like force. The symbol that glows on your neck is the conduit through which you can receive and speak to that power."

My legs buzzed with excitement at the thought of controlling magic that he spoke about like that. My feet wanted to take off in a sprint to let out the energy that was about ready to burst. "What is the power down there? If I'm the only one who has that magic, then what's the magic that the prince used with his staff when he made it appear in his hand? The Blaze Queen is famous as the strongest wielder of fire magic in the world."

"They are Cinderyn. They are born with that fire magic that emanates and festers at the heart of the Calcaedus, the mountain that Raven's Bane Castle and the Emberveil Empire are built into."

"Born of fire?" My lips pursed and my brow furrowed. I'd heard of Cinderyn, and knew the king, queen and prince were of their bloodline. But were they actually like gods?

"The closest things to gods we have. Born human, they live human lives, but they are as powerful as a thunderstorm or a hurricane at their greatest. Queen Mortriana Vissex was born a Cinderyn of Cinderyn parents. She's a pureblood and as powerful as any who have ever been before her. She wants you for your power. We cannot let you get to Emberveil. No matter what, you cannot go there." His gaze was dark, even mean, yet with a hint of sincerity.

"I think the prince is going to take me there, but it seems he's uncertain about it? I don't know. He hardly talks to me." My head hung low inadvertently. The overwhelming energy I had only moments ago sucked right out of me at the thought of the queen and the prince, and my helplessness.

"Prince Cade Phoenixfire is... complicated," Cornelius said, turning away from me to look at the stream that flowed behind the fallen mossy tree. "For the most powerful rider in the lands, he is far from... content. I suppose that's the best word for it."

"What do you mean?" My mouth salivated at the thought of learning more about the insanely handsome prince who had purchased me away from my miserable life. Gold-Marked,

Gilded Radiance, Rune Spirit, Cinderyn—there is so much I didn't know about this world. So, so much!

"Let's shelve that for another time." He spun back toward me. "Of which we have so little. Come, child, stand beside me."

I walked to his side, his head rising to my waist. He glared at the far end of the break in the Faewood, and I did the same.

"I'm going to try to recreate that same feeling of fear in you, to see if we can coax out your magic."

"You're going to what?" He didn't answer my question, at least not with words. Before us, deep within the shadowy forest, a loud crash erupted. My body tensed, jolting awake. The crash happened again, this time louder, sounding like it had toppled over an enormous tree. My limbs seized, and I panted quick breaths.

My fingers reached out for Cornelius' shell, but to my shock, they slid through empty air. "Cornelius? Cornelius?" I looked all around, but he was gone again, and at the far end of the clearing, the source of the terrifying noise revealed itself to me. My jaw clenched, and my legs screamed to run.

At the other end of the clearing, emerging from the trees, was something so terrifying that my mouth instantly dried, my legs locked, and the blood flushed from my face to my chest. Slithering out from the tree line, as wide as my arm is long, hissing low and with its devilish eyes fixed upon me—the snake that came toward me was as big as a house.

My nerves evaporated. As its massive three heads rose high before me, doubling my height, I felt as small as an ant, as insignificant as a flea, and as helpless as a legless cricket. I swallowed hard, feeling my tongue scrape the top of my mouth like sandpaper.

Its three heads fanned out like cobra heads, all six eyes staring into me, propelling me into a deep trance of fear. It crept toward me, all three of its heads slowly opening their mouths, revealing huge, curved fangs like needling scimitars. Vile green venom dripped from them as their serpentine tongues flicked in and out.

I couldn't move. I couldn't run. I couldn't even fucking swallow. I'd never been so terrified in all my life. Garris never compared to something so awful and deadly as the huge ebony snake with the sleek scales that was feet from me, staring down at me with those evil, hungry eyes.

"Protect yourself." I heard a voice mutter from the bushes.

I forced a gulp down my scratchy throat, shoving my fingers into fists. I hunted for that feeling within, that morsel of magic that had come when I needed it on the beach. My desperate search ended up dry, though, as the snake slithered through me.

"C'mon, Ash." My words were full of frustration, finding my body empty of what I sought.

The three-headed black cobra was only feet before me, its hiss sending a shiver down my back from neck to heels.

My arms shook, desperately searching for what was there.

"Call your magic!" I heard the words from the bushes off to the side. "Call your Rune Spirit!"

I dug deep, feeling for anything that felt like it did when Krakos was diving at us, its mouth full of awful dragonfire, ready to spew down upon us.

The snake's mouths opened wide, ready to strike. There was nowhere to run. I could've tried to leap over the fallen tree, but the snake was upon me, not blinking, its terrible eyes trained on me.

It lunged. Its three heads diving at me, all its fangs eager to take me, pump me with its deadly venom. I searched one last time in the milliseconds I had. But nothing. There was nothing.

And the three-headed demon of a snake attacked. It crashed into me with the ferocity of a typhoon, the power of an earthquake, and the terror of the night.

CHAPTER 13

*A*s the three-headed cobra barreled into me, my eyes closed and my arms covered my face, desperate to save myself from death. But death didn't show its sinister face then, and nothing came upon me. My eyes slowly opened to see... nothing. Under the moonlight, there was nothing... the snake was gone, disappearing like a nightmare. My hands scanned my body for puncture holes, gashes, hell... even a scratch. Nothing.

The bushes rustled beside me, and my focus snapped that direction, ready to fight. But sauntering out from the bushes was Cornelius.

"That didn't go how I'd hoped," his voice fought hard to hide his disappointment, which he did a poor job of.

My lips smacked as I shook my hands, trying to get the lingering, paralyzing fear from my body.

"It... it wasn't there." I heaved a deep sigh. My shoulders slumped, and I tried to swallow, but couldn't.

"Did you feel... anything?" Cornelius was halfway to me from the edge of the forest; his unintimidating presence calmed me.

Suddenly it occurred to me that the snake was just an illusion, an illusion caused by the disappearing tortoise. My gaze snapped back between him and where the monstrous snake had been. "You caused that. How did you...? What are you?"

"What am I? I'm your guide to staying alive. But we've got to figure out a way to get you and your magic together again."

"I tried. I really did, but there was nothing when I searched." My lips smacked as I spoke.

"You're thirsty. Go, drink from the stream." He spun slowly to face the stream behind us.

I dug my fingers into the soft, squishy moss and threw my legs over the tree, walking toward the slow-rolling stream that rippled with glowing moonlight.

My knees hit the dirt. I steepled my fingers and drove them into the frigid stream. Immediately I felt as if my spirit had been lifted to another realm. The tenseness in my body faded, sinking through my feet and escaping into the hard forest floor. My hands cupped the water, and I brought it up to my mouth, sucking the refreshing water down in two gulps. As it cascaded over every inch, I moaned deeply. It slid down my dry throat as I gasped, half from the cold, half in pure ecstasy.

The muscles in my arms returned, and I felt like I could lift the fallen tree behind me without so much as a groan. My entire core and soul relaxed.

"Better?" Cornelius dipped his head into the stream, sucking in deep gulps.

My butt fell to the ground, and my back rested against the mossy tree. A smile crossed my face. "Much."

He picked his head back up as water dripped from his dark green beak. "You felt nothing?"

"I felt like I was about to die, thank you very much!" I folded my arms over my chest and gave a fake pouty face.

"We've got to discover what it is that can awaken your Rune Spirit and call upon the Gilded Radiance. If fear can't do it, then we'll have to try something else."

"I'll do whatever you ask, Cornelius. I want to find it. I need to find it."

"Perhaps more fear…" Cornelius bobbed his head in thought. "Yes. I should've conjured five heads, not three… I should've…"

While listening to his words and watching the ancient tortoise mutter to himself about ideas of what could awaken my magic… Something felt off.

There was something out in the forest, something focusing on me. I couldn't see anything in the night forest, but the insects' chirping faded. The winds howled as they whooshed through the swaying trees, and I felt that familiar stench of fear through my nostrils and into the back of my mind.

Cornelius didn't notice anything, muttering about different methods to scare the magic into me.

I stood, glaring out into the forest, feeling the dark gaze upon me. I had no weapon, only the mysterious shelled creature beside me.

The strong wind gusted past, blowing my hair into my eyes and whipping at my neck. I brushed it back behind my ear, scanning the forest.

"I think we need to leave this place." The words left my lips before Cornelius finished talking to himself.

"What's that?" His head angled up toward me, but then, catching my drift, his head stooped, and he peered out into the dark woods before us. "Something out there?"

"Yes…"

"I see nothing." His legs stretched, and his shell raised, glaring hard into the woods.

A branch snapped. Somewhere before us in the silent Faewood, the snap broke the silence, and then another snap sounded. That one was harder, and I didn't want to find out what was heavy enough to break such a thick-sounding branch.

"Um… Cornelius… that's not you, is it?"

"No," he murmured. "I think you're correct about leaving this place..."

I turned and threw myself over the fallen tree as swiftly as I could. Another snap in the forest echoed, and then another. Whatever it was, was moving fast. I sent all my strength to my legs, knowing Cornelius could disappear. But I could not. My legs and feet moved as fast as they could. The golden light of the house glowed in the distance, seeping between the trees. It was over three hundred yards and through the dense forest.

As the snapping and breaking branches behind intensified, I heard the monstrous growl coming from my pursuer's chest and mouth. It panted, as did I, as my entire body filled with dread.

I ran as fast as my legs could carry me. My hands drove through the forest, trying to repel the branches and sharp twigs. One snapped back into my face, slicing my cheek. The warm blood dripped down my breeze-cooled cheek, but I didn't have time to worry about that.

My escape slowed to a crawl as whatever huge, destructive monster behind me shortened the distance between us. The trees around me were too dense, and my pant leg snagged on a sturdy branch.

"Shit!" My fingers fumbled to tear my pants free. "Shit, shit, shit..."

The roar of the monster awakened everything in the forest. It was so loud, so powerful, and so dreadful that the canopy above awakened with hundreds of birds and bats escaping from it, flying up into the sky, away from whatever destroyed everything in its path to reach me.

I tore my pant leg free with both hands, turning to see my pursuer. Behind me were trees too dense to run through. I'd have to squeeze, which would take time and care, and whatever was nearly upon me would just barrel through. There was no time, and there was too much distance between me and the forest house.

"You're gonna have to face it." My hands balled into clenched fists at my sides. "If I ever needed you to return, Gilded Radiance, it's definitely right now!"

I faced the danger. I barreled through the forest with the power of a hurricane. And when it emerged from the thick wood, standing on two legs in the moonlight, my mouth fell agape, my eyelids shot up, and beads of sweat poured down my brow, trickling off my eyebrows.

Looming monstrously before me, twenty yards out, was a monster that stood fifteen feet tall, with massive arms, enormous meaty hands, a solid round torso, and two stalky legs to heft its immense weight. Its eyes were dark, like two pieces of charcoal on its scarred pale face. Its mouth was too wide for its round head, its bulbous nose was blemished with flaking skin and warts, and its dark eyes were fixed completely on me.

"It's an ogre! And a huge one at that!" I heard Cornelius' voice behind me say.

I scrambled to search my core for the magic that had once come to me but had hidden like a snail sliding back into its shell. Terror shot through every inch of my body. My mind raced, going through all my options, which were far too few. Running didn't work. There was no use in trying to hide now, and with no weapon—not that I'd have any sort of chance in the Infernal Depths with a sword against that thing—magic was the only option.

"Don't run, lass." I heard a voice come. It came from the ogre, yet it didn't. The thick lips and huge, wet tongue of the ogre didn't move. But behind it, I saw a hint of movement. The ogre suddenly ducked its head, and the source of the words showed itself.

Its stench stung my nostrils, like rotten eggs and musty attic dust. A rank odor of unwashed armpits and filthy dirt-soaked clothing filled the clean forest air. Its clothing shredded and tore at its massive, muscly joints. Heavy breaths rushed in and out of its huge nose.

On the ogre's back, held up by some sort of custom saddle strapped to it, was a man. His face was gaunt, his bald head reflecting the moonlight as the birds and bats flew in a frenzy above. In one hand, the man in armor held a crossbow of fine design, with its butt perched in his armpit. He wore a tussling cape bearing the colors of Emberveil—red and gold.

He's a soldier of Emberveil? Riding that thing? But Cade's the Prince of Emberveil. Why is this man here, in the middle of the night in the Faewood? I need to get out of here, now...

"Don't run," the man with the gaunt face and beady eyes said. "It'll be a lot easier if you put your hands down and behind your back. I ain't gonna hurt ya."

"Don't trust a word that man says." Cornelius was still behind me, somewhere in the shadows. His voice was firm with me. "His name is Rone. A hunter for the queen. Wretched and ruthless he is, in every aspect of the words."

"I wasn't planning on it." I squeezed my fists tight, feeling the sweat slide between my fingers and palm. My teeth gritted as I prayed for magic. If this was going to be my last moments in this world, at least I'd go down fighting!

Holding my fists out triggered an evil snarl on the man's face as the ogre snorted through his huge nostrils.

"Not going to come along nice?" The man pulled back the bolt in his crossbow; a wide grin grew on his face. "Good. I like a good hunt. And the queen might actually enjoy getting you roughed up if you choose to fight the inevitable."

"Suck a rock!" My words slammed into his snarky tone, sending his face spiraling and twisting into a dark expression full of hate. The ogre took a powerful step forward, shaking the ground beneath its crushing weight.

I needed my magic, and I needed it right then! I had only seconds before the crossbow would undoubtedly fire, and the enormous ogre could scoop me up in one hand and crush my bones like grabbing a handful of straw.

I reached down deep, searching for my Rune Spirit, hoping desperately the golden rune would appear on my neck, but even as the lumbering ogre advanced upon me, all I found was an overwhelming sense of dread that I was about to die.

The ogre sped forward with three great strides, completely sucking the wind from my lungs as I dove behind a tree. I heard the low snap of the bowstring in the man's hand and felt the air sizzle next to my ear before the bolt plunged into the thick tree. The ogre's massive hand swatted over me as I ducked. It crashed into the trees, knocking into them with such force that an explosion of splinters erupted all around. The trees broke, and either toppled or slid down into the ground, teetering on other trees.

I ran behind another group of thick old trees, but the ogre's dark eyes were mad with rage. I didn't know if it was trying to capture me or kill me, but still, there was no magic to be found. It swatted again, its hand causing a low whooshing sound before it crashed into the trees between us. It shook the ground so hard it rumbled beneath my feet, knocking me back as the other trees crashed into the forest, revealing the monstrous face of the ogre and the sinister look of the man upon it.

Water enveloped me as my face submerged into the pool behind me. The ogre and its rider rippled through the water as I gazed up at them; the ogre taking another set of gigantic steps toward. As I emerged from the water, gasping for air, the ogre and the man were directly over me. The man nocked another bolt in the crossbow and had it aimed right at my head.

My fingers dug into the wet mud in the pool as the water dripped down my face. The man's mouth curled into a smile as he pointed the weapon at me. The ogre opened its huge hand, ready to scoop me up.

"This is it, girl." His yellow teeth barely parted as the ogre's hand crept toward me.

The dread shot down my body and limbs like a lightning strike.

I can't let him take me. I can't go to the queen. It's all going to end before my new life even starts.

My fists hit the ogre's fingers as they dug into the mud under me, lifting me helplessly into the air before the ogre's awful face and the satisfied grin of the man with the crossbow.

"Time to go." The man laughed, still aiming the crossbow at me. Beyond my fear, a rage blossomed inside me. If there was one feeling I detested more than any, it was the feeling of being hopeless and completely at the mercy of others.

"You're not taking me anywhere." The words seethed between my clenched teeth.

"You act like you have a choice, little girl."

Little girl... little girl... I hated that term so much. Those are the two words that are going to drive me into an early grave. I can't let him win. I can't let him win like Garris always won. Those words sparked something alive in me. Something terrible and ferocious, something wanting blood. I was done being a victim. I was done feeling helpless. I wasn't the little girl I used to be—chained, beaten, used—I was something more.

The water from my hair dribbled down my neck and arms, and I could feel the wetness slide between my fingers as I balled them into fists.

"Give up. You've lost." The man licked his lips, glaring at me, fully satisfied I was completely powerless at the overwhelming mercy of such a monstrous foe—or at least that's what he thought.

Something sparked alive in the wetness of my fists. The rage inside me ignited a sizzling feeling like lightning in my veins. The world funneled into a fixed gaze and eagle-like focus upon the rider wearing the colors of Emberveil. The replenishing water made me feel alive.

"I'm done being helpless! I'm done being a victim!" My fists raised to my sides as the ogre lifted me up to its eye level. In both their eyes and on their faces, a golden light reflected.

The man's trigger finger squeezed, and the bolt raced directly at me, flying at frightening speed directly between my eyes.

"Kill her!" The man's eyes were impossibly wide. The golden light pierced through my fingertips, spinning into a golden orb like an egg around me. The bolt blasted into the golden egg, incinerating into wisps of golden light like smoke trickling up from a cigar. The ogre's fingers snapped shut, squeezing with all their strength.

But instead of breaking every bone in my body, the golden orb around me stopped the thick muscles in its huge fingers. The gigantic mouth of the ogre clenched its rotten teeth, and its beady eyes narrowed. It groaned, squeezing with all its might. But instead of crushing me, it watched helplessly as I stood fully, my body enveloped in a golden light that glowed like embers smeared all over my skin.

"You're not taking me anywhere." My words were deep with spite and ill intention. The man had no qualms about stealing me away or killing me for the queen. How many other young girls had this man taken from their homes or killed because he enjoyed it? "You're not going to hurt anyone, ever again..."

My Gilded Radiance shot from my hands in two spinning pillars blasting into the ogre's shoulders and chest. It roared in pain, echoing throughout the forest as it recoiled. I fell from its hand, landing back in the water on my feet, with the cool water rising above my knees. My spell never stopped, and the two magical pillars continued spraying from my hands.

The magic burned into the ogre, and I could smell its searing flesh. But the water on my legs sent a rush of fresh energy into my magic, pulsing even more power into them.

"That's it, Ash! Keep going!" Cornelius shouted beside me.

Both pillars gushed with such raw power that they both blasted through the ogre, emerging from its back in a brilliant golden light that illuminated the forest behind. The ogre roared as my magic tore through its thick body. It fell onto its back, and I heard the man scream in pain. I left the pool, striding toward the monster, pulling the magic back into my hands. Out of the corner of my vision, I saw my reflection in the pool; a bright golden light poured out of my neck.

The corner of my mouth smirked up. I had it. The Gilded Radiance was alive inside of me, and I gushed with excitement and power.

The ogre lay motionless on the ground, all life gone from the monster. As I approached the man, he lay with his brow full of sweat and his nostrils flaring. Both his legs were crushed under the fallen beast, and his crossbow was feet from his grasp.

"You little cunt! I'll squeeze your life away with my bare hands!"

I raised my hand, brimming with golden flames. "You're not going to hurt anyone ever again."

Golden flames unleashed from my fist, engulfing the man in a blinding fire that killed not only him, but also his screams, which lasted only seconds in the blazing inferno.

Once he stopped writhing and his life left his body as well, the Gilded Radiance disappeared. All light faded from my body, and I felt my magic completely gone. Exhaustion washed over me like a tidal wave, and I crashed to my knees. My hands shook, and an aching feeling grasped my bones. My vision blurred, and my head fogged.

But there were figures coming through the forest beyond the ogre and the man of Emberveil. I squinted hard, trying to clear my blurred vision. There were over a dozen of them, taller than men, with long, pale arms; bony arms that nearly reached their ankles. They held curved swords and spears as they stalked through the Faewood.

I got upright on my knees, but that was all I could muster. All energy had left my body, and there was no magic left in me.

"Run, Ash, you've got to run!" Cornelius was fully visible next to me. His words were harsh and forceful. "Get up! You've got to run to the house!"

"I—I can't move my legs…"

"Oh no…" Cornelius gasped. "They're coming, Ash. You've got to get out of here!"

I tried to get up but collapsed to my side, barely getting a hand under me to lessen the fall. Deep exhaustion overtook me, and just before the darkness took me, I saw two men rush past me, both with swords in their hands, both shouting loud battle cries as they rushed at the encroaching monsters. One of the men had a dark mask and a staff with the head of a phoenix at its tip.

"Cade…" I moaned. "Help me…"

CHAPTER 14

*T*he battle erupted into bittersweet chaos.

Unable to move, with every ounce of energy sucked from my body, I lay helpless to defend myself or aid in Cade and Hunter's fight. The sounds of the frenzy filled the forest. Battle cries from the men echoed in my ears as they swung their sharp swords and Cade cast his fire spells at the monsters that stalked me. The monsters growled and roared as they fought, outnumbering the prince and his soldiers by over twelve to two.

Through my blurred vision, I tried to watch the madness of battle. Cade's sword flashed in the moonlight with one hand, and his magical fire staff in the other spewed magma-hot spells upon the legion of monsters. The hunters of Emberveil and their ogre were dead, and I'd been able to call my magic, but the fatigue that left me helpless and drained also left me completely and utterly vulnerable. I lay in the wet moss, left half-watching the battle with my head cocked to the side.

The last thing I saw was the world turning to fire. An explosion of sun-orange flames tore through the forest, incinerating everything in my vision. It was so blinding I shut my eyelids, trying to drown out the vivid light.

And then everything went black.

WHEN I AWOKE, having no idea how long I'd been out, the glow of candlelight pierced through my squinting eyes, and my dry lips smacked. I reached up and pulled the cool, wet towel from my brow. Rubbing my eyes and letting the room come into full focus, I realized I was in my bed in the forest house, glaring up at the beams above the bed.

I sat up quickly, startled, throwing the covers off my body. I was half-naked, with my legs bare and only my undergarments on. And there was no one in the room. Not that I expected anyone, perhaps Cornelius, though I thought the tortoise would at least be there—that is—if I hadn't created him in my dreams. The bruises on my arms and the aches in my bones screamed at me that I hadn't, though. It all was real, and my feet hit the floor, creaking the floorboards. I heard footsteps running toward my door in the other room.

The door flung open inward, and out of all the faces I expected to see, it was certainly not the prince's. Cade ran into my room, his piercing gaze half stuck in an icy glare at me, and half worriedly scanning my body for what I assumed was for injuries.

My hands tore the sheet up from the bed to cover my chest, but he didn't withdraw his gaze. No, instead, he shut the door behind him and stood with his strong arms folded over his chest, a dark expression growing on his extremely handsome face.

He wore no armor, only a thin linen shirt, exposing the muscles in his chest, the black hairs that covered it, and even the veins that ran down his neck and forearms. I felt myself moan uncontrollably. God, he was perfect. I bit my lip, forcing my lips shut, and I felt a rush throughout my whole body.

"You all right?" He forced the words out, but the agitation in his stiff body showed he was trying desperately not to show the anger I saw in him.

"I think so." Other than the pounding headache, the aching in my arms, and the scratches from the branches on my skin, I was telling the truth.

"Good," he sighed, and the anger immediately welled in like a dam breaking under the weight of heavy floods. "What the fuck... what in the name of the Infernal Depths were you doing out there in the forest? All alone? Even after I specifically told you not to leave the house!"

"I—I..." I tried to think of a lie as quickly as I could, but with my head pounding the way it was, nothing good came. Not that he would believe that a fucking invisible, god-like tortoise told me to.

"Don't even try to make some shit up." He took a powerful stride forward that made me gasp. Even when he was mad, especially when he was mad, all I could think about was making him feel better and forcing his brawny arms around me. "What were you doing out there? You almost got yourself killed! That was no mere bounty hunter out there. That was a hunter for the queen herself. You could've died or been taken."

Taken? What does he care if I was taken to the queen? Isn't that his plan as well? There's more to this prince than I realize... and that only makes me want to know him more...

"Who was he? How did he have that ogre? And what were those things that came out of the forest? They looked like half-ogre men or something like that." I noticed something on the side of the prince's neck, then—a fresh cut, still dripping blood down to his clavicle and onto his chest. "You're hurt. You're cut."

I ran to him, still holding the sheet over my nearly naked body. He put up a firm hand between us.

"It's nothing. Only a scratch. But you… how did you survive? We heard the fight and ran to where you were, but that man and his ogre were dead before we got there. Did you…?"

"Yes. I used my magic again." I couldn't believe the words that came out of my mouth were true. I still couldn't believe I actually had magic. I felt a smile curve on my face. I have magic! And I used it again!

The Blaze Prince shook his head, glowering at the floor. I could feel the tension building in the room, as if squeezing the walls in, sucking all the air from the room as I gulped. I didn't want him to be upset with me. I didn't want to be the cause of his anger, but any attention at all from him, who mostly avoided me, grumbling to himself, was something…

"Ash, listen…" The tone in his voice was a forced calm, like sails flapping in the sea winds, a break before the storm. "I don't know how else to say this to you to get you to understand— you're in danger—that magic that spawned inside you; it's going to be the end of you."

"Well, you don't seem to want to talk to me about it. You're too busy running around with Hunter and brooding over what-ever the hell it is that has you so wound up. How am I supposed to know anything when you won't talk to me? Sure, you put me up on your dragon and brought me here to the middle of the forest, to do what? Think? Aren't you taking me to your mother, the queen? What does it matter if it's you or that man on the ogre? And then you tell me I'm in danger. Of course, I'm in fucking danger. I'm always in danger. Say the wrong thing; whipped. Run; shackled. Try to escape; tortured to near madness. My life is one big fucking mistake, and you're going to lecture me about danger? What gives you the right to worry about my life all of a sudden, when Odiun put me on this earth to suffer? My entire purpose in life is to try to find little scraps of enjoyment and happiness. What do you care?"

The prince cleared his throat. "Stepmother…"

"What?" I was so taken aback by his random answer to my bombardment of rambling that it took far too long for his words to reach my heated brain. "The Blaze Queen isn't... your real mother?"

"No. And I hate it when people call her that. She's not my mother. She was my father's wife. That's all."

My chest trembled under the weight of the moment. The prince... Prince Cade Phoenixfire was... bearing his pain to me. To me! Why?

"Your father... They say he was a great man but fell in battle with the Stormscales. He died a warrior's death atop his dragon."

"I know that's what they say. That's what my stepmother, Queen of the Emberveil Empire, said."

"You don't believe that, do you?" I didn't know the prince, but I always considered myself a good judge of character. And I could tell his words were true. There was pain in his voice, deep pain.

"Ash, I'm trying to protect you. I'm trying to figure out what to do moving forward. But you've got to start fucking listening to me. We aren't in Bramblebash. This is Allovan. The closer we get to Emberveil, the more danger you're in. I thought we could hide out here, but Rone found you here, so others will too. I need time to think, but it appears we are out of that."

"Why?" I wanted to press with questions because I had so many, but I figured I'd let him roll into whatever explanation he deemed appropriate. And I didn't mind standing this close to him. His muscular stature towered over me. My arms and legs wanted to melt in the presence of such a powerful, utterly god-like man. His perfect lips, his piercing gaze, his obsidian hair flowing down the sides of his face. It all gripped me like a vice, and I wanted him. I wanted him more than I wanted anything in my life in the room that seemed to close in all around us.

"Because you're special..."

The air in my lungs squeezed, my throat tightened, and I

clutched the sheet to my chest. Special? I'd never, ever, ever heard anyone say that about me. Ever...

"I'm not special. I'm the opposite of special." My chin hit my chest, and my gaze dropped to my feet, seeing the scabs all around my ankles. "I'm nobody."

The floorboards creaked, and I heard his boots walking toward me. My heart raced in my chest, the blood in my shoulders and neck heated, and when I finally lifted my head, I found him before me. Inches between us. Nearly nose to nose. His musty smell consumed me. Every part of my body screamed to touch him, to slide my finger down his chiseled jaw, but I was left holding the sheet between us, covering my body.

He didn't speak but looked so deeply into my eyes I thought I might melt completely through the cracks in the wooden floor. Behind the closed door, both of us together in one room, my room, all I could think about was tearing those clothes off his body and feeling his bare chest pressed against mine.

"You are special. You're special to this world, and you're special to me..."

I was frozen. Petrified in his presence. He loomed over me like some kind of beautiful predator hunting his next meal. And I wanted that meal to be me. With his last words, he pulled me in so hard my chest felt like it was going to explode. I gushed for him to keep talking about me like that, even to say my name. How a man like that could say such a thing to me—I never could have imagined or dreamed.

It was just us—the most powerful man in Allovan, and me, a slave from a nowhere town as far away from important as possible. His lips—his perfect lips—were inches from mine, and I licked mine subconsciously.

"I'm not..." The words slipped between my lips like a hush. He was so breathtaking, so powerful, all I could do was stand there, wanting to drop the sheet and have him take me.

"I saw it in you the first time I saw you, even before you cast that spell."

"You what?" My head cocked slightly as I felt his breath on my mouth. God, he was going to drive me insane standing that close to me.

"I've thought about you day and night since then. You've not only awakened that ancient magic, but you've made my life a bit of a mess since we met. Not to mention you're in trouble for going into that forest alone."

"I..." I didn't know what to say. I wasn't alone. Well, I kind of was. And to promise I wouldn't do it again would be a lie. So, I decided to let him do the talking, as being that close to him was becoming my drug. He was what I needed, what I wanted more desperately than the air I needed to live. He was ravishing, deadly, and I wanted him to be mine.

"Ash," he whispered. "Things are happening in this world you don't understand yet." His hand rose, and he grabbed mine, causing me to suck in a deep breath. "I'm going to need you for what's to come. But... I can't deny I think about you more than just for Allovan. Ever since you've been in my life, it feels like I don't need anything more."

"What do you mean?" I wanted to know more. I wanted him to keep talking like that forever with me. The angry prince had simmered like a shattered plate coming back together, sealing all the broken pieces back.

"Let me show you..." His eyes closed gently. His lips pursed together, pursuing mine. My heart was beating like a drum. It pounded like an earthquake, and it felt like dragonfire erupted in my stomach.

My hands clutched the blanket between us, my shoulders tensed, and the blood in my neck heated.

And as his lips pressed to mine, all the anxiety and tension flushed away like a dam bursting open. His soft lips touched mine. I dropped the blanket and slid my arms over his neck. He was so tall he had to lean down to kiss me, anyway. His muscly arms wrapped around the bottom of my waist, and he pulled me into him. My bare stomach squeezed against his chiseled body under his thin linen shirt.

His tongue slid between my lips, and I gladly opened my mouth, sliding my tongue against his. My hands glided up from the back of his neck into his thick hair, scratching his scalp with my nails. He turned his head and drove his tongue into my mouth, exploring every inch of mine, which I couldn't get enough of. Mine licked back, wanting every inch of him.

His rough hands felt the bare skin of my back, exploring my body as I did the same to him. The kiss was the hottest thing I'd ever experienced in my life, and I thought that even if I died the next day, then at least I had that. The infamous Blaze Prince was mine in that moment. It was all I needed. It was all I wanted. I wanted him, and he wanted me. I was in heaven, and I wanted that moment to last forever. And I wanted more. I wanted all of him. Every moment of every day. He was my drug, and I was fully, completely fucking addicted. Those lips, that cock growing hard in his pants against my leg. I needed him.

Then… a knock came at the door, and all the pleasure disintegrated as he recoiled, wiping his mouth with his sleeve, coughing and nonchalantly pulling his hard-on into the crease by his belt.

God, I wanted that cock. As I wiped my mouth as well, I wanted to taste all of him.

"Come in," he said, clearing his throat. His gaze met mine for a fleeting second, hushing me, telling me that was our secret. And that secret was sure as hell safe with me. Well… until at least I could tell Bella. Bella would fucking kill me if I didn't tell her.

The door hinges squeaked as the door opened.

"My Prince," Rosa said.

"I'll be right out, Rosa." He stepped back from me, but not before his hand rose and his fingers glided down my cheek, letting his thumb touch my lips one last time before he said goodbye with his eyes. "Don't do that again."

I nodded, knowing it was a lie. But I was awestruck, smitten, infatuated. All the things. And as he left the room, closing the door behind him, I collapsed into my bed, telling myself that if all this was a dream, then I sure as shit never, ever wanted to wake up from it.

CHAPTER 15

*R*osa and Cade exchanged quick words; she whispered into his ear, and he agreed with a series of nods. He gave me a quick glance before he left the room, enough to wet my need for him, but far from enough to quench my thirst. He left like he had entered; determined and quick.

Rosa remained, standing before me, gazing at me up and down, scanning my body coldly, yet with a raised eyebrow and the slightest hint of a smile. I pulled the blanket up from the floor and covered myself, sitting on the bed as it crumpled on my lap.

"You're lucky to be alive," the old woman scolded me.

"I know…" The images of the haunting face of the ogre burned vividly in my mind. The terrifying hunter inside glimmered in its wretched, beady eyes. It was hellbent on murdering me, squashing me like an insect under its tremendous weight and muscle. The man Cade called Rone wasn't going to leave the forest without me as his prisoner. He'd have rather killed me than left me in defeat.

But I killed them.

I killed them both, and even though I had to do it, the feeling still left me feeling like a monster myself. I'd never killed anyone, or anything really. Even when I saw one of the squeaky, nasty things with the tails scurry across the room, I'd squeal myself and run as fast as my legs could carry me. That man and his ogre were dead there because I used magic again. And even though my brain told me I did the right thing, my soul felt scarred—deeply scarred—and I knew with all my heart I'd never be the same.

"You must do as the prince says." Rosa approached me and lifted my legs onto the bed. "And you need rest, dear. I'll take care of everything. You just take care of yourself…"

I wanted to deny my fatigue, but it consumed me like a huge sea wave, crashing down onto me with cool, calming forgiveness. With the prince's taste still on my lips, fighting through my brain fog, I said, "Can you get Bella for me, please, Rosa?"

"You really must rest." She tucked the thick, warm blanket over my shoulders.

"Please. I'll sleep after, I promise."

Her thoughts showed in her gaze as it darted around the room. "Very well."

Rosa left, leaving the door open an inch.

Moments later, Bella came in, closing the door behind her. Her face was stricken with worry. I could tell by her bloodshot eyes, the puffiness under them, and her flat mouth choking back tears.

"Ash…" she managed to say as she ran to me. She scooped me up to a sitting position as we embraced. "You're alive! I was so worried! Why did you go out there? What were you thinking?"

"I—I'll tell you everything." Which I did. I told her about Rone and the ogre, and my magic, and Cade and Hunter killing the monsters, saving my life.

She sat on the bed as I lay back, recanting the whole ordeal. A gamut of emotions showed on her face, with reactions of shock, bewilderment, worry, and triumph. But when I finished telling her everything, she instantly glowered at me.

I hadn't gotten to the prince, but she knew I'd left out the real conclusion to the story. "What?"

"Don't what me. I saw the expression he tried to hide when he left the room with you. And I see the same fucking expression on your face. Out with it!"

I sat up and grasped her sleeves. "I don't know what happened. But my god, Bella... I think I'm falling for him."

"What happened?" Bella pronounced the two words slowly, forcing me to spill our secret.

"He... he kissed me. He kissed me so intensely, I thought I was going to explode."

"You kissed?" Bella's eyes shot wide, and a huge grin grew on her face. "I knew something happened!"

"By Odiun, Bella. It was the hottest fucking thing I've ever felt. Nothing has even come close. My heart is so all over the place, I don't even know what to think."

"Well, slow down." She raised her palms up toward me. "He's still the Blaze Prince. You know, the most highly praised killer in all of Allovan. And, oh yeah, he's a fucking prince. But..." She raised a sly eyebrow and patted me on my thigh. "You're one lucky girl. He's as handsome as the devil. And you're getting feelings for him. I can tell by your voice."

"I—I don't know what to think. He bought me. I'm his property. He wouldn't be the first slave master to kiss his property. But... god, I would've done anything he wanted me to. If only he would've tried."

"I bet," Bella laughed. "I'm sure you would've."

I sighed, lying back on the soft pillow with a thud. "But you're right. I'm a slave, and he's a prince. Shit, he's taking me to Emberveil, or at least he was going to. I don't know why I'm getting my hopes up, or even thinking about what could happen. I've got bigger issues than thinking about him naked. That man on the ogre was going to take me to the Blaze Queen. He was going to take me to Cade's stepmother."

"Stepmother? She's his stepmother? I thought she was his mother?"

"Me too. And I don't think he wants to take me to her now, for some reason. I think... Oh god, what am I about to say? I'm such a fool..."

"What?" Bella's expression pressed it from me forcefully as she dug her fingernails into my thigh.

"He said he liked me from the first moment he saw me..."

"Shut it!" Her fist slammed into my leg.

"Ow!"

"He didn't say that..."

"He did. I promise."

Bella sat up straight with a sly, proud smirk. "You bitch. You got the Blaze Prince to like you, and now you got to kiss him."

"Bella... it was amazing. Absolutely amazing..."

That evening was so much less dramatic. It was pleasant, but in the most awkward kind of—we just acted like everything was normal, even though it was the complete opposite—way.

We ate a delicious dinner from Rosa, but it was just Bella and me. We didn't hear or see anything of Cade or Hunter. The house was eerily quiet. We only heard the winds howl from the open windows as the fire burned in the hearth. Rosa worked with her back to us, laying platters before us, refusing to answer questions. She seemed to make her point clear enough not to leave the house again.

Bella and I talked about the prince in whispers.

Where was he? What were they doing? Our imaginations ran rampant. We didn't hear the roars of the dragons, so we assumed they were out flying on them: scouring for something, fighting off the Stormscales, but most likely they were figuring out what to do with me, we both agreed.

But all I could think about was him. I wanted more than anything to be alone with him. I wanted to taste him, to dig my fingers into his back, pulling him in impossibly close. I wanted his powerful arms and hands to explore every part of me as we kissed deeply again.

I even let Bella braid my hair, putting it up, with two braids falling down the sides of my face. I wanted him to notice me. I wanted him to notice me like no other man seemed to. I never felt beautiful like that. I'd never been told someone liked me the way he told me he did. I wanted him to tell me again, so it strengthened the memory. No matter what happened, I didn't want to forget the way he spoke to me before he wrapped me in his arms.

A sharp pinch on my elbow sparked pain all the way up my arm and into my brain.

Rosa was right beside me, pulling her hand away from my arm.

"You in there?" Her tone hinted at annoyance. "If you're all done, I'll clean up. Would you like some port wine for dessert? Some more fruit?"

"Um, no. I'm fine, thanks." My hands clapped onto my happy stomach. "You've treated me enough, thank you."

She lifted our plates and carried them away.

Bella yawned, with her long arms held high over her head. "Should we go to sleep? Or are you going to stay awake? Hoping your prince is going to come walking in the door, ready to carry you in there?"

I wanted to tell her to shut up, but absolutely I wished that, and she knew it.

"How long have we been friends?" she asked.

"Ever since Garris bought me when I was four." I assumed it was true. No real reason for him to lie to me. First the orphanage, then sold off to work.

"I know you better than anyone," Bella smiled, swishing her wine in the glass next to her face. "We're family. You're all I've got. I can see you're falling for him, but don't fall too hard. He's a prince. And we are… well…"

"Orphan slaves." I finished her thought. "I know. I know."

"They say they found you on the beach as a newborn," Bella said after taking a sip of the rosy red wine. "You're quite an anomaly. Lucky to be alive. Blessed with magic. Lucky to have a prince after you."

"I suppose. I don't feel lucky."

"My parents sold me off. At least you don't have that weighing over you. Wondering why for your whole life. Like you did something wrong when you were so young you can't even remember it. It's torture. The wondering. The worrying. The guilt. At least you don't have parents that did that."

My hand went to hers, falling onto her hand on the table.

"There's nothing wrong with you. You did nothing wrong. You're the most perfect thing in the whole world."

"Thanks, Ash."

"I'm a Mist." The sigh rolled from my throat without thought. I felt my chin quiver, but I held it firm. "Abandoned by the world in every way."

"Mists are a lot more common nowadays. I guess that's good and bad. More orphans from the war. Babies found with no hint of who their parents were."

"I wish I could do something about it." I took my hand back and shoved both hands between my legs, hunching over. "I hate feeling helpless. There are so many other kids out there like I was —confused, utterly lost, hopeless. I wish more than anything that I could save them all from this world. I wish I could take a dragon and swoop into every village in every corner of this awful world and take them, buy them, whatever it took to get them out of there and free them."

"That's a wonderful thought." Bella's eyes welled with tears.

But she never said anything more than that. Because I knew it was just a fairy tale dream. And I was a slave still. Slaves don't go around being dragon riders and saving people. I had to fight to survive every day. That was my life. Even in that house in those enchanted woods, I knew that was all there was.

Magic, though. My magic was real. And with that, there was hope.

It may have been my curse, but I was determined to figure it out, master it the best I could.

CHAPTER 16

I didn't sleep a wink that night.

Tossing and turning, I felt the deep pit in my stomach of taking those lives. The twisted faces of the two, the life leaving their eyes like a sheen that would never return. Logic didn't help either. Not the prince's words, not the knowing that I did what I had to do.

I was no killer.

But, then, actually, yes, I was.

My feelings about the prince doubled down, welling in a mixed pool of swishing anxiety and nerves that were impossible to shake. I was stuck—in all the ways. I couldn't leave my thoughts, the feeling that I'd done something terrible, and hell—I couldn't even leave the house I was in.

That wasn't anything new to me, though.

Being trapped was normal.

The feeling of being free, though, wasn't.

There was a presence in the room then, in the middle of the night. Flopping over, I saw the huge tortoise with his wide, old eyes glaring at me from the side of the bed.

My legs kicked off the covers, and I sat on the edge of the bed.

Excitement shot up in me like a flurry of arrows piercing through my gloom.

"Cornelius!" I said it like he was an old friend, and perhaps he was. "You're back. I heard you in the woods, but I couldn't find you!" My voice crumbled at the words that escaped my mouth before my brain could usher them out. "Where... where were you?"

"Ash," his old voice said in a wise, croaky tone. "I'm here to guide you. I'm the wind that blows the leaves off the tree, stirs the waves of the sea, helps the clouds stroll through the sky. But I cannot become a part of this world. This is your world. Not mine."

"You're not from this world? Are you... dead?"

"Ha!" The old tortoise belted out an unusual laugh I didn't expect, and one that caused me to sit up straight. He didn't seem to notice and continued to laugh. "No, no, child. I'm not dead. However, I have been alive a long, long time."

"So that's why I didn't see you? You couldn't help me when that Rone and the ogre came after me?"

"I'm unable to aid in such a capacity. I will teach you what I can so that in the future—you wouldn't need me to. In that respect, you didn't need me then either, it appears."

"I almost died!" My butt scooted forward, and I hunched over him. "I could've been murdered, or sent to the queen!"

"But you weren't..." His tone lifted to a high note. "And I think I know why."

"Huh? You do?"

He nodded with a smirk at the corner of his old, green beak.

"You couldn't find your magic when I used my illusion to create the snake that attacked you, but you were able to when you were really in trouble. Think. What was different that time?"

"I—I was frightened by the snakes. For real, I was. But maybe part of me knew it was fake. When I was really in trouble, I..."

"No. Not that. What did you feel? What was your body doing? What changed in you?"

"I—I didn't know what to do. Rone was chasing me on that monster, and I was trapped."

"What felt different?" The tip of his beak rose and crept forward. His incredibly old and wise eyes stared deep into mine.

"I was... weak. I think. When the snakes came, I felt depleted, kinda. But when the ogre came, I fell, and I felt, kinda... strong."

He didn't press me, but there was a sparkle in his eye as he nodded slowly.

"I fell into the water." A sharp realization hit like a hammer striking an anvil. "The water..."

A proud expression grew on his face, cocking his head to the side with his eyes closed. "Ash... I believe there's more to you than you realize."

"The water..." I muttered the words, feeling the weight of them on my shoulders as they slunk. "I felt refreshed. Like I was rejuvenated, and then the magic came to me when I needed it. So what does that mean?"

"This is your first time away from the sea, is it not?"

My jaw dropped. "Yes."

"Do you know how the Blaze Prince and the Blaze Queen are fire wielders? They are Cinderyn. They command flames and are bound to them. That's why they live in Emberveil mainly. The capital is built upon the mountain that harbors the eternal fires of Allovan. And you, Ash..."

"I'm... like them? But... the opposite?" My world whirled as my head fogged. My fingers gripped the sheets as I tried to ground myself, find where I was, and remember who I was. But who I thought I was had changed so much in the last few hours; I wondered if this was all a dream.

"You, Ash... are an Aquafae. One of the Aqualorians. Or, to be more specific, part Aquafae. You wouldn't be full-bred Aqualorian and this far out of the water. Either your father or mother was an Aquafae, while the other was human."

What? Not only do I have magic... but I'm part... waterperson? I—I don't know what to think. Everything is so different... I don't even know who I am anymore... but I can't deny... it's absolutely fucking thrilling!

I didn't think my day could have possibly gotten any stranger, but that revelation shot into me like a surging lightning strike right through my temples. The electricity ran through every bone, muscle, artery; sending every single hair on my body tingling. My nails dug into the sheets at my side as sweat beaded down my brow, trickling off my eyebrow and onto my cheek.

"This has to be a dream..." It was the only explanation for how this could have all been around me. I assumed I was asleep in my bunk in Bramblebash, fantasizing away about riding a dragon with the Prince of Emberveil, taking me away to some sort of freedom. The thought of being some sort of part water god was enchanting, but a little much, I thought. It was pulling me out of the dream next to this imaginary talking turtle... er, tortoise.

"You are very much awake. And you need to learn to use the magic inside you, and quickly. You need to learn to harness the Gilded Radiance at the snap of your fingers. And time is running out. We need to get back out into the forest and keep practicing. The water is your source, and a cup of it won't do here. You need a stream, a river, an ocean to channel."

I shot to my feet. Cornelius didn't move back, but angled his long neck up to watch me.

"I—I can't. Not yet. I literally just told Cade I wouldn't. I can't lie again. Not this soon."

"What do you care what...?" The magical tortoise's eyes pulled wide. "Oh... you have feelings for the Blaze Prince. That is something I did not expect. And it will complicate things greatly."

"I do not!" My hands balled into fists, waving them at my

sides. If I fought it hard enough, then even I might believe myself, I thought. But there was no hiding it as Cornelius snickered.

"He is an instrument of your rebirth as what you're becoming," he said. "But he is not salvation. You must become your own source of strength."

My hands relaxed. I knew he was right. But damn if every fiber of my being didn't tell me otherwise.

"We cannot continue to discover your Gilded Radiance within these walls. You need the crisp air in your nostrils, the touch of sacred dirt under your feet, the splashing of cool water at your ankles."

"Can't you just give me some instructions here? I really don't want to run into another hunter in the woods all alone."

Cornelius cocked his head down and to the left. "I did not sense the presence of those hunters. Peculiar. I normally would have no trouble sensing that kind of danger coming, especially as close as they were. That is a mystery I need to research."

"I'll go tomorrow night. I need to learn, but I've got a lot on my mind and could use some rest. Actually..." My hand fell onto his ancient shell, feeling the knobs, cracks, and scars under my callused fingers. "Just you being here is helping me calm down. You have a soothing presence."

He bowed proudly.

"We could just talk here. And then I'll go with you into the Faewood."

"We do not know what tomorrow holds," he warned. "Anything could happen with so many coming now. The Blaze Queen will not be pleased with one of her own dying. And the Sythers the prince and his soldiers slew. She will want revenge for killing her creations."

"Sythers?" My brow furrowed, and my mouth flattened.

"The things that came with Rone and his ogre. After you killed him and his oaf, they came for you. They must've fallen behind or been searching elsewhere. They are one of the queen's favorite hunters. She uses dragon riders for initial attacks. They destroy with fire, and the Sythers invade and murder whatever is left."

"I only saw them for a second before I blacked out." The blurry images of the monsters that stood taller than a man with long pale arms down to their ankles rushed through my mind. "She made them?"

Cornelius nodded. "Queen Mortriana Vissex has grown very powerful over her time as queen, since the king passed. There is something unnatural about her abilities, beyond being a Cinderyn."

A grim thought stormed like dark clouds in my mind. If the prince owned me and was taking me to such an evil-sounding monster, then I truly was in danger. Bella too. "Why does Cade fight for her? I've heard stories of the things he's done, but he doesn't seem evil to me. Why would he fight for her? Doesn't he see what she is?"

"The world isn't always as simple as just doing what you believe is right. It's not black and white. Allovan is the worst sort of gray." His beak leaned in toward my face until I could smell his breath from his nostrils. It smelled like seaweed. "What do you think would happen if the prince abandoned his post as prince or tried to usurp the throne?"

"Nothing good. He'd probably be hunted like me if he failed."

"Aye, yes. The Blaze Queen holds the throne with an iron grip. She rules with terror as her weapon. Her power is unmatched, even to the prince."

I swallowed hard at another thought. A thought that made my bones shiver. "My magic. The Gilded Radiance. Why are you teaching me to use it, Cornelius?" I gulped, my throat as dry as it was back in the forest. It felt like nails going down a tube of hard, scratchy stone. "Am I... am I supposed to match the magic of the queen? Why do I have this rune on my neck? Why are you here?"

"I told you. You're special. Very, very special. And yes, you are the one who's destined to have the power to stop this mad rule of our tyrant queen. Whether you would match her prowess, I cannot say. But what I can say is that, given time, you'll be able to do things you could never even dream of. Others may look to you as their savior, their protector, a god even."

My gaze slid to the side, looking down at the back of my hand as it rubbed the soft sheets. Hours prior, magic poured out of my fingers like water flung from a bucket. My arms felt as if weighed down by lead, and my vision fogged.

"You must have the wrong person. I can't be the one you're talking about. I can't do those things. I can't fight the queen. I couldn't even protect myself from my masters in Bramblebash. How could I ever do anything like that? Sure, I killed a man. But just barely. I could've died there in the Faewood."

"But you didn't."

"No, I didn't."

"Fine. Rest up this eve," he said in a hollow voice as I watched him slowly vanish into the air, half-translucent. "Tomorrow night we will continue your training. Until then... just try to stay alive. And here in the Faewood, as far away from Emberveil as possible."

With that last word, the tortoise disappeared completely, leaving me in the room with a head full of worry and anxiety. The thing that calmed my nerves was the memory of that wonderful, exhilarating, wild kiss.

CHAPTER 17

The afternoon sun bit down hard on me, reflecting off the ground beneath our feet as the incredible, magical dragons came. Their wings gusted vast swaths of hot wind and dust into our faces as we watched. It bit at my skin as the smoldering smell of hot dragonfire returned to my nostrils.

Cade rode Krakos first, with Hunter behind on Talonor. Both dragons landed with a ferocity that would cause most to soil themselves. Their wings swept wide, shaking off the dust before recoiling into their immense bodies. They snarled, and their enormous mouths showed their vicious teeth as they lowered their bodies, and both riders jumped down.

It was midway into the day, after we'd had breakfast, and I filled Bella in on everything. Rosa always worked closely, always with an ear pointed my way.

Cade gave me a glance that pierced my heart more than it filled it. He was either fighting hard not to make eye contact, or I had done something to piss him off so badly he wouldn't acknowledge my existence. My stomach felt as if a ball of iron was twisting in it, grinding harder with every step the prince took while ignoring me.

Hunter looked at both of us, bowing his head slightly, then rushed off after the prince.

I bit my lip to not yell out after him as Cade stormed by. There was an intense energy shadowing him.

"C'mon," I finally whispered to Bella, grabbing her by the arm and pulling her. "He may not want to talk to me, but I need to know what the hell is going on."

Cade and Hunter were in front of Rosa, both clad in their brilliant royal armor, and both with their capes flapping madly behind.

"Hey." I had to force the word from my nervous throat.

Hunter turned with an upraised eyebrow, and a slight upturn of the corner of his mouth. Cade turned with stark irritation; the shadow encompassing him darkened. He glared at me out of the very corner of his eye.

"What's going on?" I asked, releasing Bella and holding both my hands out wide. My heart thumped hard in my chest, half-worried about annoying Cade, half-furious about the secrecy he kept. "While you're out playing ride the dragons, we are here, not knowing anything, trying to pretend that we are safe here. Well, we aren't. And I don't have a clue where you're going, or doing, or thinking, or hiding. And it's about time you start treating me like I'm involved in the decision making that you're secretly trying to make. I may belong to you, but this is my life, and if you're going to take me to the queen, then why don't you just tell me now so I can plan on dying?"

That got his attention.

He spun, with his huge shoulders framing me. I staggered back a step. Hunter grinned, about to laugh, but then cleared his throat, regaining his composure as he stood at the prince's side.

"I don't owe you anything," Cade said, his voice steaming. "I got you out of that hellhole of a town, and got you away from that slob. Isn't that enough?"

"I know more than you think I do." I took a terrifying step

forward, folding my arms over my stomach as a gust of wind shot through—not so much wind, with the dragons stirring alive at the way I confronted Krakos' rider.

"Is that so?" Cade asked, folding his arms as well. Rosa covered her mouth nonchalantly as she was brimming with appreciation for my dramatic callout of the prince. "What do you know?"

I coughed, not expecting to be called out myself. "You, you want me to tell you, now?"

"You brought it up. So do us all a favor and tell me what you, a Mist from some nowhere village in the southern slums, know. Go ahead. We're waiting."

I brought it up with my smart ass, always getting me into way too much trouble. I swallowed hard. I dug deep for my courage, which when I looked into the prince's glower, welling deep behind that perfect face, I found it.

"I know I have the Rune Spirit. I know about the Gilded Radiance magic that's inside of me. I know that I'm the only one with the rune on the side of my neck in Allovan, and I know that the queen wants me more than anything. There's something about the Gilded Radiance that she wants for herself. And you're the one who was charged with finding me and bringing me to her. I know that if you take me there, then I'm most likely dead. What I don't know is why she sent another hunter after me. My best guess is that you're taking too long, or she's worried about your allegiance, so she's sending others after me too. I know about the Sythers that were with Rone, and I assume there's no good reason you wouldn't have just taken me to her immediately unless there was something else going on. That's what I want to know."

I decided to keep some juicy bits to myself—like Cornelius, me being an Aquafae, and the thing that spoke to me in my head on the beach. And oh yeah, my burning desire to rush up to the prince and press my lips against his, shoving my hands under his armor, grabbing at his hard abs.

He cocked an eyebrow, thinking hard about what to say.

Rosa tossed her face all the way to the side to hide her excited cackle. Hunter turned to face the prince, folding his hands together before his belt buckle. He also waited with interest for the prince's reaction.

"How did you learn those things?" Cade had a nasty tone in his voice. "You learned how to use your magic against Rone and his ogre. How did you learn to do that?"

"Why don't you start answering some of my questions first?" I shot back with the nastiest tone I could muster.

"Easy, Ash," Bella muttered from behind me.

"You sure have a talent for getting under my skin, irritating me more than an itchy rash."

I took a bit of pride in his words but was fighting hard to reel myself back in. He was being an awful prick about some things, but by Odiun, I wanted him. I wanted him so badly.

"We are trying to figure out how much more time we have here before others arrive," he said through clenched teeth.

"Why?" The word came so quickly after his statement I felt his annoyance pulsate through the air toward me.

"Because I'm trying to save your life."

"Why?" Again, my quick response made it seem like he was about to draw his massive sword and cut my head off from my shoulders, even after the context of his words.

"You don't want your life saved?"

"Of course I do. But what do you care? Your mother is the queen, and she's the ruler of all of Allovan. Why wouldn't you just do as she ordered? You're her finest warrior after all, right? Why stall the inevitable?" I hoped I knew the answer, but I didn't want to say that in front of everyone.

"We flew the area and gathered that we think Rone was alone. He always hunted alone, hoping for a reward for bringing you to the queen himself. She probably insisted on sending the Sythers just to make sure he didn't fail. We assume he didn't tell her where he was looking. He wouldn't want competition from the other hunters."

"Other hunters?" Bella breathed. "And how did Rone find her here?"

"I'm not sure..." Cade muttered with his chin tucked to his chest. "He was one of her finest, so he had his ways." He sighed deeply, walking past me and facing the two dragons. "It matters not. His secrets died with him, and the slain Sythers of the queen won't speak of our whereabouts."

The way he walked right past me without a glance or the slightest touch made me feel as if he hated me. He hated me for causing him so much trouble. The kiss meant nothing to him, even though he said it did. Insecurity flared in me, and I shoved my hands in my pockets. Bella cupped the back of my arm gently.

"We're safe here," he said with his back to me. "But not for much longer. There's something that's making you trackable."

"Are there people who can track magic?" Bella let her arm slide down my arm and back to her side.

"Not like that. Not at great distance," Hunter said, swaying his huge sword by swiveling its pommel at his hip. "The queen could, but not miles away. If you walked into a room with her... she'd know."

"Thank you..." Bella said. "Thank you two for saving her out there in the woods."

The Blaze Prince spun, lit aflame by those words. He was angry; menacing even. His fists were balled with veins bulging, and his eyebrows forced down. "If you wouldn't have gone out into the forest, exactly like I told you not to do, then we would've sensed Rone and his convoy early. We could've had Krakos and Talonor get to the skies to fight them from above."

At the top of the prince's fist, on the underside of his arm, I saw a long, fresh gash stuffed with some herbs. It was red, swollen, and awful to look at.

"You're hurt..." I said, half-embarrassed I hadn't seen it before, when we were alone.

He turned his arm over, hiding the wound. "I'm fine."

"Let me see it." I walked toward him in front of everyone, with my hands out, eager to help.

"Stop!" The shadow returned in him, darkening the man I wanted. "Do not touch me..."

I halted in my stride, fingers stricken, and my mouth left agape. "I didn't mean to... I just wanted to help."

"I said I'm fine. It's just a scratch. And I don't need your help."

"Cade..." I muttered.

"You wanted to know what's going on? Well, now you know." The steam in his voice could've melted ice. "We're good here for now. So do me a favor and stop causing all these issues."

My lips flapped before I sensed I should've just nodded. "But if I hadn't gone into the forest, then I wouldn't have been able to find my Gilded Radiance. You can't just coop me up; I need to learn to use my magic if I'm going to live. I can't just be your prisoner."

"What were you in Bramblebash, Ash?" His words made every last ounce of pride in me fly away like birds before an incoming hurricane. "Tell me what you were."

"A slave." My shoulders hung as if a wet blanket had been thrown over them.

"And what are you now?" As he asked that, I felt not only scolded but humiliated. His words squashed me back to my reality.

"Your slave."

"Good. Maybe you should start acting like one then and less like you have any say in these matters. All your questions are wearing on my last bit of patience, and while we're here squabbling, I could better be spending my time trying to find a place to keep you alive while I figure out our next move. Now do me a favor and get into the house so I don't have to look at you and answer any more of your questions."

His gaze locked onto mine as I fought the tears back. I didn't want to give him that. I didn't want to give him the pleasure. Part of me wanted to argue—to tell him how I felt, and how I thought he felt. But the rational side of me knew what he said was true.

I was his slave, and slaves do what their masters say.

This dream of me being with him was all a fantasy.

The kiss was real, but that's all there was, and all there'd ever be.

I was a fool for falling for him.

His handsome looks had surely plucked at many girls' heart-strings. I was just his newest victim.

I spun, and Bella walked me back to the house.

The only tears that came were after the door was locked behind us, and I let my back rest against it before I slid down and cried into my knees while she held me.

CHAPTER 18

*M*y arms and shoulders burned like magma formed in my muscles.

"Digging is so much harder than it sounded," I huffed, taking a break and crossing my arms atop the handle of the shovel.

"Stop yer whining." Bella thrust the blade of her shovel into the forest dirt, heaving it out of the freshly dug hole that was eight feet long and almost four feet deep. "We're almost done. I am going to chug an entire glass of wine when we're done with this."

The sunlight sparkled through the trees like ice crystals. A summer breeze wove through the trees of the Faewood as I stomped on the shovel, throwing a load of rocky dirt out of the hole. "We're going to race with that first one, and I'm gonna leave you eating my dust."

"You're on."

"That's got to be deep enough." I wiped the dripping sweat from my brow with the back of my arm.

"Yeah," Bella agreed. "We're gonna lose the daylight soon. That'll be good enough."

The plan was simple—well, simpler than the actual 'digging

the hole' part. The dragons would incinerate the bodies of the ones that attacked me, but the armor and weapons needed to be buried… hence the giant hole in the ground.

The men had already removed all the armor from Rone and his ogre and had piled high the swords and spears the monstrous Sythers had.

After climbing out of the hole, we tossed it all in. It clacked and banged as it all landed on top of the last heap. Rone's whip was the last to get thrown in, and I spit onto it for good measure.

As we began shoveling the dirt back onto the pile of weapons, the thought of going back to the house sent a sadness sinking into my heart. I didn't want to go back to see him. I knew there was good in him. I knew he wanted me, but the way he talked to me in front of the others—it was nothing like the way he spoke to me when we kissed—but perhaps that was the way he played girls like me.

I'm so stupid. So, so stupid.

He's a handsome fucking prince, and I'm… I know what I am; nothing.

"Stop thinking about him." Bella's words cut through the clear doubt that had deep roots growing in my brain.

"How'd you know?" She could always tell, though I'm not sure why I doubted that.

"Because you get all gloomy and stop talking. Stop worrying about him. We've got more important things to worry about than that devilishly handsome ass." She sent me a sly wink, tossing another heap of dirt into the hole.

"He is an ass…" My hands tightened on the shovel handle, and I felt my brow furrow.

"He'll come around. He's just got a lot going on, and he's also halfway to treason, not taking you back to his stepmother. That's a lot to take in. I mean, we're burying evidence of the queen's men right now. Who even knows if we'll live to see tomorrow…"

Tomorrow… the thought ripped through my head like claws

raking down granite. I told Cornelius I'd go with him tonight back into the forest. If Cade finds out... he's going to do me in himself...

"We're stuck in quite the situation." I heaved another load of dirt in; my shoulders throbbing. I drove the shovel tip into the dirt, leaving it erect in the dirt and turning to Bella. "I'm sorry. I'm sorry I got you into this mess."

She tossed her shovel to the ground. Looking deep into her eyes as she faced me, the blue of her eyes reminding me of the far-off sea. Her sandy blond hair was still thick and gorgeous even after shoveling dirt.

"Ash, look at where we are. Look all around us. We're in the Faewood. Isn't it incredible? It's even better than the paintings and songs. We flew dragons to the top of a mountain! We flew through clouds like goddesses. I don't want to die, but if it comes, then I'd rather die like this than back there with that fat bastard telling me what to do, selling us off to his friends. Don't apologize for any of this. It's like a dream. It's all like a wonderful, marvelous, impossible dream... So, thank you. Thank you for bringing me."

"I'm glad you're here. I think I might be losing my mind if you weren't here with me."

She smiled a brilliant smile with her perfect teeth. "Now c'mon. There's wine that deserves to be drunk!"

We left the shovels and all that metal beneath the ground. We sauntered back to the house, humming tunes and admiring the beauty of such a breathtaking forest just before the brink of twilight.

We slammed our wines before dinner, with Bella winning. I tried, but my mouth wasn't big enough, leaving red streaks trickling down my chin. She swallowed with a mighty smack of her lips. I swallowed the last bit down, leaving Rosa with an irritated yet slightly amused look. She scratched her temple, turning back to the kitchen to finish the last of the wonderfully smelling buttery meal.

The food was placed on the table with Cade and Hunter nowhere to be found. They'd taken the dragons to Odiun knows where, doing who knows what. Hopefully, they were still trying to find a way to get out of the hunters' sights and figure out how to postpone the inevitable... my knee bobbed thunderously under the table, rattling the silverware before Bella and me.

"Dig in," Rosa said with no hint of a smile.

"Rosa..." Her name squeaked out of my throat far more mousy than I intended. For some reason, I felt nervous, like a wet rag was being wrung out in my stomach as she turned to acknowledge me.

"Yes?"

"What do you think is going to happen? You seemed to have known Cade for a long time. Do you have an idea?"

"Enjoy your dinner." She turned and walked back toward the stove. "Try not to worry about those things. The prince has everything in hand."

"I hope so," I muttered, taking the fork and prodding the tender beef coated in aromatic rosemary.

"She keeps things tightly sealed," Bella whispered.

"As do the both of you," Rosa responded quickly with her back still to us from the other room.

Bella's face flushed like she'd been caught sneaking out of the forge at night. "How did she hear me?"

"I hear everything," Rosa said, stirring a wooden bowl with a spoon.

We finished supper with no more talk that Rosa's ears were eager to hear. And with all the digging, feeling like I'd shoveled a thousand pounds of dirt, I was eager to get some sleep before Cornelius arrived.

Bella and I both said our goodnights, and I took a quick bath before slipping under the covers. The soft blanket and pillow warmed my soul, sending waves of glee down from my tingling scalp to the tips of my toes.

My eyes closed, as heavy as they were, and I drifted off into a deep slumber.

Yet, I awoke after an impossible amount of time to decipher, only knowing my body required at least three more full days of sleep.

Rolling over, I found the two glassy orbs that were the tortoise's eyes in the room's corner. It was dark in my room, but I could clearly see the outline of his shell cast against the shadow of the room. The lights of his eyes glimmered like streaks of light reflecting off amber in a dark cave.

"Cornelius..." I sat up in bed and lit the candle on the side table. The room glowed in candlelight as his vast body strode over to the bedside.

"Are you ready, child? You have used your magic a second time, but more practice is needed, and time is running out..." The tone of his voice was far more dire and urgent than his normally slow drawl.

The backs of my hands wiped the sleep away from my eyes, and I threw the covers off, swinging my legs over the side of the bed. I nodded eagerly. My body begged for sleep, but I knew he was right. There was no time. I needed to become something that could defend myself when trouble came next.

"Follow me, then."

I put on my pants and shirt and followed him to the wall. Touching his rough shell, we walked through it together and out into the forest veiled in sparse moonlight. Thunder clapped far in the distance.

We walked deep into the forest, leaving the safety of the house behind. My heart raced as my gaze darted around the darkness, scanning for another hunter waiting for me to show myself and give them the chance to strike. But there was nothing, and the insects continued to chirp and buzz everywhere. We went so deep into the forest that the canopy darkened the ground, making each step over roots and fallen trees more precise.

"Let me help." Cornelius' shell shimmered with a soft amber light between the plates. I stepped back as the light caught the rest of the shell, pouring a warm glow from it. My jaw slacked.

"You really are full of surprises…" I muttered, waving my hand over the golden rays that poured from his body.

"This is good." He turned to face me, and I stood with my shoulders squared to him. "Now, step into the creek."

I was so fascinated by the magical light that glowed from his shell that I didn't notice the creek that flowed right behind me. I slipped off my shoes, stepped back, and walked into the cool water that rose above the scabs on my ankles.

My eyes closed, and I went into a safe place inside myself. The water cooled the forever-lasting pain from the shackles that bound me. The moan left my lips as a summer wind washed through the Faewood, causing my hair to blow from my chest to my back.

"What do you feel?" he asked calmly, yet with that hint of urgency still there.

"Calm."

"Good. Now, search for the Gilded Radiance. Feel for the Rune Spirit that lives in you. It's there. Somewhere. It's deep down, but the more you practice feeling it, the stronger it will become. Like a bud growing into a vibrant, lush red rose. It should feel like it's a part of you, yet separate. Like coming home to a sister you never knew you had, but feel that deep connection instantly."

"A sister?" My stomach sank at the thought of never having a family. Never knowing my mother, not having a face to remember. Never having met my father, never having had him catch me when I fell, or even wrapping his arms around me to make me feel safe in this wretched world. "A sister? I would welcome one of those."

"Name her, and when you feel her, get to know her. Tend to her feelings and emotions, because she will help you grow more powerful than you can imagine..."

And as if I were sifting through dirt, searching for that one diamond that would make me wealthy and change my life, as soon as I searched myself for what he described, it appeared like a flawless diamond that sparkled like every star in the sky combined.

"There..." I uttered, all of my focus shifted onto that spot deep within, somewhere between my belly button and my sternum. It was like a golden sunflower blossoming inside me, warming my insides with its exquisite, blissful light. "There she is... I feel her."

"What's her name?"

"Eden," the name came without a single thought. "Her name's Eden."

"Good job, Ash. Excellent..."

CHAPTER 19

"*S*peak to it. Breathe with it. Feel that connection like it's the sea's waves washing over you, purifying your spirit, and replenishing what was taken from you."

Cornelius' ancient, powerful voice reverberated between my ears as my eyelids were shut tight and I searched deep inside, feeling Eden like a ghost that was never there, but yet, always as well. She slumbered like a magnificent dragon waiting patiently to be awakened.

Eden. She feels as powerful and magical as a waterfall in the middle of an ancient forest. My brain tingles as if she's trying to speak to me. She's like a long-lost friend I never knew, but has walked beside me my whole life.

Holding my hands out wide, the feeling of the Gilded Radiance flowed through me like a second blood. My feet planted into the stream, the fresh forest air streaming in and out of my nostrils, I felt like a new woman—one birthed from the womb the moment my shackles popped off back in Bramblebash—and I knew and dreamed I'd never go back to the life I grew up in.

My soul was breaking the chains. My dreams were beginning to come true, and the magic inside me beckoned to be set free.

"Open your eyes, child."

I opened my eyes at Cornelius' command, and standing before me, twenty paces out, was the hulking ogre with a scowl as mean as sin, and the small, ruthless man Rone perched on his back.

I didn't flinch, my heart didn't race, and I didn't have the feeling to turn and run. It was another of the magical tortoise's illusions, but it was enough to remind me of what being hunted felt like and to remind me of the imminent confrontation with the Blaze Queen.

"He's here to take you away." Cornelius was directly next to me, his long neck guiding his head to my hip. "He's here to kill Bella and to take you back in chains to the queen."

My teeth gritted with a clenched jaw. The scabs on my ankles tingled in the cool water, reminding me of so, so many years of no semblance of self or freedom. The scars on my back tightened as I moved my hands before me, aiming them directly at the giant ogre and his rider. Their faces twisted in disgust and rage. The veins in the ogre's thick muscles bulged, and Rone flicked the menacing whip, causing the scars on my back to shudder in remembrance.

"If you want to keep what is yours, then you have to fight!" Cornelius' words were as commanding as I'd ever heard them. He may have been old, but there was a tempered spirit in there. Wise as he was and humble, his words caused the hatred in me to grow like an incoming storm, causing the calm sea to stir into massive, crashing waves.

Staring at Rone, glaring into his beady, soulless eyes, a light grew from my chest, flowing into my shoulders and down my arms to my fingertips. It was as if gorgeous sunlight emanated from my body, flowing down to my hands.

"Show the queen what it means to try to come for you and for Bella. Show her the rage that's built up within you all those years.

Show them what will happen if they come and try to take you again, because if they do, everything ends. Your story, Bella's life, and every bit of your new freedom dies. Show them you're not a slave anymore. You're not that little girl getting hurt and beaten. You have power now. You have control, and you're never going to let that go, ever again…"

"Never again…" As the words squeezed through my clenched teeth, the surge of my magic nearly buckled me. Feeling like every drop of blood in my body rushed to my fists, the golden light before me erupted into what looked like staring with tired eyes into the sun just after first light.

The Gilded Radiance exploded from my hands like lantern fuel set ablaze. My magic left my fingertips and shot through the air at Rone like an inferno. The magical flames tore through the gap between us, exploding into Rone and the ogre, and as it collided with them, they didn't react or recoil. Instead, they vanished, disappearing into the air like phantoms.

Shocked, my hands dropped, and the golden flames fizzled, dissipating like drops of water on hot lava rocks. The light faded from my fingers almost instantly, leaving only a hint of light flowing back up my arms into my shoulders.

"Good, good. Excellent." Cornelius' head bobbed beside me.

Where Rone and the massive ogre had stood was transformed into fire. Fire that burned the trees, singed the leaves, and caused smoke to rise into the night sky.

"How did that feel?"

"I—" I couldn't find the words. All that came to my mind was, "That was the coolest thing I've ever felt." My gaze snapped to his. "I want to be able to do that again."

"You will. You must form a bond, a connection, with Eden. She will be your guide, and your connection to your Rune Spirit. She will grow strong as long as you keep practicing and… stay alive."

The thrill twisted in my body to the staggering reminder of what I was up against. Still a slave, at the mercy of that asshole prince and his powerful dragon. I had no freedom except my magic, which made me feel like I was free; even if I wasn't.

Someday I'd finally be free, or I'd die trying.

As I glared out at the flames that scorched the ground, sending their heat rising to the forest canopy, a thick raindrop splattered on the tip of my nose. Thunder clapped in the distance.

A stark, drawn-out yawn pressed out from my throat. My limbs dragged once again, yearning for a soft mattress to rest upon.

"Am I always going to get this exhausted using my magic?"

"No," he said quickly. "And yes. As you get more used to expelling your magic, your body will adjust, and you will retain more of your strength. But…"

"But?"

"But we will increase the potency of your spells, which may negate your body's resilience to the loss of energy."

"So I'll get better at dealing with the zap my magic puts on me, but I'm going to be casting stronger spells, so my body's going to have to adjust." If I wasn't so exhausted, the thought of stronger spells would've had my mind racing at the possibilities. But that late into the night, and after an already body-aching day of shoveling, all I could focus on was rest.

"Let's go again." He said the words, and I wanted to resist, but even in my brain fog I knew the queen wasn't going to give me the time I needed to get as strong as I needed to be. I sighed deeply and shook the fatigue out of my shoulders.

A series of raindrops hit my hair as the sound of fat droplets struck the dry ground all around me.

"Ready?" Cornelius asked in his wise, croaky voice. "This time, call your Rune Spirit without my assistance. Now you know how to call forth Eden. So, pick a target and unleash her."

Beside the dying flames, dampening lower and lower from the raindrops, lay a fallen tree, weathered with aged-worn bark that cracked like a nut's shell.

"There." I pointed.

"Very well. Make it a strong one. Your body has to learn to cope with the release of such energy. It's like teaching your body to run faster and farther. You've got to start pushing yourself. We don't have much time."

I didn't respond but raised both arms, pointing my hands at the fallen tree. My arms shuddered and surged with fresh energy as I felt the connection with Eden, still fresh. The golden light poured out of my skin as the rain fell harder, and the thunder intensified, bursting in the night sky all around.

My fingertips glowed with the dazzling light, and my mind readied a burst of my magic onto the tree. All I felt was the magic; it coursed through me with a thrilling, surging feeling. It pounded like fiery blood. My heart thumped hard like a beating drum in my chest, and sweat wetted my palms.

I was ready to send the magic streaming out of my fingers at the tree, ready to increase the flames, ready to let all the pent-up rage and frustration of such an awful childhood out. I was ready to unleash my rage!

"Ash…" Cornelius said, with a nervous edge in his voice.

It was immediately followed by the ear-pounding sound of Krakos' roar.

"He's coming…" the tortoise said, but as the magic drained from my hands and arms, crawling back into my body, I glanced to my side to find Cornelius had vanished.

I swallowed hard as the enormous black dragon flew into the sky directly above, Cade mounted on its back, a furious look harbored in his dangerous eyes.

I staggered back as the winds from the dragon's wings forced down upon me like a typhoon's fury. Tree limbs broke under the powerful wings and tail of the dragon as it lowered into the forest.

Oh no. He's going to be absolutely furious with me for being out in the forest again. What do I do? What do I say?

But I knew there was no excuse for my actions. He strictly forbade me from going back out into the Faewood, and I did it almost immediately after.

Just when I thought everything had finally turned around for me...

Krakos landed, his serpentine eyes glaring at me as if he knew as well. Cade leaped down immediately, striding toward me, sword in hand, muscles bulging under his linen shirt, clinging wet to his body from the rain.

He stopped six feet away as all my breath hid deep in my chest. His mouth was a flat line, and the wrinkles in his brow furrowed. His long black hair clung to the muscles in his neck and chest. Lightning struck in the far distance behind him as his sturdy frame didn't flinch. Krakos let out a deep growl from deep within.

"Cade..." I said in a breathy, shaky voice.

"I don't even know what to say..." His voice, however, was as close to a furious roar as he could muster without the volume of his voice rising. "I told you not to return here. And here you are..."

"And here I am." My gaze tore away from his, unable to look at his mean glower, but trying with all my might not to just stare into his handsome features, his perfectly muscled chest and cut abs under the soaked shirt.

"What the fuck am I supposed to do with you, Ash?"

I knew exactly what I wanted him to do with me. I wanted him to wrap me up in his powerful arms, pull me in tight, and kiss me with the ferocity he carried within him. But that would never happen again, I knew...

He turned to look at the scorch marks in the forest behind

him. At the sight of the magic I'd used, he forced his eyes closed with an angry snort from his nostrils.

"How did you learn to do that? And don't lie to me." The way he spoke to me made me feel as if he had some hidden insight into me, like the invisible string that connected us from our cores was being plucked like a lute string. I worried that if I lied to him, the string would snap from the tension, and whatever connection we had would be severed forever.

But I couldn't tell him the truth. At least… I couldn't tell him the whole truth.

"I need to practice. And I can't do it cooped up in that room. How do you expect me to learn to use my magic if you won't let me try it? Shit. You hardly even talk to me. Do you know how it works? Were you ever going to help me figure out how to use it?"

He didn't respond but stood like a statue in the growing storm.

A chill ran up my spine from the deluge, but if we were going to fight, then I'd let the furnace inside of my rage.

"I didn't think so. All this talk of trying to figure out how to get me to survive your stepmother, and you never even thought to guide me. You just go off with Hunter on your 'save the magical slave' adventures, leaving me to worry, stress, and have no insight into how I might be able to use this magic to fucking help!"

"You're infuriating," he said after a pause. He strode forward a step with his finger aimed my way. "It's not all about you. There are so many factors at play here. Yes, you have the Gilded Radiance, and you're the Gold-Marked, but just me keeping you here and not taking you to the capital has serious implications on not only me, but all of Allovan. If you knew the whole picture, then you wouldn't be acting this way."

"Then fucking show me the whole picture!" I took a terrifying step toward him, out of the creek, leaving the tip of my nose inches from his finger. "I can help. I'm not just an armor-polishing, sandy slave. I'm more. I can help, but you've got to talk to me."

His finger dropped, and it felt as if all the minuscule courage poured out of me as he took another step in. I smelled my own hot breath reflecting off his enormous chest. I had to tilt my head up to look at him.

Cade moved to speak, but the words caught in his throat, unable to escape his perfect lips. He either didn't know what to say, or my ability to drive men into a mad fury intercepted his words.

"Say something!" My fists balled at my sides as the rain streaked down my face, dripping down my neck.

"God," he breathed. "You drive me wild." His tone softened, striking me like his fingers were gliding along the string that bound us together. "The things I want to do to you…"

My balled fists instantly relaxed to my fingers cocking out in shock. My gritted teeth loosened as my bottom jaw dropped in awe, finding no words.

He took the final step, closing the gap between us, and my heart sank down to my heels. His powerful, muscle-clad arm with streaks of tight veins slid around my side and wrapped around my back. The prince pulled me to him, our chests pressed together, with my breasts against him, showing out the top of my shirt. His gaze drifted down, and a moan slipped through his lips.

"God Ash, I want you. I've wanted you for so long now."

His free hand rose and brushed my wet hair back behind my ear. Every single hair on my body grew erect instantly at his touch.

"You do?" I knew I wanted him. I wanted him and whatever he'd give me, but I wanted to hear him say it again. My core begged for him to say it again.

"I want you, Ash." His arm around me pulled me in tighter, his head cocked, his lips devilishly close to mine.

"Then take me," I whispered as lightning crashed again. "I want you."

The rain increased, landing in sharp, warm droplets as he pressed his lips against mine, kissing me deeply. His lips parted, and his tongue slid into mine, exploring each other in the same way I dreamed of. His wetness touched mine, and my arms wrapped around him, feeling the sharp definition of the ripped muscles in his back.

We kissed in the rain of the Faewood for what felt like a blissful eternity. But as soon as his hands gripped the bottom of my shirt, rising it up over my shoulders as our lips parted, my core dripped with excitement. He took my shirt off, laying it on a fallen tree to our side, then he took his off.

My heart beat like a deep drum in my chest. I felt like I was in a fever dream but never wanted to wake. His wet shirt slid up his rock-hard body before hiding his face, and when he yanked it over, his wet black hair flung down, spattering on his chest. I squeezed my thighs together to attempt to control the overpowering urge to leap up onto him, wrapping my legs around him.

Instead, he kissed me again, then his lips left mine and his soft lips hovered past my cheek onto my ear, nibbling at my earlobe. Goose pimples stiffened all the way down my body as he kissed and sucked on my neck afterward. A moan left my lips, closing my eyes with my face aimed up at the rain. I felt his hand rise from my hip, up my rib cage, and then cup my breast. The moan turned to a deep groan of raw pleasure as his mouth drifted down to my nipple; his wet tongue circling it, kissing and sucking gently on it.

"Cade..." I gasped, steam vapors coiled up from his hot shoulders.

He lifted his head as I opened my eyes again, staring at the most handsome, breathtaking man I'd ever seen in all my life.

"Yes?" He gave no smile, but the wild animal inside, the hunter, glared at me as if he wanted to take me as his trophy.

"Show me how much you want me." The power I felt from those words from a simple slave girl from a nowhere town, saying them to such a powerful lord, made me feel like a princess in my own right. "Because I want you. I want all of you." A deep heat welled inside me, almost burning my insides from a growing passion I'd never experienced before.

A wry smile hit the side of his mouth, and he put his hand around my back, drifting to my ass, squeezing it in his huge hand, pulling me into his thigh. And there it was, unmistakable against my stomach, under his tightening pants; he was hard, shoved tight into the side of his pant leg. His other hand went below my belly button and undid the buttons that held my pants up. My breath caught, and my hand went to his abs, feeling the definition between each muscle.

His fingers loosened my pants, and as their waistband dropped a couple of inches, his hand slid under my underwear. I couldn't breathe; the anticipation was killing me, and I wanted him to touch me. I wanted him to touch me deeply. My legs separated slightly with a smooth sidestep, and his strong fingers went into my pants and touched my clit. Wet and smooth, his fingers rubbed around it gently as the guttural moan poured from my mouth. He kissed me deeply, forcing the moan inside. Hot breath escaped my nostrils as he played with me, pleasuring me in a way that cascaded down my entire body to my toes.

"God, I want you," he breathed after pulling away. "I want you, Ash."

"How much do you want me?"

"I want you more than anything."

"Then take me," I moaned as the pleasure of his fingers overcame me. I took him by the wrist and shoved his hand down further under my pants as I separated my legs further. His fingertips played with me before separating me, sliding in, and an intense shiver ran up my whole body. He kissed me again, and then without warning, his hand pulled away, causing me to gasp.

But he put both muscular arms behind me and lifted me up with both hands on my ass. I wrapped my legs around his huge core instinctively. He lifted me as if I weighed nothing. He turned and set my butt onto the fallen tree.

"Take your pants off." His words were commanding, as if I were one of his soldiers. The rain couldn't cool my heat. I was the hottest I'd ever been in my life, and I thought I saw steam coming from us, but I was just so absolutely lost in his majesty that I sat back on the tree on my elbows, gazing up at the mountain of a man as he undid his belt buckle; his cock forming a huge crease in his pants.

I slid my pants down my legs, but with a grunt, he grabbed them and pulled them down. They slipped past my scabbed ankles, and he tossed them to the ground. My bare legs scratched against the tree bark under me, but I couldn't give two shits. Leaning forward, I pushed his hands back from undoing his belt, and I grabbed the reins. I snapped his belt from the belt loops like a whip, tossing it away.

As I undid his pants, I gazed up at him, slick from rain on his chiseled body. He stared back as his chest heaved. His pants slid down, and I was left staring at it. Thick, and nearly as big as my forearm, I slowly wrapped my fingers around it. His raw power was intoxicating. As I stroked it slowly, my fingers barely able to wrap around it, he groaned like an animal, and for the first time, I felt like the hunter. My hand slid from the head of his cock down to the base, and as I did so, it grew even bigger, with a thick throb and another groan from his lips.

All the shit he'd put me through the last couple of days was brushed so far out of my mind that all I could think about was the gushing bliss of having him naked before me, and as I lay back, spreading my bare thighs, exposing myself to him, he leaned over me, and I raked my fingernails down his chest, dusted with dark hair.

It was more than lust growing. I felt a connection, a bond

building between us. I didn't know if it was real or just a figment of the deep passion that was like a new drug. But I never wanted anything as much as I wanted him in that moment. And I wanted it to last forever.

He moaned as he touched me, sliding his fingers along my lips down there, and just as he pressed the huge tip of his cock to me, he paused.

"Ash, I've never felt these feelings for anyone like I have for you."

I pushed my fingers hard into his lips. "Stop talking, and take me."

He drove himself into me, and sliding in as wet as I was, I screamed. It was a scream of such pleasure it flirted with pain. He was so massive that my core erupted into a shaking exhilaration.

"God, I want you. You're so beautiful." His voice was soft, but with a growl behind it.

"You feel unbelievable," I moaned, wrapping my hands over his shoulders and digging my nails into my back, pulling him into me. His cock slid in further, and I gasped. The heat of him being inside me was so intense my instinct was to pull away. I thought I was going to combust into flames right then and there.

A wince caught the corner of his eye.

Steam flooded my vision.

"Take me," I moaned. Pulling his face to me, I kissed him deeply, sliding our tongues against one another's. My body shook with overwhelming pleasure as he pushed himself into me deeper and deeper. I bit his lip from the intensity. I'd never felt anything so good in my life, and I couldn't bear it. For a moment, I thought I was back in the forge, heat exuding from every inch of the place.

He started to thrust, and his cock sliding against my walls drove me into near insanity. Cade held onto the tree on both sides of me, his powerful arms with rivers of veins as he rocked inside me. My legs spread as he thrust into me, grunting like an animal, beads of sweat dripping from his brow, evaporating into steam on my breasts.

An irk of pain fell from his mouth.

"Cade…" I moaned.

He had his way with me on top of the fallen tree, him gripping it while my head fell back onto it. The overwhelming sensation of all of him inside me overpowered the creeping pain that grew. Sweat poured down my brow, and a dryness caught my mouth, which I licked to wet.

"Ash?" He cocked an eyebrow and winced again as he continued to fuck me.

"Don't stop," I begged.

"Ash…"

My hands grabbed his sides and pulled him into me as he pulled away. "I'm close…" I moaned as a scream caught in my throat from the intense feeling crawling all over my skin.

"Ash, you're catching…"

I didn't hear his words. "Don't stop, don't stop."

He grabbed my hands forcefully and pulled them off his wet body.

As he pulled himself out of me, deep confusion tore through me. I was so close, and he was as hard as nails.

I rose up, glaring at him, and his eyes peeled wide at me. He was staring at my body, and as I looked down, still distraught from frustration and near anger, fear overtook all those sensations.

My stomach and legs had flames covering them. I looked at Cade, who looked as pale as a ghost. His tan skin whitened to an ash gray, and his face looked gaunt.

My hands hurried to put out the flames as steam poured off my skin. My mouth and throat went as dry as dirt, and I gasped for breath.

"Ash…" Cade groaned as he buckled to his knees before me.

"Cade!" I leaped down to my feet from the tree, naked as the day I was born, but all strength had left the muscles in my body. I fell onto my side, weak, frail, and as vulnerable as a babe.

My head fogged with darkness, swirling to overtake me. The last words I heard before the blackness consumed me were, "Ash... you're... an Aquafae? You didn't tell me... I didn't..."

And then there was nothing... only darkness.

AQUAFAE

Passage from the Tomb of the Elements. Chapter 6, verse 2.

Where fire destroys, ravages and wipes away traces of history, it also invigorates life. It rejuvenates, washes away the freezing cold, and heats the meals that nourish us.

Yet, while fire enhances life—water, is life.

The Aqualorians are as old as time itself, presumably, for as long as oceans covered the majority of our world, there were the Aquafae to swim the currents, sway the tides, and truly inspire man.

Where the Cinderyn burn and rage with a burning desire for power, the Aqualorians are the temperament to their flame. A monsoon will always triumph over the inferno. And as so, the Aquafae inspire hope, peace, and tranquility.

As a river runs endlessly through the mountains, valleys and forests, so does the spirit of the water elementals of Allovan. None other know the strength that lies under the vast, crashing waves.

It is said the great water spirit Dydrus once spoke to man,

saying, 'he who knoweth and speaks with the streams and seas, knows the great wilderness beyond the stars, and with that knowledge, one dwells inward to peace, to calm, to pure and utter perfection.'

-Written by the Prophet Dantris Oireillus. 676 of the Ember Age.

CHAPTER 20

I awoke groggy and disoriented, the world around me hazy and unfocused. A sharp pain throbbed in my chest, making it difficult to breathe. As my vision cleared, I realized I was standing in knee-deep water, the coolness contrasting the burning heat I had felt just moments before.

Panic surged through me as I looked around, but the serene sound of the stream calmed me slightly. I glanced down to see my legs glowing pale in the moonlight, caked with mud, but alive. Beneath the surface of the water, I felt an unusual warmth emanating from my skin, and slowly, I turned my gaze to see Cornelius standing at my side, his shell reflecting the shimmering water.

"What happened?" I managed to croak, my throat dry as parchment.

"Stay calm, Ash," he said, his voice steady and soothing as always. "You were in shock and nearly burned up. I pulled you into the creek to save you from the heat."

The memories flooded back—the intensity of our kiss, the feeling of him inside of me, on top of me... and then the consuming heat. I bolted upright, splashing water, and scanned the area for Cade. "Is he all right? Where is he?"

Cornelius gestured toward the fallen tree where we had been moments before. My heart raced at the thought of him, confused by what had transpired. I glanced over, and there he was, lying on the bank, white as a ghost, with a look of shock plastered across his face.

"Ash…" His voice was strained, barely above a whisper. The sight of him like that sent a wave of relief washing over me.

"What's wrong?" I called out, still unsure of the severity of what had happened. I labored up from the water and stumbled toward him. But I could see it etched on his face: something had changed.

"You…" he began, looking up at me with bewildered blue eyes. "You're an Aquafae?"

I nodded slowly. "I just learned of it. My father was an Aquafae, a sea lord." The truth hung heavy in the air, thick with consequence.

The look on Cade's face transformed from shock to something deeper, more troubling. "You're one of the Aqualorians…" His voice trailed off, as if he were speaking to himself then.

"And you're a Cinderyn…" As I said the word, it hit me like a brick in the mouth.

He nodded, still trying to shake away the cobwebs. "Yes, I am…"

"Our species cannot mate," he said, his voice barely above a whisper. The words hung in the air like a dark cloud, heavy and oppressive.

I felt a pang of sadness in my chest, a deep ache that seemed to radiate through my entire body. "What does that mean?" I asked, my voice trembling slightly.

Cade looked away, his jaw clenched tightly. "It means we can't be together, Ash. Not like that. Our bodies are too different, too… incompatible."

I felt a lump form in my throat, and I swallowed hard to keep the tears at bay. "But we were just…" I trailed off, unable to finish the sentence.

Cade nodded, his expression grim. "I know. But it can't happen again. It's too dangerous."

I wanted to argue, to fight for what we had just shared, but I could see the resolve in his eyes. He had made up his mind, and there was no changing it. I felt a deep sense of loss, like a piece of me had been ripped away.

Just then, the unmistakable sound of mighty wings filled the air. The trees shook, and leaves scattered as Hunter and his dragon, Talonor, descended nearby. Talonor's stone-gray scales shimmered in the moonlight, and his wings created a powerful gust that whipped my hair around my face. I squinted against the wind as Talonor touched down with a thud that sent vibrations through the ground. Hunter dismounted quickly, his armor clanking with each movement. His expression was etched with concern as he took in the scene before him.

"What happened here?" he asked, his gaze flicking between Cade and me.

Cade stood up, his expression hardening. "Nothing. We were just… training."

Hunter raised an eyebrow, clearly not buying the explanation. "Training? Half-naked in the forest?"

Cade's jaw tightened, and I could see the muscles in his neck tense. "Oh, fuck this. Let's burn the bodies and be over with this night."

I watched as Cade and Hunter mounted their dragons, the powerful beasts taking to the sky with a thunderous roar. I felt a profound sense of loss as I watched them disappear into the night, the silence of the forest closing in around me. Bella rushed to my side seemingly from out of nowhere, her eyes wide with concern.

"Ash, what happened? Are you all right?" Bella asked, her voice laced with worry.

I nodded, but the tears that welled up in my eyes betrayed my true feelings. "I'm fine, Bella. Just... just give me a moment."

Bella wrapped her arms around me, providing the comfort I desperately needed. I leaned into her embrace, letting the tears flow freely. The weight of what had just happened pressed down on me, making it hard to breathe.

"What happened, Ash?" Bella asked, her voice filled with concern.

I took a deep breath, trying to steady myself. "Cade and I... we were together. But then something happened. I burned up, and Cornelius had to pull me into the creek to help me after."

Bella's eyes widened in shock. "You were burning up? Why? And who's Cornelius?"

I sighed, knowing I had to tell her the truth. "Because I'm an Aquafae, Bella. My father was a sea god, and that makes me one of the Aqualorians. And Cade... he's a Cinderyn. Our elements are too different. We can't be together like that, I guess. I didn't know..." And the realization of me saying Cornelius' name meant I knew I had to spill the beans. I took a deep breath, trying to find the right words to explain. "Cornelius is an enchanted, old, wise, kinda quirky, magical tortoise. He's been helping me learn about my magic and my true heritage. He's been seeing me at night, and he's the reason I keep coming out into the Faewood."

Bella's eyes widened in disbelief. "A magical tortoise? That sounds... incredible."

I nodded. "It is. But it's also complicated. I just learned I'm one of them, and Cade and I... we... it was the most amazing thing in my life... ever... before it all came crumbling down. Now I feel like I'm all alone in a dark abyss."

Bella's expression turned to one of sympathy. "I'm so sorry, Ash. This is all so much to take in."

I sighed, feeling the weight of the situation pressing down on me. "I know. But I have to figure out a way to deal with it. I can't just give up."

Bella squeezed my hand reassuringly. "You're right. We'll figure this out together. But first, let's get you back to the house. You need to rest and recover."

I nodded, grateful for her support. As we made our way back to the house, I couldn't shake the feeling of loss and confusion that hung over me. The thought of not being able to be with Cade was painful, but I knew I had to focus on the bigger picture. I had to learn to control my magic and figure out a way to protect myself and those I cared about.

As we approached the house, I could see the smoke rising from the pile of bodies being incinerated by the dragons. The sight sent a shiver down my spine, a reminder of the danger that still lurked around us. The rancid smell of burning flesh drove us running to the house, slamming the door behind ourselves.

I felt I needed to talk to Bella, while Rosa watched with wicked curiosity. But it would have to wait. My lips quivered so hard I knew I wouldn't be able to speak through my gasping breaths.

I made my way to my room, feeling the exhaustion of the day catching up with me. As I lay down on the bed, I couldn't help but think about Cade, about the connection we shared and the pain of knowing we couldn't be together. But I also thought about Cornelius, about the magic within me and the potential it held. I knew I had to embrace it, to learn to control it and use it to protect those I cared about. I couldn't let the pain of my past or the challenges of my present define me. I had to be strong, to fight for what I believed in and for those I loved.

I thought about the thrill of his lips kissing my neck, the feeling of him inside of me, and the agony of us being torn apart.

With that resolve, I closed my eyes and let sleep take me, but not before the gushing tears soaked my pillow.

CHAPTER 21

*A*s the first rays of sunlight crept through the window, casting a soft glow over the room, I stirred from my fitful sleep. My head felt heavy, and my limbs ached—physical remnants of the emotional turmoil that had consumed me the night before. The sound of mighty dragons roaring in the distance pulled me from my reverie, and I pushed myself to get out of bed, even though a deep sadness weighed down on me. Cade had flown off so abruptly after our failed attempt at intimacy, leaving me with a profound sense of loss and confusion.

I dressed quickly, pulling on my pants and a loose shirt, tucking my unruly hair behind my ears. The thought of facing Cade after what had happened made a knot form in my stomach. But I knew I couldn't hide away forever. With a deep breath, I stepped out of my room and into the main hall, where the scent of fresh bread and brewing tea filled the air.

Rosa was already bustling about the kitchen, her eyes flicking briefly to me before turning back to her work. Bella sat at the table, her hands wrapped around a mug of steaming tea. She looked up as I entered, her eyes filled with concern.

"Good morning, Ash," she said, a small smile playing on her lips.

"Morning," I replied, forcing a smile in return. I took a seat next to her, accepting the cup of tea Rosa offered me with a nod of thanks.

The sound of heavy footsteps outside drew our attention, and a moment later, Cade stepped into the house. He looked tired, his hair slightly disheveled, and his usual confident stride replaced with a weary slump. His eyes met mine briefly before he looked away, his jaw clenched tightly. Hunter followed, also looking as though no sleep had found him that night.

"Morning," he said curtly, his voice distant.

"Morning," I replied, feeling the tension between us like a physical force.

Rosa set a plate of food in front of Cade, and he ate in silence, his gaze fixed on his plate. I tried to focus on my own breakfast, but the knot in my stomach made it difficult to swallow.

"Where were you last night?" Bella asked directly of Cade. Her tone was innocent enough, but I could see the underlying concern in her eyes.

Cade looked up briefly, his expression guarded. "Out. Taking care of things that needed handling."

"Like what?" Bella pressed, her eyes narrowing slightly.

Cade let out a sigh, setting down his fork with a clatter. "Things, Bella. Just things. You don't need to worry about it."

Bella opened her mouth to respond, but I cut in, wanting to defuse the tension. "Leave it, Bella. It's fine."

Bella shot me a look, but I gave her a small nod, signaling to drop the subject. She sighed but complied, turning back to her own breakfast.

As we ate in awkward silence, I couldn't help but steal glances at Cade. His brooding presence filled the room, making it hard to breathe. I could see the turmoil in his eyes, the internal struggle playing out behind his stoic façade. Despite everything, my heart ached for him, yearning for the connection we had shared so briefly.

After a while, Cade stood up abruptly, pushing his chair back with a scrape. "I'm going out again," he declared, his voice tinged with frustration.

"Where are you going?" I asked, unable to keep the concern out of my voice.

Cade paused, his gaze flicking to me before he looked away. "There are questions that need answering. I can't find them here in the forest."

A flare of anger sparked within me, fueled by the pain of his rejection. "So you're just going to leave again? Without any explanation?"

Cade's jaw tightened, and he turned to face me, his eyes flashing. "I don't owe you an explanation, Ash. You're my slave, nothing more. I should've never thought anything otherwise."

His words stung like a physical blow, and I felt tears welling up in my eyes. "Fine. Go. I don't care anymore."

With that, Cade turned on his heel and strode out of the house, leaving a heavy silence in his wake. Bella looked at me with sympathy, reaching out to take my hand.

"I'm sorry, Ash."

I shook my head, blinking back the tears. "It's fine. I knew I couldn't expect anything more from him."

Rosa cleared the table quietly, her eyes flicking between Bella and me. She offered no words of comfort, but her silent presence was soothing, nonetheless.

Bella squeezed my hand, her voice soft. "Let's go back to your room. We can talk more there."

I nodded, grateful for her support, and followed her back into my room, but not before Bella grabbed a bottle of red wine from a cabinet.

"You always know how to make things better," I said with a

small smile, taking the bottle from her, popping the open cork and drinking from the bottle with a thick gulp.

She gave me a playful nudge. "That's what best friends are for. Now, tell me everything."

We settled onto the bed, each taking a long sip from the bottle. The wine was sweet and rich, a welcome distraction from the turmoil of my thoughts.

"So, tell me. What exactly happened between you and Cade last night?" Bella asked, her eyes wide with curiosity.

I sighed, letting the memories wash over me. "We were together, Bella. In every way. It was... incredible. But then something happened. I burned up, like my body was on fire. Cornelius saved me, pulling me into the creek just in time."

As Bella and I sat huddled together in my room, sharing a bottle of wine, I took a deep breath and recounted the events of the previous night. Bella's eyes widened with curiosity and concern as she listened intently, taking occasional sips from her glass.

"It started in the forest," I began, my voice trembling slightly with emotion. "Cade found me there, and we... we kissed. It was like nothing I've ever felt before, Bella. His lips were soft, yet firm, and when he touched me, it was like an electric current running through my body."

Bella's eyebrows rose as she took another sip of wine, hanging onto every word. "Go on," she urged.

"He undressed me, and then himself," I continued, feeling my cheeks flushing at the memory. "We were standing there, skin to skin, as the rain poured down on us. He kissed every part of me, Bella. It was like he was exploring my body, and I felt so alive, so desired."

Bella's gaze never left my face, her eyes filled with intrigue and a hint of envy. "And then?" she prompted.

"He lifted me up and set me on a fallen tree," I said, my voice growing softer as she relived the moment. "He kissed me deeply, and then… he was inside me. It was intense, Bella. I've never felt anything like it. But as we continued, something happened. I could feel the heat building inside me, consuming me."

Bella leaned in closer, her grip tightening on the bottle. The sound of her sweaty hand on the bottle caused a subtle squeal. "What do you mean, heat?"

"It was like my skin was on fire," I explained, my voice laced with fear. "I could see steam rising from my body, and the pain was unbearable. I tried to ignore it, to push through it, but it was too much."

Bella's eyes widened in shock. "That's terrible, Ash. What happened next?"

"Cade noticed something was wrong, and he started to pull away," I said, my voice trembling. "But it was too late. The heat intensified, and I passed out. The next thing I remember is waking up in the creek, with Cornelius standing next to me."

Bella shook her head in disbelief. "This is all so… overwhelming. I can't believe you went through all of that alone."

I offered a small smile. "I wasn't alone, Bella. I had Cornelius, and I have you. You're here for me now, and that means everything."

Bella wrapped her arms around me, pulling me into a tight embrace. "I'll always be here for you, Ash. No matter what happens, we'll face it together."

As Bella and I continued to share the bottle of wine, we delved deeper into our fears and hopes for the future. Bella expressed her worries about what would happen if the queen found them, and I shared her determination to learn to control my magic and protect those I loved.

"We can't let the past define us, Bella," I said, my voice filled with resolve. "We have to fight for our future, for our freedom. I won't let anyone take that away from us."

Bella nodded, her eyes filled with admiration. "You're right, Ash. We'll find a way to overcome these challenges together. We always have." She left the room after giving me a soft kiss on the cheek and a squeeze of my shoulders. The soothing of her arms calmed me before she left. The warmth of the wine also had a calming effect that helped me drift off into a deep, needed sleep.

I woke up to the sound of rustling in my room. Startled, I sat up, my heart pounding in my chest. The room was dark, save for the soft glow of the moonlight filtering through the window. As my eyes adjusted to the dim light, I saw the silhouette of the vast shell between the window and me.

"Easy, child," came the familiar, wise voice of Cornelius. "It's just me. I came to talk to you, Ash," he said, his voice tinged with urgency. "There are things you need to know, and we have little time."

I rubbed the sleep from my eyes, trying to focus. "What things? What's going on?"

Cornelius paced slowly back and forth, his shell reflecting the moonlight. "The Blaze Queen is growing stronger. She has sent more hunters after you. They are not far behind. You and Cade must work together to defeat her, despite your differences."

I scoffed, crossing my arms over my chest. "Defeat her? Work together? After everything that's happened? Cade can barely look at me, let alone work with me."

Cornelius stopped pacing and turned to face me, his eyes glowing in the dark. "You must try, Ash. The fate of Allovan depends on it. The queen seeks the power that lies within you. If she gains control of it, all will be lost."

I swallowed hard, the weight of his words settling over me like a heavy blanket. "But how? How can we work together when we can't even be in the same room without arguing?"

Cornelius sighed, a sound like distant thunder. "You must find common ground. You both share a desire to protect those you care about. Use that as a starting point. Together, you are stronger than the queen. Apart, you will both fall."

I nodded, feeling a renewed sense of determination. "What do I need to do?"

"You need to increase your abilities and the potency of your Gilded Radiance. That is the key. You have to become stronger in every way, and the prince can help with that."

"If he can even look at me." My stomach seemed to sink into the floorboards beneath the bed.

"Yes, we will need to figure out a way past your current... situation with the Blaze Prince." Cornelius cleared his long throat. "But regardless, we need to get you training more. You've made progress, but Queen Mortriana Vissex is the most powerful being in all of Allovan, you're nowhere near ready to defend yourself against her yet."

"You're right." I swung my feet to the side of the bed, standing quickly. "And if Cade doesn't want to help me, then fuck it, I'm not just going to lie around here moping. You don't want to talk to me? But you want to tell me to stay put and not work on protecting myself and Bella? Well, Cade, then you can suck a rock. Get me out of here, Cornelius. I've got magic to use!"

CHAPTER 22

here were multiple reasons for me to disobey Cade's orders to stay in my room. I needed to learn to use my magic, and I had to be out in the forest, near the water, to do that. But there was something deeper at play too—something about Cade's recent behavior nagged at me. He had been such an asshole, treating me like I was nothing more than his property instead of the person I was becoming. I didn't mind defying him; not this time. I was tired of waiting for someone to rescue me. If there was a chance to gain power, to harness this magic within me, I had to take it.

"Where do you think you're going?" Bella's voice broke through the dense air, yanking my arm, as she'd surely been waiting outside my room under the night sky.

"I need to practice," I replied, my voice steady, though my insides twisted with uncertainty. "I can't just wait here and hope for things to get better. I need to learn to use my magic."

Bella interrupted, shaking her head vehemently. "Cade didn't leave you here to go off by yourself, and he forbade you from doing this again."

I turned to her, frustration bubbling to the surface. "I've got to do this, Bella. I can't rely on someone else to protect me all the time. I've got to learn to fight. I've got to be ready when the time comes!"

"You're right," she admitted, stepping closer. "But that doesn't mean you have to do it alone. I want to come with you. I want to see your magic!"

"Bella, listen!" I stepped back from her, feeling my nerves surge. "I don't want to get you hurt. I don't want to put you in danger again. You have no idea what I'm up against..."

"It's not just you anymore!" she argued back, her voice firm as she crossed her arms. "We're in this together. I can't sit back and let you face whatever is out there alone. You've already saved me once, and I'll be damned if I'm not strong enough to help you fight back."

I opened my mouth to protest, but stopped. The fierceness in her glacier-blue eyes reminded me of the bond we shared through our tumultuous past. If she wanted to be by my side in this and was willing to fight, who was I to deny her that?

With a reluctant sigh, I relented. "All right... But you need to promise me that if things get too dangerous, you'll run."

"Deal." A smile slipped onto her face, and I felt a spark of hope rekindle.

I stepped back, turning toward where the ancient tortoise had been in the moonlight, as he'd disappeared again at the sight of Bella.

"Cornelius, she's with me. Please, can you show yourself to her, to help me?"

He sighed, the sound rippling through the air.

As Bella stepped forward, he materialized into view. His head extended from his shell, revealing the wise, old eyes that seemed to see right through me every time we spoke. In the light of the full moon, his body glistened with a faint yet staggering aura.

Bella gasped.

I suppressed a grin—that was nothing compared to what I felt the first time I saw him.

"Easy there," Cornelius spoke, his wise old eyes looking Bella over. "You're with the Gold-Marked, and that's good enough for me. But you should know, she's about to take us into great danger. Are you ready for what may come?"

Bella swallowed hard, but nodded. "I am." A resolute expression coated her face, and if I didn't know any better, I'd think she was about to charge into battle.

Her bravery made me feel even more nervous, but with Cornelius and two of us, I thought we could manage. I hoped we could.

"Good. Then let's begin," he said, turning away from us and starting off into the night.

Bella and I followed, and as we ventured deeper into the thick of the Faewood, the only sounds that filled the air were our footsteps, the distant hooting of an owl, and the creaking of old trees that rose tall into the starry sky. I glanced over at Bella. She looked so determined. Her long blonde hair was pulled back into a ponytail, and beneath the light of a thousand stars, her skin glistened. I wished I looked half as courageous as she did at the moment.

We walked for what felt like hours in complete silence except for the crunching of leaves and the slight muffle our footsteps made in the bleak night. I worried; worried that Cade would find out and be even angrier than before. When it came to him, my insides quivered with uncertainty, but as the thought of him left my mind, it was replaced with the feeling of powering through this journey—the drive to learn, and butterflies of excitement— that was all I needed.

"This way," Cornelius said, veering off the path and into a thick area of the forest where moonlight couldn't puncture through the canopy above.

The deciding factor in keeping going was seeing a sparkling

creek ahead, winding like a silver serpent through the trees. The surface shimmered with the soft reflection of the moon and stars.

Cornelius stopped beside the creek and turned to face us. "The water will help you greatly. Take off your shoes."

Bella and I sat on the bank and complied, wincing as the cool water seeped between our toes.

"Now, listen closely. The Gilded Radiance has been unlocked inside of you, and it's long been dormant. To summon it, you must first feel for Eden within you. Feel that connection, that bond that I told you about. She will help you. And when you're ready, picture an orb of golden light in the center of your chest."

I closed my eyes, taking a breath as the cool water lapped against my ankles, and I felt for the sister I never had, this magical being that was me, but also not me.

She was there again—that rich, warm streak of golden light pulsing inside of me. I smiled to myself.

"I feel her," I whispered.

"Excellent," Cornelius said. "Now, when you're ready, summon her. Imagine that orb blooming, getting bigger, brighter, until you feel its heat radiating throughout your body. When you're overcome with it, release it."

I nodded and closed my eyes. I took several deep breaths as the cool creek water lapped higher onto my calves. My insides churned with excitement and nerves. This was it. The moment of truth. I felt for Eden, that stable streak, and imagined a glowing flower opening inside my sternum. A warmth grew from deep within me, making me feel powerful, and charged with electric potential. The golden orb expanded, and with each breath, it grew bigger, heavier, nobly bright. I clasped my hands over it, feeling like a maiden about to give birth to a powerful future queen.

"Now, release it," Cornelius whispered.

I opened my eyes and screamed, thrusting my hands outward, palms facing the thick black forest in front of us.

A brilliant pulse of golden magic erupted from me, exploding into the night. The force of it knocked me backward, sending me falling into the creek with a splash. The magic ripped through the air, cutting into the blackness and puncturing the silence of the forest.

As the golden light dissipated, I felt a rush of power coursing through me. I gasped, sputtering as I stood up in the waist-high water. The cool liquid soothed my burning skin, and I felt incredibly alive, energized in a way I never had before.

"Ash!" Bella shouted, her eyes wide with a mix of excitement and concern as she rushed to the water's edge.

"I'm okay," I assured her, stepping carefully toward her. "I'm fine."

Cornelius moved beside me, his eyes glowing in the moonlight. "You did well, Ash. Your magic is strong, but remember, it comes with a cost. You pushed it too far, too fast."

I nodded, feeling a mix of elation and exhaustion wash over me. "I know. I just got caught up in the moment."

"You must be careful," Cornelius warned. "Too much and you'll be left vulnerable, just like what has happened the last few times. Use only as much as you need, and leave some in the reserves."

Something tingled at the back of my brain; an eerie, troubling notion. Like a scratch I couldn't itch. Even past my exhaustion, it was as if something was pulling me deeper into the forest, beckoning for me to come, and it was overpowering.

"What?" Bella asked with both eyebrows raised. "You look like you've seen a ghost."

"There's something over there," I breathed. The chirping of crickets and the flutter of bird wings overhead dimmed.

Cornelius' head followed my gaze, and his wise eyes narrowed, but he didn't peep a word.

"Follow me." I trudged down the middle of the stream, the

cool water replenishing my depleted energy as we stalked deeper into the night forest.

The night was eerily peaceful, the forest creatures silent as if holding their breath. I felt that tingling sensation at the base of my skull, an ominous foreboding that something sinister lurked nearby.

Twenty minutes into our search, the sound of rushing water grew louder, and the forest opened up to a small clearing where a waterfall flowed gracefully over jagged rocks into a deep pool below. The moonlight illuminated the mist rising from the waterfall, creating an ethereal atmosphere.

And there, standing in the shallow pool, was the most breathtaking creature I had ever seen. The waterfall fell onto its massive body, rolling down its wings like a river.

It was a dragon, its scales a brilliant shade of blue that shimmered in cascading waves of hues, glistening under starlight. The creature was immense, easily half the size of Krakos, with graceful curves and a sleek, muscular build. Its eyes, a striking shade of emerald, scanned the surroundings, locking onto us momentarily before baring its pearly white teeth.

"Oh my god," Bella breathed, her grip on my hand tightening.

I felt transfixed, unable to tear my eyes away from the stunning creature. Its scales were wet and glistening, each one reflecting the moonlight like a polished gem.

Cornelius seemed to sense my intention. "Ash, we must go. Now."

But I couldn't move. The dragon was the most beautiful thing I had ever seen, and a part of me yearned to approach it, to touch its sleek scales and feel its power.

The dragon emerged from the waterfall, shaking its massive head, and a burst of cool mist enveloped us. It roared, the sound like thunder in the night sky, and spread its wings, which were a deep indigo shade. With a powerful flap, the creature launched into the air, its eyes fixed on us. Its wild eyes pierced me so deeply that my knees wobbled and I couldn't look away, even if I wanted to. It was incredible. The most majestic thing I'd ever seen.

I felt a rush of adrenaline as the dragon's gaze bored into me. Then, with a final, piercing look, it turned and soared into the night sky, its wings carrying it away.

I stood, transfixed, watching the dragon until it disappeared from sight.

"Come on," Bella urged, pulling me from my trance. "Ash, I have a feeling that's not the last time we're going to see that dragon."

"Why do you say that?" I hoped her words were right, but she always had a knack for those things. Getting feelings that were right, even when I swore by Odiun she had no way of knowing those things.

"Just a feeling." She winked, but then noticed something on the ground. She knelt, plucking a small white flower, showing it to me before placing it in her pocket.

I grinned. Bella, always finding beauty in this ugly world.

With a deep breath, I followed her and Cornelius back into the dense forest, the image of the blue dragon etched into my mind. As we walked, the excitement of what I had just accomplished buzzed through me, along with a sense of unease about the mysterious dragon.

We returned to the house in silence, each lost in our thoughts. Bella bid me goodnight with a hug and a whispered word of encouragement, and I retired to my room, my mind racing.

Sleep eluded me for a long while as I stared up at the ceiling, replaying the events of the night. The power I had unleashed, the breathtaking beauty of the blue dragon in the forest—all tangled together in my thoughts.

CHAPTER 23

The late afternoon sun dipped below the tree line, casting a warm, golden glow over the horizon. Bella, Rosa, and I sat on the porch, watching as the sky turned a beautiful shade of orange and pink. The forest was alive with the sounds of birds chirping and insects buzzing, creating a serene atmosphere that seemed to wash away the stresses of the day.

My mind, however, was elsewhere. I had been wondering all day where Cade and Hunter kept disappearing to. They would fly off on their dragons and return at some undisclosed time, day or night. I couldn't shake the feeling that they were keeping something from me, and it gnawed at me like a persistent itch.

As if on cue, the sound of powerful wings beating the air filled my ears. I craned my neck to see Cade and Hunter descending from the sky, their dragons' massive forms casting long shadows over the forest. Krakos and Talonor landed with a thud that shook the ground, sending vibrations through the porch.

Cade dismounted first, his body slumped with fatigue. His normally impeccable armor was smudged with soot, and his hair was disheveled. He pulled off his black wolf mask and handed it to Rosa without a word, then trudged inside, leaving a trail of muddy footprints in his wake.

Hunter followed suit, looking equally worn out. He gave us a curt nod before heading inside, his armor clinking with each step.

I couldn't take the suspense anymore. I jumped up from my seat and followed Cade inside, my heart pounding in my chest. I found him in the dining room, slumped over a plate of food, shoveling it into his mouth with a wicked hunger.

"Where were you?" I demanded, my voice trembling slightly.

Cade looked up at me, his eyes bleary with exhaustion. "We were looking for answers," he said vaguely, before turning back to his food.

My frustration bubbled over. "Looking for answers where? And what kind of answers? Why won't you tell me what's going on?"

Cade sighed heavily, pushing his plate away. "It's complicated, Ash. I can't just... explain it to you."

"But I deserve to know!" I cried, my voice cracking with emotion. "I'm not just some pawn in your game, Cade. I'm a person, with feelings and thoughts and a right to know what's going on in my own life!"

Cade's jaw tightened, and he looked away. "I can't tell you everything, Ash. Not yet. Just... trust me, okay? I'm doing this for your own good."

I scoffed, crossing my arms over my chest. "Trust you? How can I trust you when you keep lying to me, keeping secrets from me?"

Cade's eyes flashed, and he stood up abruptly, his chair scraping against the floor. "I'm not lying to you, Ash. I'm protecting you. There's a difference."

With that, he turned on his heel and strode out of the room, leaving me standing there in stunned silence. I felt a mix of anger, frustration, and hurt all churning inside of me. How could he expect me to trust him when he kept me in the dark about everything?

I spent the rest of the evening stewing in my thoughts, trying to make sense of the whirlwind that was my life. Bella and Rosa did their best to distract me, but my mind was consumed with thoughts of Cade and the secrets he was keeping from me.

As night fell, I retreated to my room, my body heavy with exhaustion. I crawled into bed, pulling the covers up to my chin as I stared up at the ceiling. My mind was a jumbled mess of thoughts and emotions, and I couldn't shake the feeling of unease that had been plaguing me all day. Cornelius didn't appear that night, so I took the opportunity to rest after using my magic the night before, and the spectacular sight of the blue dragon in the waterfall.

Just as I was about to drift off to sleep, the sound of the door creaking open startled me. I bolted upright, my heart pounding in my chest as I scanned the dark room.

And there he was, standing in the doorway, his silhouette outlined by the soft glow of the moonlight streaming in through the window.

Cade.

I blinked, rubbing my eyes to make sure I wasn't seeing things. He stepped into the room, closing the door behind him with a soft click.

"What are you doing here?" I whispered, my voice barely above a breath.

He didn't answer, just stood there, his eyes locked onto mine. I could see the war raging inside of him, the struggle between what he wanted and what he knew was right. The air between us was thick with tension, filled with unspoken words and unfulfilled desires. His gaze was intense, piercing through me, as if he could see the very essence of my being.

And then, without a word, he moved toward me. I watched, transfixed, as he crawled onto the bed, his body moving with a predatory grace that sent shivers down my spine. He slid under the covers, his hands gripping my hips gently yet firmly, the warmth of his touch sending jolts of electricity through my body.

My breath hitched as I felt his warm breath against my thighs, his fingers hooking into the waistband of my underwear. Slowly, almost painstakingly, he tugged them down, his eyes never leaving mine. I lifted my hips to help him, my heart pounding wildly in my chest, a mix of anticipation and anxiety surging through me.

He pressed a soft kiss to the inside of my thigh, and I let out a soft gasp, my body tensing with anticipation. He trailed kisses up my leg, each one more intense than the last, his hands gripping my hips tightly as he moved closer to my center. Every touch, every caress, felt like a flame igniting my skin, burning away all doubts and fears.

And then, with a soft moan, he buried his face between my legs, his tongue sliding against me in a way that made me see stars. He licked my clit expertly, sliding it in wet circles around it, causing my legs to quiver and me to moan his name. I gripped the sheets tightly, my body arching off the bed as wave after wave of pleasure washed over me. His mouth was hot and wet, his tongue moving in ways that left me breathless and gasping for more.

Each stroke of his tongue sent shivers of ecstasy coursing through my veins, building up a fire within me that threatened to consume me whole. I could feel the heat radiating from his touch, the raw power that flowed between us, connecting us in a way that transcended mere physical pleasure.

His hands explored my body, each touch deliberate and filled with desire. But as the heat built inside of me, so did the pain. The same burning sensation that had consumed me before rose, threatening to overwhelm me.

I tried to ignore it, to push through it, but it was too much. The heat was unbearable, and I could feel myself losing control.

"Cade, stop," I gasped, pushing at his shoulders.

He looked up at me, his eyes clouded with desire, but also concern.

I shook my head, tears stinging my eyes. "It's too much. I can't... I can't handle it."

He pulled away, sitting up on his knees. His chest rose and fell with his ragged breaths, and I could see the struggle in his eyes. His face was pale, with droplets of sweat streaking down his chiseled face. "I'm sorry, Ash. I didn't mean to... I just... I couldn't help myself. I've been thinking about you all day, and I... I needed to be close to you."

I reached out, cupping his cheek in my hand as I struggled to catch my breath, feeling completely depleted. "I know. And it was... incredible. Until it wasn't."

He leaned into my touch, his eyes closing briefly. "I'm sorry. I never meant to hurt you."

I shook my head. "You didn't hurt me, Cade. Not really. It's just... we're too different. We can't..."

He nodded, understanding dawning in his eyes. "I know. I just... I wanted to try. I had to know if there was a way..."

I offered him a small, sad smile. "I wanted it too. More than anything. But we can't force something that's not meant to be."

He sighed, pulling away from my touch. "You're right. I'm sorry, Ash. For everything."

With that, he slid out from under the covers, standing up beside the bed. He looked down at me, his expression torn.

"Goodnight, Ash," he whispered before turning and walking out of the room, the door clicking shut behind him.

I lay there, my body still tingling with the remnants of pleasure, but my heart aching with longing and confusion. I wanted Cade more than anything. But our elements were too different. We were too different.

And as I lay there, staring up at the ceiling, I couldn't stop the tears from falling. I cried for the feelings that could never be, for the man who had stolen my heart, but could never truly be mine.

I cried until the tears ran dry, and exhaustion claimed me, pulling me into a fitful sleep plagued by dreams of fire and ice, of love and loss. And when I woke in the morning, it was to a bitter realization.

I loved Cade Phoenixfire. And that love was destined to break me. I couldn't tell him, though. He was too withdrawn, too distant, too resilient. And of course, he was my new master, and I was his slave. He couldn't defy his stepmother forever, and I knew the end of us would be devoid of all hope for me.

But I refused to let it. I refused to let the circumstances of our birth, of our elements, define us. I would find a way. Somehow, someway, I would find a way for us to be together.

And with that thought burning in my mind like a beacon, I rose from my bed, ready to face whatever the day may bring. Because I was a survivor—a survivor that would one day be free —and I would not be broken.

CHAPTER 24

The first rays of morning sunlight crept through the window, casting soft rays of golden light on the wooden floorboards. The night had been a torment of restless thoughts, and I felt the weight of my emotions pressing down on me like a heavy blanket. Even though Cade's touch had ignited a fire within me, the realization that we could never truly be together extinguished it just as quickly, leaving a void in its place. The reality of our situation—of what we couldn't deny—was a bitter pill to swallow.

Finally, I threw off the covers and swung my legs over the edge of the bed, my bare feet cold against the hardwood floor. With a heavy sigh, I rose and made my way to the window. As I looked outside into the pale morning light, my heart sank. The dragons were gone, and so was Cade.

I didn't want to think too much about where he had gone this time, or what he would do. I couldn't bear another moment of worrying about the man who my heart refused to stop loving, even if every fiber in me screamed it was impossible. The ache inside of me was only growing stronger as I thought more and more about him... about us. I needed a distraction.

Rosa was sitting quietly on the porch, a steaming mug of tea in hand, staring off into the peaceful surroundings. She seemed so serene, so at ease, like she had all the time in the world. I envied that about her.

Pushing the thoughts of Cade aside, I made my way to the porch, easing myself into the chair next to Rosa. She glanced my way but said nothing as I sat down.

I took a breath, the cool morning air filling my lungs as the birds chirped melodically in the trees. "Where do you think they've gone this time?" I asked, breaking the silence, though my voice was heavier than I intended.

"Eh. Who knows?" Rosa responded simply, taking a long sip of her tea. "Those two are always running off ta' only the gods know where."

"I just... I hate waiting," I confessed, staring out at the forest, my eyes tracing over the spot where the dragons had been. The anxiety gnawed at me like a persistent itch, never letting me relax completely.

"They'll be back," Rosa assured me, though her tone didn't betray any confidence. "They always come back." She took tobacco from her pouch on the side table and stuffed it into her pipe. Sparked it with the lit candle on the table and puffed. The wrinkles at the corners of her mouth deepened as she sucked in the smoke, then blew it in a plume before her.

I nodded, even though the words did little to soothe me. Cade always felt like a storm ready to unravel, and the unpredictability of his behavior left me feeling uncertain about everything. Just then, Rosa rose, but I reached out, grabbing her hand gently before she could walk away.

"Wait, please." My words were softer now, weighed down with desperation. "Can you stay with me for a moment? I... I have questions. Questions about Cade."

Rosa hesitated, her brow furrowing as she looked down at our hands. "I don't think it's wise to meddle in their affairs, Ash. The prince and you is not my concern."

"But he is my concern," I pressed, my grip tightening. "I need to understand him. He means so much to me, even if I can't have him. I know that sounds foolish, but there's something about him that... I can't just let it go."

She gave a deep sigh, one side of her mouth twisting. "What do ya want me to tell ya?" Rosa asked, pulling her hand free to sit back down. She folded her arms over her chest, peering at me through narrowed eyes.

"Anything you can. I just... I feel so lost. He's so withdrawn and angry. I want to know why. What happened to him? Why does he seem so tormented?"

Rosa sighed heavily again, glancing off into the distance before turning back to me. "He lost his father in battle with the Stormscales. His father was a powerful rider in his own right. When he fell, Cade was left to shoulder a heavy burden..."

"A battle?" I asked, drawn in by the gravity of her words. "What happened?"

Rosa leaned back in her chair, her eyes becoming distant as she recalled the past. "His father led a charge against them, but during the attack, witnesses say he was wounded. The Blaze King fell from his dragon Scorpius. None thought the king would ever die, especially Cade. He admired the king. Cade deeply misses his father. The king meant everything to him, and when he died, I think a piece of Cade died too. So, all he was left with was the queen, who ascended the throne by the Rite of War. While there is a current war, the spouse of the king may ascend the throne if the firstborn isn't fit to, until the war is done, and that kin will be crowned." She paused, a flash of bitterness crossing her face. "His stepmother is not what he needed, though. Mortriana was never the nurturing type. Chaos breeds chaos, and the queen is a conniving, spiteful woman."

"I can't imagine what that's like." I shook my head, my heart aching for him. "I never met my parents. Garris used to tease me, saying my mother was a whore and my father was just some drunken nobody. But I always dreamed of what they looked like —my imagination filled them with grand stories, images of strength and adventure. I imagined them as dragon riders, heroes of the realm, fighting against dragons in the sky, rescuing me from the wretched life I felt so trapped in." Hearing about Cade's father hit hard. An actual hero. Fallen in a battle that spiraled his son's life out of control.

"This Garris doesn't know a bloomin' thing what he's talking about," Rosa said, her voice quiet yet firm. "I'm sure your mother and father were good souls. Because you're one." She put her leathery, kind hand on mine, causing my eyes to water and my lips to quiver. "You may never get to hear stories about them, but they're a part of you. All the characteristics you possess—it was in their blood. Don't let anyone tell you otherwise."

"Thank you, Rosa." My throat tightened. "I used to make up adventures for my parents, imagining they were out there flying on dragons and saving the world. It's sad to know they'll never come for me, just like I feared. And that every time Garris opened his mouth, he was betraying the truth of such a beautiful outcome. But at least I hope they died for someone worth fighting for, right?"

"That's exactly it." Rosa's eyes softened, and there was a warmth in her gaze I hadn't noticed before. "And you are worth fighting for, Ash. No matter what circumstances brought you here, you have magic and power that others envy. Each day you grow stronger. Don't let anyone dim that spark."

"Can you tell me more about Cade?" I leaned forward, my curiosity growing. "What was he like before… his father died?"

Rosa glanced away, her fingers tracing the rim of her pipe. "He was carefree. Lighthearted even. One might say he was like a breath of fresh air. The prince of the Emberveil Empire, adored by all."

My heart sank again. "And then everything fell apart?"

"Exactly," she said solemnly. "He became a shadow of himself; burden-laden by the weight of the empire, and life pushed onto him at such a young age. His stepmother... Mortriana Vissex. I don't know what kind of madness consumed her, but she's driven Cade into a corner. The pressures of royal life are immense. He fights so hard against expectations, against the dark legacy of his stepmother. Everything became a performance to him. He had to be tough, ready to fight against everything and everyone at all times."

"I don't want to think of him as that kind of person." I shifted nervously in my seat, wishing for the prince whom I had kissed, who had held me so close. "He isn't that guy now."

"No, he's not. But it takes time fer' someone like him to open up. And you may have to be the one that helps him break through those barriers." Rosa suddenly leaned in close, watching me intently. "But I will say this, Ash. The obstacles in front of ya are monumental, and he may never be able to give you the life you dream of. You should focus on what's in front of you, and that's the Blaze Queen."

"I want to fight for him." My voice was stronger than I expected, though it still surprised me.

"That may be a fool's errand." She waved her hand at me dismissively, and I sensed she was blocking something in the back of her mind. "You have to keep your head together. You cannot let your feelings surmount the reality. Your feelings blind you to danger, but if you could break through to him, you might get a chance at something more than just survival."

"I know he cares about me in a way. I know he does." Warmth unfurled in my chest. It felt real, but the lingering doubts flipped back to the front of my mind.

"I know you're scared. Scared of losing him. You can't look at him without thinking about how much he means to you. I've watched you, you know. The way you look at him when you say things in the room before. How you light up even just when he walks back in. It's obvious to me you have feelings for him." Rosa took a moment, dropping her eyes before she continued. "But you have to remember, as much as he may care about you, he has a surprise loyalty to his stepmother and his empire that runs far deeper than you can imagine. The stakes are high."

The truth echoed in me, and as I lowered my chin, shame fueled my prior anger. "I'm just another burden to him, aren't I?"

"With everything happening—oh child… even if you think he cares for ya back, he may need to see it. The truth is, no true feelings can come out of this at this time. This is war. Hard, dirty, terrible war." She leaned back in her chair and crossed her arms, hardening her gaze. After a breath, she leaned in again, and she lowered her voice; her words were fierce yet soothing. "What you need right now is to be steadfast, Ash. Do what the prince needs. Not what you want. Let him see what you're capable of, and you might break through."

Inside, I felt myself trembling, but I pressed on. "Rosa, can you help me? Please. I want to know how to be with him, even if I can't like before. Even if I have to fight for it. Even if it will be a torturous path." She was right; my feelings for Cade were consuming me. Every gesture, every word from him punched like knives, but I couldn't let go.

Suddenly, Rosa caught me in a gaze so intense I nearly flinched. "You presume I can help you, but… child, I can only say what I know." Deliberately slowly, she leaned back in her chair. Her gaze dropped slightly before she spoke again. "Even if I tell you how his heart can be won, you have to carry the responsibility."

My pulse quickened. "I can handle it. I'll do anything."

Her eyes riveted on mine again, and her expression hardened. "The truth behind the Blaze Queen is a terrible one. It plagues Cade with a cruel fate, a fate where he believed love doesn't belong. Ever since the king passed, I feel something has taken the queen. A darkness in her heart, like a demon buried in her soul. Cade's troubled, but not lost in darkness like his stepmother, but that darkness in her heart is spreading. I fear the prince thinks he is undeserving of love, and happiness will never find him."

I gasped. "What?"

"He thinks that love is a luxury. If you can show him that love and care is strength," she said, her voice laced with a bitter humor, "it might work. His life has been one tough mountain to climb since his father disappeared. The woman you have to win him over from isn't easy. She is powerful, calculating, and she has everything else knotted around him. But in her quest for power, she often overlooks the power of what she can't comprehend."

"The power of …?"

"Love. Love finds a way. Love conquers all," Rosa said with a gentle nod. "All those ancient sayings we've heard time and time again… all those clichés about love. They're true. If destiny deems you two to find a way, then it will. But until then…" she stood slowly, ashing her pipe. "…maybe you should stop sneaking out at night. You're digging yourself into a hole that's gonna be awfully hard to get out of." She walked off to build the fire in the ovens and prepare breakfast, leaving me with a knot tied tightly in my stomach.

CHAPTER 25

*T*he soft glint of afternoon sunlight trickled through the dense canopy above, casting a dappled pattern of light and shadow on the forest floor. The Faewood was quiet, save for the occasional rustle of leaves and the distant call of a bird I couldn't quite place. I needed this walk, needed this space.

After my conversation with Rosa, I couldn't sit within the confines of the house any longer, not with how heavy my heart weighed with thoughts of Cade, with the overwhelming confusion that clouded my mind. I had thought coming to the Faewood would offer me freedom, but all I had found was more chains—chains in my heart, chains in my mind, chains I couldn't seem to break.

Rosa's words replayed in my head. 'You have to show him that love and care is strength...' She had made it sound so easy, but nothing about Cade Phoenixfire was easy.

I kicked lightly at a fallen branch as I walked, half-contemplating the choices that seemed to spiral endlessly in front of me. Two paths lay at my feet, two impossible choices, neither of which led to the freedom or life I had dreamed of as a child.

If I stayed, I could fight for Cade. I could show him that

together, we were stronger. My feelings for him were undeniable, but with every interaction, it became clearer how tangled his life was, how heavy the weight of his obligations crushed him day after day. Cade wasn't free. He was a prisoner too, locked behind his stepmother's iron expectations.

But stepping onto that path meant accepting that we could never truly be together. His magic, his Cinderyn fire, was the opposite of the Aquafae magic in my blood. No matter how much I yearned for him, there were some things not even love could overcome. I thought of the heat that had nearly consumed me when we were together, how it threatened to destroy me—destroy us—if we tried again.

My other choice was...to run.

I paused at the edge of the creek I had come to so often. The steady bubbling of the water soothed me, just as it always did. I crouched, dipping my fingers into the cool stream, letting the water flow over my skin. Run. The word echoed through my mind, as shaky and unstable as the current in the creek.

If I ran, I could disappear. Maybe not forever, but long enough to create a new identity. Hiding the golden rune on my neck would be the first step. I'd need to blend in somewhere far away from Emberveil, far from the queen's spies, the dragon riders that crisscrossed the skies, and even further from Cade. I could finally be free... or at least free from this nightmare that had me chained to destinies I never asked for.

But that thought hung heavier in my chest than I expected. Free from Cade. The possibility of such a thing made my stomach twist in knots. Yes, he was infuriating—cold, consumed by duty—but I couldn't just shut off my feelings like flicking a switch. What we had, however brief, had ignited something in me—something precious and fragile. Could I really walk away from that? From him? Or worse, from the possibility that he might care?

I looked upstream, considering where I might go. Perhaps I

could slip away under the cover of night and find a small village on the edges of Allovan, one nobody cared about. A forge some-where along the coast, perhaps. Maybe I could hide among the fishermen and laborers. I could paint or do anything, really. So long as I put as much distance as possible between me and that blasted crown resting on the Blaze Queen's head.

But then there was Bella. Bella trusted me. We shared every-thing—we were sisters in all but blood. If I left... no, when I left... she would be stuck with Cade and whatever fate was coming for us like a raven circling the sky.

How could I leave her behind? She was the only solid, true thing I ever had. Running meant leaving behind the only person I cared about, and I wasn't selfish enough to doom her to whatever happened. Guilt stewed inside me—it burned away at my thoughts until the flirtation with the notion of freedom grew weaker, smaller.

Maybe I could take her with me?

Could we find that small, peaceful life together, both of us vanishing into the unknown? But then again, the Blaze Queen's reach was long and sharp as a blade. She would never stop hunting me—not until she held my magic in her hands, no matter how well-hidden I thought I'd be. I'd only be trading one cage for another: a lifetime of running, of hiding, of constantly looking over my shoulder while shoving my former life into the abyss.

I stood, shaking the water from my fingers, and turned back toward the trees. I didn't know where my feet were leading me. All I knew was that this forest, as beautiful as it was, felt like it was swallowing me whole. I was suffocating under the weight of choices that had no clear endpoint. Stay or run? Fight or flee? Cade or solitude?

A noise caught my attention—a soft rustling not far ahead. I squinted into the distance and saw a figure atop a boulder just around the bend in the path.

Cornelius.

Of course. The wise old tortoise was sitting serenely on the moss-covered rock, as if waiting for me. His huge shell caught a stray beam of sunlight, reflecting an almost magical shimmer across the clearing. His usually slow movements seemed oddly purposeful today, his eyes watching me closely as I approached.

"Do you get tired of appearing out of nowhere?" I asked, climbing up the boulder and plopping down beside his shelled body.

Cornelius chuckled—a low, rumbly sound like waves crashing against the shore. "You make it sound as if I have other places to be, child."

I swung my legs over the edge of the boulder, letting them dangle in the open air as I stared into the trees. "I don't know what to do, Cornelius."

For once, he seemed quiet, listening as the wind picked up around us, ruffling the leaves. I wasn't sure he had an answer, and somehow, the silence made my words flood out of me like an overflowing dam. "I'm stuck. I'm... torn." I sighed, feeling the weight of everything I'd kept bottled up pressing down on my shoulders. "I could leave, you know. I could run. Start over somewhere far away. But Bella... I can't leave her. And Cade? I..." My voice broke. "I don't know where I stand with Cade. He's—he's confusing. He's torn too, between what he wants and what he thinks he's supposed to do. He's complicated."

"And you're wondering if you should stay and fight for him," Cornelius said, his eyes twinkling with an old, knowing sincerity.

I nodded, feeling the knot in my throat tighten. "It's not just him I'm fighting for. It's... everything. My freedom, my power, a world where I don't have to be afraid." My voice cracked under the weight of it all. "And if I run, it might all go away and I'll be free... but what kind of freedom would that even be?"

"You and your friend, Bella," Cornelius began, adjusting himself on the boulder as his shell shifted slightly, "are strong. You both have a will to survive that few people possess. That much is obvious. But... you also have goodness. A spark that's worth fighting for. If the world you envision can be created, you have to be here to work toward that."

His words made me think about the girl I was back in Bramblebash, a girl who only ever thought of surviving each day, scraping by on what she could. Her will to fight, to create something better hadn't flickered into life until she'd seen Krakos raining down fire, the possibility of death forcing something inside her to bloom. I was still that girl, but there was more to her now. There was a fire burning, a need to change the world.

"I want that world, Cornelius," I said, tracing the outline of a leaf with my finger. "I want to be free, and I want to help others find freedom too. But...is it worth it? The path... the fight... it all seems so improbable."

"I cannot see the future," Cornelius said with a wisdom that seemed both ancient and comforting. "Nor can I see into the prince's heart." His beak tilted slightly, as if he were gazing at something beyond the forest. "I can see the turmoil that battles within him, however. He's torn between two worlds."

"You're talking about the Cinderyn and Aqualorian powers, aren't you?" I whispered, feeling a familiar ache in my chest as I thought of Cade and what we could never have.

"It's not just that," Cornelius murmured. "It's who he must abandon to choose his path. He's lost so much already, and the queen demands those closest to those in power get thrown beneath the wheels of the carriage, so to speak. The things she asks of him... they weigh heavily on him, and I can see it in his eyes."

"If only he'd talk to me." I sighed. "Maybe if he'd actually tell me what's going on, maybe I could help him..."

"He thinks he's protecting you," Cornelius said, his voice as gentle as the rustling leaves above. "He thinks that by keeping you at a distance, he can find the way forward, keeping you safe, and at the same time not losing his own aspirations, and promises."

These answers didn't make anything easier. Cade, the son of the Blaze King, the future guardian of the empire—he had the entire weight of the world on his shoulders. It should have made me feel small, insignificant, but instead, it sparked something inside me.

"What happens if I stay?" I asked, my eyes locked onto Cornelius. "What can I change? What can we change together?"

Cornelius sighed deeply, his shell glinting. "I won't lie to you —the path isn't an easy one. But together, with the prince fighting by your side, there is a chance. A chance to end this civil war. A chance to create a new world, a world where people don't live in fear."

"And if I leave... if I run..."

"You could save yourself." His wise old eyes met mine. "But others will suffer. The war will rage on. The queen will continue her reign of terror, seeking ultimate power. And who's to say she won't capture you, eventually? No matter how well you hide, magic like yours leaves a trace."

A shiver ran down my spine at the thought of the queen's cruel hands stretching toward me, seeking to siphon my power for her twisted ambitions. Could I really hide forever? Did I want to—knowing what it could cost others?

I paused, my thoughts spiraling. "And Cade? If I run, what will he do?"

Cornelius was quiet for a moment, as if choosing his words carefully. "He believes he must ascend the throne someday, that he can help Allovan more with absolute power. With his duty to the crown, he will do what he thinks is best for his people, even if it makes him miserable."

"Miserable? You mean he'll give me up to his stepmother? That he'll turn me over if I escape?"

The pause in his eyes spoke more than his words. "Yes, child, there's a chance he will turn to his stepmother's bidding. The queen seeks immortality, and the power locked inside you might just be the key. And if she achieves that, then saving you from her clutches will mean facing a whole different beast. It makes this fight so much harder."

My breath caught in my chest. The idea of Cade turning me over... it hurt more than I could explain. But I had to hear it. I had to face what that might mean and how devastating it could be for all of us.

With that thought, and my fingernails tapping on the mossy rock, a new grit formed deep down. The thought of him turning me over was perhaps the final straw. Not only could I not allow the queen to continue in her brutality of our world, but I had to convince Cade to do the right thing, even if it meant tossing away our feelings, and never sharing a kiss with him again.

"What are you thinking about, child?" Cornelius' brow furrowed as he thought. "Something inside of you is screaming, but I can't hear the words."

I'm tired of being the victim. I'm tired of being used for other people's gains. I deserve more. I deserve to be happy, even if I have to fight to get it. Bella deserves the world, and if I can... I'm going to fight to make it a better world for her. She's stuck by me, and I'll tear down Calcaedus itself if that's what it takes!

"I'm going to stay, Cornelius. I'm going to stay til the end. Not just for him, not just for me or Bella, but for everything. I've got to do what I can to help all the people who share our world. I'm done being put in chains. Someone, or something, gave me this magic for a reason. And although I don't know what the reason is exactly, I've got to follow my heart. And my heart is screaming for Cade. I choose... to fight!"

CHAPTER 26

The forest around me blurred into a haze as I marched back to the house, determination fueling each step. I had to talk to Cade. I had to convince him that I could help, that I was more than just a pawn in his stepmother's twisted game. The realization that I had a choice—that I could fight or flee—had crystallized into a fierce resolve. I was done running. I was done being a victim.

As I approached the house, the sight of Bella and Rosa washing clothes together outside brought a wave of comfort. Their presence grounded me, reminding me of the strength we had together. I paused for a moment, watching them work in harmony, their laughter echoing through the air. It was a simple, peaceful scene, a stark contrast to the chaos that seemed to follow me everywhere I went.

Just as I was about to step forward, a thunderous roar reverberated through the sky, shaking the very ground beneath my feet. I looked up, my heart pounding in my chest, as two massive shapes darkened the horizon. Krakos and Talonor, their powerful wings slicing through the air like black and gray blades, descended with a grace that belied their enormous size.

The scales on Krakos shimmered like obsidian under the sunlight, reflecting an almost blue tint as he spread his vast wings wide. His fearsome maw was lined with teeth as sharp as daggers, and his eyes were an unnatural red that seemed to burn with an eternal flame. Talonor, by contrast, glistened with stone-gray scales that caught the light in a softer glow, his sleeker form no less imposing. Massive curling horns adorned the sides of his head, and his eyes were a milky white cloud, almost ethereal but commanding. The sheer strength and power emanating from these beasts was palpable, a force of nature that could level mountains and tear through the skies like a storm.

As the dragons landed with a thud that sent vibrations through the earth, Bella and Rosa dropped their laundry and rushed to my side, their eyes wide with concern. Cade and Hunter, astride their respective dragons, looked worn out and haggard, their bodies slumped with exhaustion. Their faces were etched with lines of weariness, but there was no mistaking the determination in their eyes—a resolve that matched my own.

"Ash, what's happening?" Bella asked, her voice laced with worry.

"I don't know," I replied, my gaze fixed on Cade as he dismounted Krakos, his movements slow and deliberate.

As Cade approached, his eyes met mine, and I was struck by the liveliness in them. There was a spark, a flicker of something that I hadn't seen before. He looked tired, yes, but there was a determination in his gaze that matched my own resolve.

"Cade," I began, my voice steady despite the butterflies fluttering in my stomach. "I need to talk to you."

He hesitated for a moment, his gaze flicking to Hunter's before returning to me. "Ash, I—"

"Please," I interrupted, taking a step closer. "I need to understand what's going on. I need to know why you've been so distant, why you've been keeping things from me."

His jaw tightened, and for a moment, I thought he would

refuse. But then he sighed, running a hand through his dark hair. "I found something, Ash," he said, his voice low. "Something that might help us."

My stomach squeezed like pincers grabbing hot iron at the thought he was going to finally tell me the truth.

Bella, Rosa, and Hunter had gathered around us, their faces etched with curiosity and concern. Cade glanced at them briefly before continuing.

"We've been looking for something, well, someone, my father told me about when I was a boy. But I found him! I've been searching for an old mystic deep in the heart of the Faewood," he explained, his eyes never leaving mine. "His name is Myrathyn. He's a great keeper of knowledge of the old world. My father told me that when he was a young man and at a critical point in his life, needing guidance and resolve, his father told him to find Myrathyn. And with everything going on right now—my step-mother, the war, the constant battles, and now you... I needed answers."

My eyebrows rose in surprise. "A mystic? Why would you keep that from me?"

He hesitated again, blinking hard and turning his head. "I'm not always good at... opening up. I've always been the strong one. The leader of armies. I didn't need you to know, and I wanted to keep you safe." He turned and raised his arms toward the house behind me. "Because this house is magical, Ash. It's protected by a barrier put on it hundreds of years ago by my people. It keeps you safe while you're inside."

"That's why you were telling me to stay inside at night all that time," I realized, embarrassment coloring my cheeks. "Why didn't you tell me that? Why keep it a secret?"

His eyes met mine again, and there was a sadness in them that I hadn't noticed before. "Because I didn't want to burden you, Ash," he said. "Because I thought I could protect you from all of this. If only you would just listen..."

I shook my head, my heart aching with a mix of frustration and understanding. "You can't protect me from everything, Cade," I said, my voice firm. "And you shouldn't have to. I want to help. I want to fight beside you."

His gaze softened, and for a moment, I thought I saw a flicker of hope in his eyes. But then his expression hardened, and he looked away. "We need to go back to the mystic," he said, his voice distant. "He was in a deep slumber when we found him, and we couldn't wake him. But I think you might be able to."

I nodded, my resolve strengthening. "Me? Why me?" But then the realization of the Gilded Radiance within me sparked alive, changing my tone. "Let's go then. I'll try to awaken him!"

Cade glanced at the others, his expression grave.

Bella stepped forward, her chin held high. "We're ready, Cade," she said, her voice steady. "We'll follow you."

Rosa nodded in agreement. "Take them, Cade. Get your answers."

Hunter clapped a hand on Cade's shoulder, a small smile playing on his lips. "You've got your team, brother," he said. "Let's go wake him up, and hopefully we'll get the answers we need. The answers we've been praying for..."

As we made our way to the dragons, anticipation surged through me. This was it—our chance to change the course of our fates. Together, we could face whatever lay ahead. Together, we were strong.

Just as we were about to mount the dragons, a sudden snarl ripped through the air, followed by a chorus of growls that sent a shiver down my spine. Krakos and Talonor reared up, their massive wings flapping as they snarled in response, their eyes flashing with fury.

"What's happening?" Bella cried, her eyes wide with fear.

Hunter drew his sword, his gaze scanning the surrounding forest. "Who is it? The Stormscales?"

Huge dark clouds flew above the dragons from behind,

looking like a mist enveloping them. The mists crashed onto the dragons as we all staggered back in confusion. Both dragons' bodies sank to the ground. Their enormous wings pinned under the weight of the gray mists. Wait, that isn't mist... it's nets!

The dragons howled in anger as they were stuck, trapped beneath the nets that covered them, little blue flowers sewn into the stitching of the nets.

Cade growled, his eyes narrowing as he looked at the forest. "No. Those are dragonpearl nets. Only one person owns those. My stepmother... Once those pearls hit their scales, it makes their scales lock together! They can't move!"

As the words left his lips, a horde of monsters emerged from the trees, their long arms and bony forms making them look like shadows come to life. Their glowing eyes fixed on us; their weapons raised. I recognized them by the sparse white fur that covered their inhuman bodies. After all, I helped bury them.

Cade unsheathed his sword, with a fierce determination in his eyes. "Sythers! We need to fight," he said, his voice like thunder. "We need to hold them off."

A lone Syther, the tallest of the over two dozen, strode forward, hefting a massive spear with a curved blade, finely sharpened on one side and jagged with barbs on the other. Its eyes were a berserking red; like the deep color of fresh blood. One arm raised the spear, and the other hand fell almost to its ankle. It lifted its head up and barked up to the sky. Its bark was shrill and ragged, like a dying wolf's.

Dread washed down from my mind to my feet, sinking fear deep inside of me. Glancing all around, I saw we were greatly outnumbered, and the two dragons were pinned and nearly motionless under the dragonpearl nets. How are we going to get out of this? I shook off my fear and reached down for Eden. She was there. Distant... but there.

"The girl," the Syther croaked, his white, scraggly beard hitting his chest as he spoke. "Give us the girl."

We all looked to Cade to respond. He didn't blink, glaring angrily at the lead Sythers, a full two heads taller than the prince.

"We will finish what you did not," the Syther said, inching toward us slowly. "The queen wants her prize. She wants the Gold-Marked. And you, Prince, have disgraced your queen and your legions."

"How did you find us?" Cade finally spoke, his voice a shell of his normal battle cry.

"We always find what we're after. It's only a matter of time before we find our prey."

Behind the lead Syther, the others muttered. It took me a moment, but in their jumbled mess of echoes, I clearly heard they were repeating the word 'prey'. All of them. Every single one repeating the word like drums from the underworld, as if Rone himself was orchestrating their chant.

"Give us the girl, and we will let you live. You will have the queen to suffer to, but you may live, even reprieve your role after your... penance..." A wicked smile of yellow, sharp teeth gleamed in its mouth as he smiled wide.

"You're not taking her!" The Blaze Prince bellowed. "She's mine. You will not have her."

I grabbed the back of his arm subconsciously, feeling his power build back from the drained man who'd dismounted his dragon.

"Then you will die," the Syther said, lowering his weapon and pointing it at us. "Then you will all die."

Hunter's blade swiped the air. "Not before we cut your disgusting head off your miserable body!"

"Then so be it." The Syther snarled, taking a lumbering step forward. "You've chosen death, and we, the queen's Sythers, will gladly reap it upon you."

"Get back in the house," Cade muttered to me. "Get Rosa and Bella inside now! The Sythers can't get inside while the spell is still up."

"Still up? It can come down?" I asked, my core full of fright, not for me, but for Bella and Rosa.

"It'll stay up long enough for us to kill these animals," Cade said. "Now go!"

"No." I turn, feeling his anger at me grow. "Bella, get Rosa inside! You'll be safe there!"

Bella ran without a nod, grabbing Rosa and leading her to the house.

"I'm not going anywhere," I growled. "I'm fighting now. No more hiding, no more running, no more escaping. We're doing this together from now on."

Whether the prince decided to welcome my help or not fight it any longer, I didn't know. But what I did know was, I was finally in the fight. For real this time, and I'd have to use all the lessons that Cornelius taught me. It was fight or die then, and I sure as hell wasn't ready to die just yet...

CHAPTER 27

The Sythers charged, their gaunt forms slicing through the air with a sinister elegance. The lead Syther, distinguished by its size and brutal snarl, dashed across the stretch between them and lunged at Cade with its jagged spear and unnatural speed. Cade, unperturbed, planted his feet firmly and raised his sword, deflecting the attack with a clang of steel against iron.

In an instant, Cade's hand flared with an orange glow, and as he clenched his fist, flames erupted from his hand. His phoenix head staff materialized, its ruby eyes shimmering as if alive. With a swift movement, Cade raised the staff, sending a torrent of fire blazing toward the Sythers. Several of them howled in pain as the flames licked their bodies, but they pressed forward, undeterred.

Hunter, agile and precise, darted between two Sythers, his sword carving in a deadly arc. One Syther fell with a gurgling cry, clutching its throat as blood spurted from the wound. Hunter spun, his dagger finding its mark in the chest of the second Syther. The creature collapsed to the ground, its lifeless eyes staring up at the sky.

I stood my ground, my heart pounding in my chest like a

drum. This is it, Ash. You're fighting beside Cade and Hunter. This is your chance to prove you're not just a helpless slave. Eden pulsed inside me, her golden warmth filling my core. I focused on the power within, visualizing the golden light expanding, growing larger and brighter.

Don't overdo it, I reminded myself sternly. Use only as much as you need. Remember Cornelius's words.

A Syther rushed at me, its curved blade glinting in the sunlight. I thrust my hands out, and a brilliant pulse of golden light erupted from me, sending the creature stumbling back. The gold-hued radiance enveloped the Syther, lifting it high into the air before dropping it with a sickening thud onto the ground. Its bones crunched as its body hit the earth, and the creature lay motionless.

That's it, Ash. You can do this. You can defend yourself.

"Keep fighting," Cade shouted, his voice cutting through the chaos. He was a whirlwind of fire and steel, his sword and staff moving in harmonious tandem. A Syther lunged at him, but Cade sidestepped, bringing his sword down in a brutal arc that severed the creature's head from its body. The head rolled, spattering blood in circles below it. The Sythers charged, their gaunt forms slicing through the air with a sinister elegance. The remaining Sythers hesitated for a moment, their eyes fixed on the lifeless form of their comrade. But their momentary shock only fueled their rage, and they redoubled their efforts, surging forward with renewed ferocity.

Cade and Hunter fought with relentless skill, their movements fluid and precise. Cade's staff sent arcs of fire scorching through the air, while his sword deflected and struck with deadly accuracy. Hunter's dual-wielding of sword and dagger made him a formidable force, darting between the Sythers with lethal grace.

I focused on harnessing Eden's power, channeling it into controlled bursts of golden light. Each blast sent Sythers reeling, their advance temporarily halted. *Stay steady, Ash. Don't let the adrenaline overwhelm you.* I reminded myself, maintaining a steady flow of magic.

We have to keep pushing. I glanced at Cade, seeing the determination in his eyes despite the strain on his face. This fight was crucial—it was about more than just survival. It was about proving that we could stand against the queen's forces, about showing that we were capable of resisting her tyranny.

A Syther lunged at me, its spear aimed at my heart. I sidestepped, feeling a surge of adrenaline as I raised my hands. A golden orb pulsed from my palms, hurling the Syther back with a force that sent it crashing into a tree. The tree shivered, and the Syther slumped to the ground, unconscious or dead.

Bella is inside. She's safe. But if we fall, they'll get to her. They'll get to Rosa eventually. I can't let that happen. The thought of Bella and Rosa being in danger fueled my resolve. I couldn't let the Sythers win. I couldn't let the queen take me!

Cade let out a grunt of pain as a Syther's blade sliced across his arm. Blood seeped from the wound, but he didn't falter. With a roar of defiance, he held his staff upward, sending a column of fire engulfing the Syther. The creature screamed in agony, its body consumed by the flames.

Hunter stumbled, narrowly avoiding a spear that whizzed past his ear. He gritted his teeth, his grip on his weapons tightening as he launched a renewed assault against the Sythers surrounding him.

I channeled another burst of magic, this time lifting a Syther off the ground and flinging it into a group of its comrades. The impact sent them all tumbling to the ground in a tangle of limbs and fur.

We're making progress. We're holding our own. But as I scanned the battlefield, I saw that the Sythers were relentless. For every one we felled, another took its place, their numbers seeming endless.

I focused on the golden light within me, drawing on its power to fuel my attacks. I focused on my power, but tried to keep it controlled. It would only take one wrong burst to send me to the ground, depleted and helpless.

Each burst of my magic sent Sythers reeling, their advance momentarily halted. But the Sythers were learning. They attacked in coordinated waves, their movements more strategic. They seemed to anticipate our attacks, their defenses tightening.

Cade let out a cry of pain as a Syther's blade found its mark, slicing deep into his thigh. He stumbled, and for a moment, I thought he might fall. But with a surge of sheer willpower, he steadied himself, his eyes blazing with renewed determination.

He's hurt. He can't keep going on like this. Concern for Cade surged through me, but I couldn't let it distract me. I had to keep fighting, had to keep pushing.

Hunter, seeing Cade's injury, redoubled his efforts, his attacks growing more desperate. He fought with a ferocity that was both awe-inspiring and terrifying, his strikes finding their marks with brutal efficiency.

I channeled another burst of magic, this time lifting a Syther off the ground and flinging it into a group of its comrades. The impact sent them all tumbling to the ground in a tangle of limbs and fur.

Keep going, Ash. You can't falter now. I focused on the golden light within me, drawing on its power to fuel my attacks. Each burst sent Sythers reeling, their advance momentarily halted.

The battle raged on, the air thick with the scent of blood and the terrible smell of burnt flesh. The Sythers seemed to multiply, their numbers barely dwindling despite our relentless assault. Cade's injury was taking a toll on him; his movements were slower, his breaths more labored. Hunter fought valiantly, but fatigue was setting in, his strikes becoming less precise.

I channeled more of Eden's power, careful not to overextend myself. Just enough, Ash. Control it. I focused on the golden light within, shaping it into controlled bursts that sent Sythers tumbling back. The glow from my hands illuminated the battle-field, casting eerie shadows on the twisted faces of our enemies.

Cade, grimacing in pain, managed to send another torrent of fire from his staff, incinerating a group of Sythers that had been advancing on him. Hunter, breathing heavily, dispatched another Syther with a swift strike to the heart.

But the numbers were against us. For every Syther we felled, more seemed to replace them from the trees. Their attacks grew more coordinated, their tactics more cunning. They anticipated our moves, adapting and countering with chilling precision.

A Syther with a fearsome snarl lunged at me, its spear aimed at my chest. I stumbled back, channeling a burst of golden light that sent the creature crashing into a boulder. As I turned back to the battle, I saw Cade, his face pale and drawn. He was injured, and even with his ferocious will, his strength was waning. His thrusts were labored, and his fire magic more erratic, more desperate.

We have to get him out of here. I looked around frantically, assessing our options. But where can we go? The dragons are pinned, and we're surrounded.

As if sensing my thoughts, a group of Sythers encircled me, their eyes glinting with malice. Cade was struggling to keep his footing. Hunter was fighting valiantly but was overwhelmed also. The lead Syther stepped forward, its eyes narrowed as it raised its spear.

"There's nowhere to run, Gold-Marked. We are here for you. The others may die, but the queen wants you. She wants you so badly."

"The queen can go to the Infernal Depths and rot there for all I care!" My fists were balled up, radiating with golden magic. "I'm not going anywhere."

"Who said anything about you going anywhere?" the lead Syther snarled with an awful smirk.

My stomach fell to the ground, and terror rushed through my

limbs like red rivers. "What do you mean? Speak, or I'll incinerate you from the inside!"

"The queen is coming for you," it growled, its voice a chilling echo. "She's done waiting on Prince Cade to do his duty. She's coming... for you..."

My heart sank as the reality set in. My limbs went numb, and my heart pounded like a hammer striking hot iron on an anvil. We were in trouble, deep trouble. The house was no longer a safe hiding place. We were outnumbered, and Cade was injured. The fight was far from over, but the odds were stacked heavily against us.

My mind raced, desperate for a solution, a way out. But as I looked around, all I saw were Sythers, their eyes glinting with a dark promise of death.

And as the lead Syther advanced, its spear poised to strike, I knew that this battle was far from over. But the outcome, at least for now, was grim.

I had to get out of this mess and help Cade. But there are so many of them... I can't let these monsters kill them. I can't let them win. But there are so many of them... and they're so relentless. I can't lose now. Not after all I've been through. I've got to find a way... There's got to be a way...

CHAPTER 28

I stood surrounded by Sythers, their long arms and feral snarls sending a chill down my spine. Cade and Hunter were in their own battles, both fighting valiantly, but blood was trickling down Cade's armor, staining it a deep crimson. I clenched my teeth, trying to hold back the panic surging through me. I had magic—Eden's golden radiance—but I was gasping for breath, worried I wouldn't have enough strength to face down the horde of enemies before me.

"Cade!" I yelled, my voice trembling with a mixture of fear and desperation.

He responded with a roar, a flare of flames exploding from his staff, but there were too many Sythers between us. Hunter was also pinned down, his dagger flashing as he fended off multiple attacks.

The lead Syther stepped closer, its eyes glinting with a cruel malice. "Don't worry," it sneered, "we won't kill you. But you're not going to enjoy the pain you're going to endure before the queen finds you."

"I'm not giving up," I growled, clenching my fists as the golden light pulsed within me. "And I won't let you hurt the others."

The Syther laughed, a sound that grated against my very soul. "You're weak, girl. Weak for a woman, and weak even for a slave. Why does the prince hide you like he does? You're not pretty for a human. I wouldn't even feed the stringy meat off your bones to my Sythers. You may fight with your magic, but you're tired, exhausted from magic, and now you're mine. The queen will reward me greatly for this. But please... don't give up. I want to enjoy this!"

As the Syther advanced, I prepared for the onslaught, steeling myself against the impending attack. My heart hammered in my chest, a relentless pulse that echoed through my entire being. Suddenly, I saw a glimmer beside me, and there, appearing for a flicker, was a shimmer of Cornelius. His wise eyes met mine for only an instant, and his words cut through the chaos of the battle.

"Ash, run. Run as fast as your legs can carry you," he said, his voice low but urgent.

Before I could respond, Cornelius vanished, but in his place, an illusion of Rone mounted on the back of an ogre materialized behind the Sythers. They were stunned, their eyes widening in fear as they launched their attack on the fearsome beast and hunter with his whip snapping.

"Run!" Cornelius's voice echoed in my mind, and I turned, dashing into the forest, branches whipping my face as I ran. My heart raced as I sprinted, my breath ragged and desperate. Sharp branches scratched my arms and legs, leaving stinging trails of pain. Eventually, I heard the Sythers roar in rage at the illusion, racing into the forest after me. They crashed through the trees like a monsoon ripping in from the sea. A spear zipped through the air, narrowly missing me as it slammed into a tree with a resounding thud.

My mind was a maelstrom of terror and regret as I fled deeper into the Faewood, the image of Cade and Hunter battling valiantly against the Sythers seared into my memory. Each step I took away from them felt like a betrayal, yet the wisdom of Cornelius' command reverberated through me: Run.

The underbrush whipped against my legs, and the sting of scratches from low-hanging branches barely registered through the adrenaline coursing through my veins. My breath came in ragged gasps, the air burning my lungs as I pushed my body to its limits, driven by the primal instinct to survive. The golden light of Eden pulsed within me, a reminder of the power I held—a power I was only just beginning to understand.

As I sprinted through the dense forest, the sound of pursuit grew fainter, but the fear of being caught never waned. My heart pounded in rhythm with my frantic footsteps, a drumbeat of flight echoing in my ears. The Faewood around me was a blur of green and brown, a testament to the speed at which I moved—a speed I had not known I possessed.

The cool, rushing water of a brook came into view, and I skidded to a halt, my boots slipping on the damp earth. I bent over, hands braced on my thighs, as I fought to catch my breath. The gurgling water seemed to mock my desperation, its tranquil melody a stark contrast to the tumultuous pace of my heart. I was alone, wounded, and far from safe, yet the brook whispered of peace and serenity—a sanctuary amidst the chaos.

Bella's face flashed before my eyes, her glacier-blue eyes filled with trust and affection. I had promised to protect her, to keep her safe from the horrors that plagued our world. And here I was, running for my life, while she was left to face the darkness alone. Guilt gnawed at my conscience, threatening to pull me under just as surely as the Sythers' nets had ensnared Krakos and Talonor. Cade and Hunter were back there fighting for their lives, and there I was, forced to run. But there was no time for thoughts of their safety, I had to worry about my own.

Just as my breathing slowed, I heard a familiar, terrifying voice in the dense forest. It was the lead Syther's voice, and fear gripped me anew as he emerged from behind a tree.

"Where are you running to? There's nowhere to hide from me and from the queen. I've marked your scent. I'll follow you to the ends of Allovan now."

I stood my ground, summoning every ounce of strength and determination within me. "Well, I'll have to take that disgusting nose right off your face then," I said, my voice steady despite the fear churning in my gut.

The Syther hulked forward, his eyes narrowing as a wicked grin spread across his face. "You're nothing, girl. Tiny, frail, puny."

The lead Syther lunged with a swift, vicious motion. I braced myself for the inevitable impact. My hand shot out, fingers splayed, and to my astonishment, they closed around the sharp blade's tip. The golden light Eden provided pulsed strongly, radiating from my palm and encasing the spearhead in its brilliant glow. The Syther's eyes widened in shock as the momentum of his attack halted abruptly, his mighty strength rendered useless against the force of my magic.

The golden light intensified, seeping into the spear and crawling up its length toward the Syther's clawed hand. Panic flashed across his grotesque features as he felt the relentless power consume him. His fur smoldered, the light spreading across his body, igniting an ethereal fire that burned bright. His screams echoed through the forest, a sound that would have once terrified me but now served as a testament to my own strength.

"You'll never harm another woman," I repeated, my voice carrying the weight of my resolve. "I won't let you." The words were more than a promise; they were a vow to protect myself and those who couldn't defend themselves against the cruelty of the Blaze Queen's army.

The Syther's body convulsed as the golden flames danced across his form, his cries growing more desperate with each passing second. I watched, unflinching, as the creature that had intended to bring me pain and suffering crumpled to the forest floor, a husk of what it once was. The golden light receded, leaving behind nothing but the metal spearhead and the charred remains of the spear's wooden staff.

After a moment standing over his body, I spat on his corpse, showing my final farewell to the monster. Then, I heard a rustle in the forest. The other Sythers were coming, and not far off. I darted into the dense thicket of the Faewood. My heart pounded in my chest, not just from exertion, but from the adrenaline of battle and the thrill of victory. I was no longer the helpless girl from Bramblebash; I was a force to be reckoned with, a beacon of power that could finally stand up for myself and others. And it felt incredible!

Branches whipped at my face and arms, but I barely felt the sting of their slender fingers against my skin. My focus was singular—escape and regroup with Cade and the others. I could hear the Sythers crashing through the underbrush behind me, their snarls and growls growing ever fainter as I put distance between us. I didn't dare look back, knowing that any moment wasted could mean the difference between life and death.

Suddenly, a searing pain tore through my side, and I stumbled, a gasp of pain escaping my lips. A spear, thrown with deadly accuracy, had grazed me, leaving a burning trail of agony in its wake. I pressed a hand to the wound, feeling the warm trickle of blood seeping through my fingers. The Sythers were gaining on me, their determination to capture me—or worse—fueling their pursuit.

I pushed myself to run faster, the forest around me blurring into a mass of greens and browns as I weaved through the trees. My breath came in ragged gasps, my lungs aching with the effort, but I refused to give in to the fatigue that threatened to overwhelm me. I refused to become another casualty in the Blaze Queen's relentless quest for power.

As I sprinted deeper into the forest, the sound of the Sythers' pursuit gradually faded away, replaced by the gentle babbling of a nearby brook. I paused for a brief moment, leaning against the rough bark of a tree as I caught my breath and assessed my injury. It was painful, but I would survive. I had to.

But just as I felt a glimmer of hope, the ground beneath me gave way, and I tumbled down a steep embankment. My body rolled and bounced uncontrollably, the world around me nothing but a dizzying whirl of sky and earth. When I finally came to a stop at the bottom of the cliff, I lay there, dazed and in pain, with the coppery taste of blood in my mouth.

The last thing I remembered before darkness consumed me was the distant roar of dragons, a sound that filled me with both hope and a deep, pervasive dread. The Blaze Queen was still out there, and she would not rest until she had claimed the power that pulsed within my veins. But the darkness took me, and there was no Cade or Cornelius to protect me.

CHAPTER 29

The brisk air bit into my skin as I stirred awake, the damp earth beneath me sending a chill through my bones. I groaned, my side throbbing with a dull, insistent ache. Gingerly, I touched the wound where the spear had grazed me, hissing at the sharp pain that shot through my body. The blood was dried and crusted, clinging to my skin like a grim reminder of the battle I had fled.

I tried to stand, but my legs wobbled, and I stumbled, falling back onto the forest floor. The world spun around me, the shadows of the trees merging into a dizzying blur. I was alone, surrounded by the eerie silence of the Faewood, the only sounds being the distant hoots of an owl and the rustling of leaves above.

A heavy weight settled in my chest, a mixture of guilt, fear, and self-doubt. How could I have been so foolish to think I could fight alongside Cade and Hunter? I'm just a slave girl from Bramblebash, unremarkable and weak. What good is my magic if I can't protect those I care about?

Tears welled up in my eyes, blurring the moonlit forest around me. I had failed. I had run, leaving Cade and Hunter to face the Sythers alone. I'm no warrior, no savior. I'm a burden, a liability. The Blaze Queen is coming for me, and there is nowhere I could hide, nowhere I could run that she wouldn't find me.

I hugged my knees to my chest, rocking back and forth as despair washed over me. The weight of my failures pressed down on me, threatening to crush me beneath their weight. I was just a pawn in a game I didn't understand, a game where the stakes were too high, and the odds were stacked against me.

"I can't do this," I whispered, the words tasting like bitter ash in my mouth. "I'm not strong enough. I never will be."

Just as I was about to give in to the overwhelming hopelessness, a soft, familiar voice cut through the darkness. "Ash, you are stronger than you think."

I looked up, wiping the tears from my eyes, and saw Cornelius standing a few paces away. His deep yellow eyes with streaks of fiery oranges and reds glowed in the moonlight, a beacon of hope in the darkness.

"Cornelius," I said. "I can't do this. I'm not strong enough. I failed them. I failed Cade and Hunter. I failed Bella."

Cornelius moved closer, his sturdy tortoise legs carrying him with a slow, comforting gait. "You did not fail, Ash. You fought bravely, and you survived. That is a victory in itself."

I shook my head, the weight of my failures pressing down on me. "I ran. I left them behind. The Sythers said the queen is coming for me. I can't face her. I'm just a slave girl from a miserable small town. I'm not strong enough to go on."

Cornelius's voice was gentle yet firm. "You had to run, Ash. You were outnumbered, and Cade and Hunter could not have reached you in time. If you had stayed, you would have died, and the dragons were incapacitated by the nets. I'm glad you listened to me. You did the right thing. You survived."

His words did little to comfort me. The image of Cade, injured and fighting valiantly, flashed through my mind. I had left him behind, left him to face the Sythers alone. "I can't fight the queen. I'm not strong enough. I never will be."

Cornelius' gaze was steady and unwavering. "You are strong, Ash. You are still alive, and that is a testament to your strength. You killed the lead Syther. That was a huge accomplishment, and I am proud of you."

His words sent a ripple of warmth through me, a flicker of hope in the despair that threatened to consume me. But the doubt lingered, a shadow that refused to be banished. "How can I be strong when I couldn't protect them? When I couldn't protect Bella?"

Cornelius's voice was filled with wisdom and patience. "Strength is not just about physical prowess, Ash. It is about resilience, determination, and the will to keep going even when the odds are against you. You have shown all of these qualities and more. You are strong because you continue to fight, continue to seek a way forward despite the obstacles in your path. Strength is not the absence of fear or weakness, but the ability to face them and keep moving forward."

His words struck a chord within me, a spark of hope that grew into a flame. I was still alive. I had survived. I had faced the Sythers and emerged victorious. Maybe, just maybe, I can face the Blaze Queen someday. Maybe I can be the Gold-Marked, the one destined to wield this magic and help those in need.

But the doubt still lingered, a stubborn shadow that refused to be banished. "But how can I face the queen? She is powerful, ruthless. I am just a slave girl from a shit town. How can I hope to stand against her?"

Cornelius' gaze softened, filled with a gentle understanding. "You are more than just a slave girl, Ash. You are the Gold-Marked, the one chosen to wield the power of the Gilded Radiance. The queen fears you because she knows the power you possess—the power that could bring an end to her tyranny. That is why she seeks you, why she will stop at nothing to capture you."

His words ignited something within me—a spark of defiance

and determination. Maybe I'm not just a slave girl. I'm the Gold-Marked, chosen to wield the power of the Golden Rune on my neck. I have a destiny, a purpose. I could not let fear and doubt hold me back. I had to embrace my strength and face the challenges ahead.

"But how can I face the queen when I can't even protect those I care about?" I asked, the doubt still gnawing at the edges of my newfound resolve. "How can I stand against her?"

Cornelius's voice was calm and reassuring. "You will learn, Ash. You will grow stronger. You have already taken the first step by acknowledging your strength and facing your fears. With time and practice, you will become a formidable force, capable of standing against the queen and protecting those you care about. But remember, you do not have to do this alone. You have allies, friends who will stand beside you and support you in your journey."

His words filled me with a newfound sense of purpose and determination. I was not alone. I had allies, friends who believed in me and would support me in my journey. I had to embrace my strength, face my fears, and continue to grow and learn. With their help, I could face the Blaze Queen and bring an end to her tyranny.

Cornelius extended a sturdy leg, offering it to me. "Come, let us get you on your feet. You have a long journey ahead of you, but you are not alone. I will be with you every step of the way."

I reached out, gritting my teeth against the pain in my side, and gripped his leg. With a grunt, I pulled myself to my feet, the world spinning around me for a moment before steadying. I took a deep breath, steeling myself against the pain and the doubts that still lingered in the corners of my mind.

"Thank you, Cornelius," I said, my voice filled with gratitude and determination. "I will not give up. I will face my fears and continue to grow and learn. I will become the Gold-Marked and bring an end to the queen's tyranny."

A soft smile spread across Cornelius's face; his eyes filled with pride and encouragement. "That is the spirit, Ash. Now, let us get you to safety. You are injured and depleted from using your magic. You need rest and healing."

He led me through the moonlit forest, his sturdy tortoise legs carrying him with a slow, comforting gait. I hobbled along beside him, each step sending a jolt of pain through my side. But I gritted my teeth and pushed forward, refusing to let the pain hold me back.

We walked for what felt like an eternity, the darkness of the forest engulfing us as we made our way deeper into the Faewood. Eventually, the sound of rushing water reached my ears, and we emerged into a clearing bathed in the soft glow of the moonlight.

A magnificent waterfall cascaded down the side of a cliff, the water shimmering in the starlit night. The waterfall fed into a pristine spring, its surface seemingly incandescent under the celestial light. The sight was breathtaking—a sanctuary of peace and tranquility amidst the chaos and turmoil of my journey.

I stumbled toward the water, my legs giving way as I reached the edge of the spring. I collapsed into the water, letting the cool liquid envelop me. The coldness was a shock to my system, but it also brought a sense of relief and rejuvenation. I let myself sink beneath the surface, allowing the water to wash away the blood, sweat, and tears of my fight. The water felt like magic in itself, soaking into my body, making me feel whole again, pieced back together. It felt something like I would imagine a father holding a child in his arms would feel like; a foreign feeling that I'd never had, and never would...

As I lay there, letting the cool water lap around me, I felt a ripple of water splash into my face. I blinked, opening my eyes and peering into the depths of the spring. And that's when I saw it—a massive shadow moving behind the waterfall.

My heart leaped into my throat as I glared at the waterfall, the shadow growing larger and more distinct. Cornelius gasped and turned to me, his eyes wide with alarm. "Ash, get to your feet! You need to run!"

But I was frozen in place, my limbs heavy with fear and exhaustion. The shadow emerged from behind the waterfall, its form becoming clearer with each passing moment. And then I recognized it—the same dark blue dragon I had seen nights prior with Cornelius. Its body was immense, its scales shimmering in the moonlight, and its eyes burning with a primal, predatory intensity.

The dragon growled low, raising its head high above me, its jaws snapping in the air. Fear gripped me, paralyzing me as I watched the beast approach. It moved closer, its massive form towering over me, the scent of dragonfire wafting from its nostrils. I could see every detail of its form—the sharp scales, the powerful indigo wings, the fearsome teeth.

But this time, seeing the dragon, I saw more than just menace in its form. The dragon stepped fully into the moonlight, and its scales, though shadowed in indigo and navy, rippled with silver-blue veins that pulsed like rivers beneath the surface. Mist curled around its feet, as if the waterfall obeyed its presence. Its wings were vast, webbed with a glimmer that mirrored starlight on still water, and as it breathed, the air thickened with the scent of rain and sea salt. Something stirred deep inside me—a resonance, like an echo in my bones—as though a current long buried had risen. The dragon tilted its head, its gaze locking with mine, and for one suspended breath, I wasn't afraid. It felt like recognition. Like we were two tides pulled by the same unseen moon.

I am going to die if I keep running, I thought to myself, a realization dawning within me. I've got to be brave. For me. For Bella. For Cade. For Hunter. I can't keep running. I can't keep hiding. I have to face my fears and stand my ground.

With a deep breath, I summoned every ounce of strength and courage within me. I raised my hands, holding my palms out to the dragon, which snarled and flashed its teeth. It lowered its head, gazing deep into my eyes, its breath hot against my skin.

I took a tentative step forward, my heart pounding in my chest as I reached out a trembling hand. "Easy girl, easy..." I murmured. The dragon's mean, unworldly, emerald eyes narrowed, a low growl emanating from its throat as it pulled its head back and snapped its jaws at me.

My heart leaped into my throat, but I refused to back down. I took another step forward, my hand still extended. "Easy girl..." I repeated, my voice gaining a hint of confidence. The dragon snarled again, but this time it didn't snap its jaws. Instead, it lowered its head, allowing me to touch its snout.

The moment my hand made contact with the dragon's scales, a surge of energy coursed through me. It was a sensation unlike anything I had ever experienced—a mixture of power, warmth, and a deep, primal connection. The dragon let out a low rumble from deep within its chest, its eyes softening as it bowed its head to me.

A wave of confidence washed over me, a realization that I was capable of more than I had ever imagined. Maybe I can do this. Maybe I can be the Gold-Marked that's destined to wield this magic and help people. Maybe I can be free after all...

I stepped back, my gaze never leaving the dragon's eyes. With a newfound sense of purpose and determination, I walked to the side of the dragon, climbing up its wing and straddling its back. The dragon's scales were warm and smooth beneath my touch, its powerful muscles rippling with each of its movements.

Cornelius cheered from the side, his eyes gleaming with pride and excitement. "Ash, you did it! You did it! I can't believe it! You did it!"

The dragon flapped its wings, the sound like a massive ship's sails biting and cracking in the sea winds. It lifted off the ground with a powerful surge, flying high into the night sky, the rush of wind sending my hair whipping behind me.

As the dragon soared through the air, the cool night wind whooshed around me, invigorating me with a sense of freedom and empowerment I had never known before. The moonlit landscape below was a tapestry of shadows and silver light, a breathtaking sight that filled me with awe and wonder.

The dragon's wings beat a steady rhythm, and with each powerful stroke, I felt more alive, more determined than ever. The fear and doubt that had plagued me earlier seemed to fade away.

I looked down at the vast expanse of the Faewood Forest, the dense canopy a sea of dark green under the silvery moonlight. The wind rushed past my ears, carrying with it the distant sounds of nature—the rustling of leaves, the murmur of wildlife, and the haunting calls of wild creatures.

As we ascended higher, the air grew cooler, and the world below became a distant memory. The dragon's powerful body moved with grace and precision, each wingbeat carrying us further into the night. I clung tightly to its scaled back, feeling every muscle tense and release with each movement.

The dragon's breath came in hot, rhythmic bursts, the smell of brimstone and fire mingling with the crisp night air. Its scales were smooth and warm under my touch, their deep blue hue shimmering in the moonlight like an otherworldly gem.

I leaned forward, digging my hands into the dragon's scales to steady myself. The creature responded with a low rumble, its massive body vibrating beneath me. The sensation was both exhilarating and grounding, connecting me to the beast in a way that transcended mere physical contact.

"I'm up here," I whispered to myself. My voice was carried away by the wind. "I'm flying. I'm free!"

CHAPTER 30

The cool night air rushed past me as I soared through the sky on the back of the magnificent blue dragon. The moon hung high, casting a silvery glow over the landscape below. The forest was a dark, dense mass, broken only by the winding ribbon of the river that snaked through the trees. The sight was a breathtaking beauty that seemed almost unreal.

But as we approached the clearing where the house stood, the scene below shifted from serene to harrowing. The ground was littered with the bodies of fallen Sythers, their twisted forms a grim reminder of the battle. Some lay with deep sword wounds, while others were charred beyond recognition, their blackened skeletons left like obsidian statues.

My heart pounded in my chest as I scanned the area, searching for any sign of Cade and Hunter. Fear gripped me as I worried I might find their lifeless bodies among the carnage. But as I circled lower, I saw no sign of them. The dragon descended gracefully, her wings flapping in powerful strokes that sent gusts of wind swirling around us. As we touched down, the ground trembled slightly beneath us. The dragon let out a low rumble, her eyes scanning the area with a primal intensity.

The door to the house burst open, and Cade and Hunter dashed out, their eyes wide with shock and concern. To the north of the house, their dragons roared, their massive forms freed from the nets that had ensnared them. Krakos and Talonor reared up, their jaws snapping in the air as they snarled at the new arrival.

The blue dragon responded in kind, her deep growl resonating through the air. I quickly slid off her back, my hands raised in a calming gesture. "Easy, girl," I murmured, trying to soothe the beast. "They're friends."

Cade and Hunter approached cautiously, their eyes fixed on the new blue dragon. Bella emerged from the house next, her face stained with tears. She ran to me, her arms wrapping tightly around my neck. "Ash!" she cried, her voice choked with emotion. "I thought you were... I thought..." I'd never felt her hold me so tightly, I thought my head might burst off my body!

I hugged her back, feeling the weight of her relief and joy. "I'm okay, Bella," I reassured her, though the dried blood on my clothes and the gash on my side told a different story.

Rosa joined us, her face a mask of relief. "Thank Odiun," she muttered, her voice low and grateful.

Cade and Hunter stood a few paces away, their expressions a mix of awe and bewilderment. "Ash," Hunter began, his voice filled with disbelief. "Is this... is this your dragon?"

I nodded, with a sense of pride and accomplishment swelling within me. "Her name is Errax," I explained. "I heard it in my head as soon as I mounted her. It was as if she was introducing herself to me. It wasn't in our language, but I understood it. Like we have a communication in our thoughts if we try hard enough."

Hunter let out a low whistle, his eyes wide. "You've bonded with a dragon," he said, his voice laced with admiration. "I can't believe it."

Bella looked at me with newfound respect, her tears forgotten in the wake of this revelation. "We all thought you might be... but you're here, and you've bonded with a dragon!" she exclaimed, her voice filled with wonder.

Cade, who was dead silent, only glared at me and the dragon, and I couldn't tell what thoughts were going on in his head. It was a coin toss with him, but my stomach twisted and tied in knots waiting... Cade stepped closer, his gaze intense. Without a word, he reached out and embraced me, his powerful arms wrapping around me, pulling me close. His warmth enveloped me, and I felt a sense of safety and belonging that I had never known before. "I'm so glad you're alive," he murmured into my hair. "I was so worried..."

I melted into his embrace, feeling the weight of his worry lift from my shoulders. "I was worried about you too," I replied, my voice muffled against his chest. "You were injured against them. I thought the worst might have happened."

He pulled back slightly, his eyes meeting mine. "The illusion of Rone and the ogre gave us enough time to free the dragons. We ran and cut the nets while they were distracted," he explained. "Krakos and Talonor incinerated the remaining Sythers. How... how did you do that?"

"Can't a girl keep her secrets?" I laughed. "You hold yours as tight as a fisherman holds onto his prized new catch..."

Cade's face flushed, something I'd never seen, or thought I'd see. He cleared his throat, changing the subject. "We need to figure out our next move," he said, his voice taking on a more serious tone. "Now that we know the queen is coming, we need to be ready."

I nodded in agreement, my mind racing with the implications of our situation. "The mystic," I said, remembering the conversation we'd had before the attack. "You said you found him, that he might have answers. We need to go see him."

Cade's expression grew grave. "Yes, but it won't be easy. The journey to his sanctuary is treacherous, and the queen's forces will be on the lookout for us. But it's our best chance to find out how to defeat her and end this war."

Hunter stepped forward, his determination clear in his stance. "We're with you, Cade. Whatever it takes."

Bella, who had been quietly listening, spoke up. "I'm coming too. I'm not staying behind again."

Rosa bowed. "I would argue that y'all need rest and time to heal, but I know you know the queen, my prince. Do what you must. Find the mystic."

"Rosa?" I asked, worried for her safety. She was mostly distant, but I cared for her, not wanting to leave her. "What will you do?"

"I know these woods pretty darned well by now," Rosa jostled her belt with pride. "These old bones still know a trick or two. I'll head into the Faewood and wait out the storm."

"What if the queen finds you?" I tugged at her arm.

"If she finds me, then she finds me. I've lived a long, full life. If it's my time, then it's my time. But like I said, I've still got a few tricks up my sleeve... But know that we're with you, Ash. We believe in you..."

A swell of gratitude filled my heart as I looked at my friends, their faces etched with resolve. Together, we stood a chance against the overwhelming odds. "Thank you," I said, my voice filled with emotion. "All of you."

Cade turned to me, his gaze steady. "Ash, you need to rest and heal. Even though you have a dragon now, you don't know how to fight on one, and you'll need your strength for something like that."

I understood his concern, but the thought of delaying our mission felt like a luxury we couldn't afford. "I'm okay," I insisted, though the throbbing pain in my side said otherwise. "We need to move quickly."

Cade's expression softened, but his voice was firm. "You've been through a lot, Ash. Just a couple hours of rest. The queen won't come yet. I know her. She'll wait for word from the Sythers, or lack of a word. She rarely leaves the castle, not unless absolutely necessary."

Hunter shifted uneasily in his stance. "The Syther did say she would come."

"She will," Cade agreed. "Trust me. I know her. She will come, but we have time. Maybe a day, maybe a week. Either way, we need to be ready, but Ash needs food and rest. A couple of hours, and then we'll be off on our way."

I relented, seeing the wisdom in his words. With a sigh, I nodded.

Cade gave a small smile, a rare sight that sent a flutter through my stomach.

As we made our way back to the house, I noticed Errax watching me intently. I paused, turning to the magnificent creature. "Thank you, Errax," I said, my hand reaching out to touch her snout gently. "For everything."

Errax let out a low rumble, her emerald eyes filled with an understanding that transcended words. The connection between us was palpable, a bond that went beyond mere friendship. She was my dragon, and together, we would face whatever challenges lay ahead.

Inside the house, the atmosphere was tense but focused. Bella and Rosa began gathering supplies, while Hunter and Cade discussed our route and potential dangers. I sat at the large wooden table, watching them with a mix of awe and admiration. Despite the dire circumstances, there was a unity among us, a sense of purpose that bound us together. Rosa rummaged food together for me in the kitchen.

Cade returned to my side, his expression serious. "Ash, I need to speak with you."

I looked up at him, a sense of unease settling in my stomach. "What is it?"

He hesitated for a moment before continuing, his voice low. "I need you to understand the risks involved. The mystic's sanctuary is deep within the Faewood, near the Brakenstone Ridge Mountains. The journey itself will be dangerous, and there's no guarantee that the mystic will even help us. I hope you can wake him, but I'm not certain of it."

I swallowed hard, the gravity of our situation sinking in. "I understand, Cade. But we have to try. We can't just sit here and wait for the queen to find us."

Cade's gaze softened, and he reached out, tucking a strand of hair behind my ear. The gesture was surprisingly tender, sending a shiver down my spine. "You're right, Ash. We have to try. But I need you to promise me something."

"What is it?" I asked.

"Promise me you'll stay close, that you won't take any unnecessary risks. We can't lose you, not now."

His words stirred something deep within me, a warmth that spread through my chest. "I promise, Cade. I'll stay close."

Rosa brought me a bowl of stew that I devoured.

He nodded, his expression easing slightly. "Good. Now, let's get you cleaned up and rested. You'll need your strength for what lies ahead."

As the others continued their preparations, Cade led me to the back room where a basin of warm water awaited. I winced as I removed my clothing, the dried blood pulling at the wounds on my side. Cade's eyes darkened with concern as he took in the extent of my injuries.

"Let me help you," he said, his hands gentle as he cleaned the wounds with a damp cloth.

I hissed at the sting of the water, but Cade's touch was soothing, his hands surprisingly gentle for someone of his size and strength. As he worked, I found myself studying the lines of his face, the way his hair framed his firm jaw, and the intensity in his piercing blue eyes. There was a depth to him, a complexity that I had only begun to scratch the surface of.

"Thank you," I murmured, feeling a warmth spread through me that had nothing to do with the injuries.

He looked up, his eyes meeting mine. "You don't need to thank me, Ash. I'm just doing what needs to be done."

But there was more to it—a connection that went beyond mere necessity. As his hands brushed against my skin, I felt a spark, a warmth that sent shivers down my spine. There was a moment of silence, a pause where the world seemed to still around us.

"Cade..." I began.

But before I could finish, he stepped back, breaking the moment. "You should rest now," he said, his voice steady, though I could see the faint flush in his cheeks.

I nodded, feeling a mix of disappointment and relief. "You're right. I should."

He helped me into a fresh set of clothes, his hands lingering for a moment longer than necessary. As I lay down on the bed, he pulled the blankets up over me, his eyes softening. "Sleep well, Ash. We need you at your best for what lies ahead." He leaned down with his lips leading the way. They pressed against mine, and a warmth shot through me like a tidal wave. The warmth had the opposite reaction I would've expected; it made my head spin and my vision soften. I'd been through hell and back, and the claws of slumber raked at me deeply.

As I drifted off to sleep, my mind was filled with thoughts of Cade, of our journey, and of the challenges that awaited us. The road ahead was uncertain, filled with danger and unknowns. But with Cade and the others by my side, I felt a sense of determination and hope that I had never known before. Together, we would face whatever came next.

CHAPTER 31

*M*orning light filtered through the window, casting a warm glow over the room. I stirred awake, the memories of the previous day flooding back like a tide. The throbbing pain in my side served as a stark reminder of the battles we had faced and the challenges that still lay ahead. I stretched, wincing slightly as my wounds pulled taut, and swung my legs over the edge of the bed.

The house was already abuzz with activity. Bella and Rosa were gathering supplies in the kitchen, their whispered conversations carrying through the air. Hunter was sharpening his sword with a steady, rhythmic sound, while Cade stood by the window, his eyes scanning the horizon with an intensity that made my heart race.

I slipped out of the room, my bare feet padding against the wooden floor. As I entered the main room, all eyes turned to me. Bella rushed over, her glacier-blue eyes filled with concern. "How are you feeling?" she asked, her hand gently brushing against my arm.

I offered a reassuring smile. "I'm okay. Still a bit sore, but I'll manage."

Rosa handed me a mug of steaming tea, the scent of herbs filling the air. "Drink this. It will help with the pain and heal your wounds faster."

I took the mug gratefully, the warmth seeping into my palms. "Thank you, Rosa."

Cade turned from the window, his eyes meeting mine. There was a seriousness in his gaze that sent a ripple of unease through me. "We need to prepare to leave soon. The queen's forces will be looking for us. We can't be here when they find the Sythers' bodies. We need to distance ourselves from this place, and the mystic is quite a ride away. If he's still slumbering in the same place we found him. "

Hunter stood, sheathing his sword with a metallic clang. "Bella and I will gather the rest of the supplies. Rosa, do you have everything you need?"

Rosa nodded, her eyes flickering to me for a moment. "Yes, I have what I need. I'll be heading into the Faewood. I know the forest well; I'll be safe there."

I felt a pang of worry for Rosa, but I knew better than to argue with her. She was a strong woman, resourceful and determined. She had been a loyal ally to Cade, and I respected her deeply for it.

"Rosa, thank you for everything," I said, my voice filled with gratitude. "You've done so much for us. I can't thank you enough."

Rosa's lips curved into a small smile. "It's been an honor, Ash. You're destined for great things. I have faith in you. Good luck to you all. Show the queen a thing or two for me. I'll be waitin' when you need me again. And Cade, if we don't meet again, it's been the pleasure of my life serving you. I believe in you. Stay true to who you are, and show this world the true meaning of the word hope."

She walked over to Cade, placed both hands on his temples and brought his head down so that she pressed her aged lips against his brow. He nodded with a serious look of full appreciation for her. With a final nod, Rosa slung her pack over her shoulder and headed out the door, disappearing into the dense foliage of the Faewood. I watched her go, a mix of admiration and sadness swirling within me. She was a woman of few words, but her actions spoke volumes.

Cade approached me, his expression softening slightly. "It's time to learn how to call your dragon. Now that you're bonded with Errax, she can somewhat hear your thoughts. Keep it simple and clear. Call her in your mind."

I took a deep breath, focusing my thoughts on Errax. I pictured her magnificent form, her deep blue scales shimmering in the sunlight. Come, Errax. I thought, my mind reaching out to her.

For a moment, nothing happened. Doubt crept in, but then, a distant roar echoed through the forest. The sound grew louder, and I felt a surge of excitement as Errax emerged from the tree line, her massive wings flapping powerfully. She soared toward us, a breathtaking sight that filled me with awe and pride.

"She's coming!" I exclaimed, my heart racing with excitement.

Errax descended gracefully, her powerful form landing with a thunderous impact that shook the ground. She lowered her head, her emerald eyes meeting mine with a look of fierce loyalty. I approached her, my hand reaching out to touch her snout gently.

Errax let out a low rumble, her eyes filled with understanding. The connection between us was palpable, a bond that went beyond mere friendship. She was my dragon, and together, we were unstoppable.

Cade watched the exchange with a mix of awe and admiration. "You have a natural talent for this, Ash." He turned to Hunter and Bella, his voice taking on a serious tone. "Hunter, take Bella with you on Talonor. Ash needs to focus on learning how to ride Errax. Bella will ride with Ash someday, but not yet, not while she's training."

Hunter nodded, his gaze shifting to Bella. "Come on, Bella. Let's get you settled on Talonor."

Bella cast me a quick glance, her eyes filled with a mix of excitement and apprehension. I offered her a reassuring smile, knowing that she was in good hands with Hunter. Bella approached the dragon, but stopped, knelt and plucked a clover from the grass. She eyed it in the sunlight. She shrugged with a smirk and put it in her pocket.

I giggled. I loved when she did things like that. There's truly no one else like her.

As Hunter and Bella made their way toward Talonor, Cade turned back to me. "All right, Ash. Let's get you mounted on Errax. Without a saddle and reins, you're going to have to command her by speaking into her mind and shifting your body weight to signal directions. But most importantly, trust Errax. She was born to fly; let her instincts guide you. But don't fall off."

I felt a surge of nervous excitement as I approached Errax. Her massive form was both intimidating and awe-inspiring. With a deep breath, I climbed onto her back, settling into a comfortable position behind her powerful shoulders.

"Now, remember, keep your commands simple and clear," Cade instructed. "Errax knows what she's doing. Trust her to fly."

I nodded, focusing my thoughts on Errax. Fly, Errax. I thought, my mind reaching out to her.

With a powerful surge, Errax launched into the air, her wings flapping with a force that sent my hair whipping behind me. The sensation was exhilarating, a thrill that sent shivers down my spine. I gripped her scales tightly, feeling every muscle tense and release with each powerful stroke of her wings.

I glanced over at Cade, who was flying alongside me on Krakos. His expression was serious, his eyes scanning the horizon with keen intensity. Hunter and Bella flew behind us, their forms silhouetted against the brightening sky.

Errax flew differently than Krakos. She was smaller, more

agile, with shorter wings and slender. I felt like a bolt of lightning in a bursting storm. The feel of my thighs around her felt awkward, but I told myself I'd get past that feeling. Soon, I'd be zigzagging in circles around Krakos and Cade.

"Remember, keep your commands simple and clear," Cade called out, his voice barely audible over the rush of wind. "Let Errax guide you."

I nodded, my heart pounding with a mix of excitement and nervousness. I focused my thoughts on Errax, feeling her powerful muscles ripple beneath me. Faster, Errax. I thought, my mind reaching out to her.

Errax responded with a surge of speed, her wings slicing through the air with a precision that took my breath away. The sensation was exhilarating, a thrill that filled me with a sense of freedom and empowerment I had never known before.

As we soared through the sky, I reveled in the scent of dragonfire, the heat of the flames mingling with the crisp morning air. The sensation was invigorating, a reminder of the power and majesty that lay within the magnificent creatures we rode.

Cade flew beside me, his expression serious but steady. "You're doing well, Ash. Keep it up."

His words filled me with a sense of pride and determination. I had come so far, from a slave girl in Bramblebash to a dragon rider, wielding magic and facing the Blaze Queen herself. It was a journey that had tested my limits, pushed me to the brink, and yet, here I was, soaring through the sky on the back of a dragon.

Cade's voice cut through the rush of wind, his tone serious. "Ash, listen to me. The queen is coming. We can't avoid her forever. But you must not engage with her. Not yet. You are not ready. Trust me on this."

I felt a shiver of unease at his words, a stark reminder of the danger that awaited us. "What should we do if she comes?"

"If the queen comes, we need to keep our distance," Cade said, his voice firm. "Do not engage with her under any circumstances.

Even with your newfound magic, you are no match for her. She wields ancient powers fueled by malice and ambition. We must outmaneuver her, not fight her directly."

I nodded, understanding the gravity of the situation. The idea of facing the Blaze Queen, a figure of terror and darkness, sent a chill down my spine. But Cade's words were clear: engage only if absolutely necessary, and even then, trust him to handle the situation.

"And if she doesn't listen to reason?" I asked, my voice barely audible over the rush of wind.

Cade's eyes darkened, a storm of emotions swirling within them. "Then we pray to Odiun that she will. And if that doesn't work, leave the queen to me. I know her better than anyone. I know her weaknesses, her motivations. Trust me, Ash. I will do everything in my power to protect you and bring an end to her tyranny."

His determination was contagious, filling me with a renewed sense of purpose. We flew on, the landscape below a blur of greens, browns, and the occasional sparkle of water. The sun ascended higher in the sky, casting a warm glow over the world.

The journey to the mystic was fraught with uncertainty, but as I looked at Cade, Hunter, and Bella, I felt a deep sense of unity and resolve. Together, we would face whatever challenges lay ahead. Together, we would find a way to overcome the Blaze Queen and restore peace to Allovan.

As we flew, the sky darkened, clouds gathering on the horizon. The air grew cooler, and the scent of rain filled my nostrils. The distant rumble of thunder echoed through the sky, a portent of the storm to come.

"Storm's coming," Cade called out, his voice carrying over the wind. "Stay close, Ash."

I nodded, focusing my thoughts on Errax. Stay close to them, Errax. Storm's coming. I thought, my mind reaching out to her.

Errax growled low, her wings flapping powerfully as she

adjusted her course to stay near Krakos and Talonor. The storm clouds grew darker, the rumble of thunder growing louder with each passing moment. The first drops of rain fell, cool and refreshing against my skin.

Cade scanned the horizon, his eyes narrowing as he searched for a suitable shelter. The landscape below was a dense, unending expanse of forest, the trees towering and ancient. There was no sign of civilization, no towns or villages in sight.

"We need to find a cave or an overhang," Cade shouted. "Somewhere we can take cover. It's too dangerous to fly in lightning storms."

I nodded, my heart pounding as the storm grew fiercer. The rain poured down in sheets, soaking us to the bone. The wind howled, whipping around us with a force that threatened to dislodge us from our dragons' backs.

Errax let out a low rumble, her wings beating steadily against the storm. I could feel her unease, her instincts urging her to find shelter. I focused my thoughts on her, reaching out with my mind. Find shelter, Errax. Somewhere we can take cover.

Errax responded with a surge of speed, her wings slicing through the rain-soaked air. She dove lower, scanning the forest below with keen intensity. I clung to her scales, my heart pounding as I scanned the landscape for any sign of shelter.

A thunderous roar echoed through the sky, and I looked up to see a bolt of lightning slice through the dark clouds. The air sizzled with electricity, with the hairs on the back of my neck standing on end.

"Over there!" Cade called out, pointing toward a distant cliff face. "I see an overhang!"

Hunter and Bella followed closely behind, Talonor's wings flapping powerfully against the storm. We dove lower, the dragons angling toward the cliff face. As we approached, I could see the overhang, a natural shelter carved into the rock by centuries of wind and rain.

Errax landed first, her powerful body settling onto the rocky ground, her powerful wings folding against her body. I dismounted quickly, my feet splashing in the puddles that had formed on the ground. Cade, Hunter, and Bella followed behind, their dragons landing with a thunderous roar.

We rushed inside the cave, grateful for the shelter it provided. I looked around the cave, marveling at the natural beauty of the rock formations and the intricate patterns etched into the walls. The sound of rain echoed throughout the hollow interior of the dark cave.

"I'll get to making a fire," Hunter said, scanning the darkness. "Once the storm passes, then we'll continue our search."

Bella said something that caused my breath to catch in my throat then. She said, "Ash... watching you ride your dragon... it was like I was in a waking dream. I can't believe it. You're a dragon rider!"

I couldn't begin to describe how I felt in that moment. The best I could think was that I was about to die from excitement and pride. It was as if a bright ball of light was building inside of me, brushing away the worry, self-doubt and shame of my past, paving the way for the new me, and I loved every morsel of it...

CHAPTER 32

The sound of rain echoed throughout the cave, creating a soothing rhythm that seemed to wash away the tension from our bodies. Hunter was diligently at work, gathering dry wood and igniting a fire with his flint and steel. The warmth of the flames spread through the cave, casting long shadows that danced on the rocky walls.

The cave itself was deeper than it first appeared, carved over centuries by the flow of water that still trickled faintly down its walls in glistening threads. Moss clung to the damp stone, and ancient mineral deposits created strange, spiraling patterns on the ground—like the cave was telling a story in forgotten runes. The air was cool and heavy with the earthy scent of rain-soaked stone, but the firelight gave it a golden glow, as if holding back the chill of the storm outside. A narrow tunnel yawned off to the left, its darkness untouched by the fire, while the far wall curved into a shallow pool where rainwater collected, perfectly still and reflecting the flickering flames like a mirror to another world. It felt like a place outside of time—a sanctuary both wild and sacred.

As the fire crackled and popped, Cade stood up and extended

his hand toward me. "Ash, come with me," he said, his blue eyes gleaming in the firelight.

I hesitated for a moment, glancing at Bella and Hunter, who were preoccupied with warming themselves by the fire. Then, tentatively, I took Cade's hand. His touch was warm and reassuring, sending a wave of anticipation coursing through me. He led me deeper into the cave, where the darkness became a shadowy veil.

"I can't see where I'm walking," I whispered, my heart pounding. The darkness was disorienting, and I clutched Cade's hand tightly, trusting him to guide me.

In response, a soft red glow illuminated the space around us. Cade's magic staff, with its intricately sculpted phoenix head, materialized in his hand, casting a warm, comforting light onto the surrounding cave walls. The red glow danced on the rough rock surfaces, revealing intricate patterns and formations that told a story of ancient times.

"Where are we going?" I asked. My heart beat like a drum, and a growing heat spread through my core, making me acutely aware of every touch and movement.

Cade didn't answer immediately, but his grip on my hand tightened slightly. "I want some privacy," he finally said, his voice low and filled with a warmth that sent shivers down my spine.

The deeper we ventured into the cave, the more my nervous anticipation grew. The sound of the storm outside faded into a distant murmur, replaced by the steady beat of my own heart and the soft rustle of our footsteps on the cave floor. The air grew cooler, and the scent of damp earth filled my nostrils.

Eventually, the light of the fire was completely out, leaving only the warm red glow of Cade's staff to guide us. The darkness seemed to press in around us, but the light from the staff created a cocoon of comfort and warmth, a sanctuary amidst the enveloping darkness.

Cade came to a stop and turned to face me, his eyes reflecting the flickering light of the staff. I couldn't read his expression entirely, but there was a softness in his gaze that made my heart flutter. "Ash," he began. "I need to tell you something."

"What is it?" I asked, my voice quivering slightly with anticipation.

He took a deep breath, his eyes never leaving mine. "I'm falling for you, Ash. I can't stop thinking about you. Every moment we're together, every touch, every glance... it means something more to me. I've never felt this way before, and it's both exhilarating and terrifying."

His words sent a shiver of excitement and uncertainty shuddering inside me. I had been feeling the same way, drawn to him in a manner that was both thrilling and frightening. The tension between us had been building—a slow burn that was now threatening to ignite.

I could feel the heat in my core spreading, the sensation of desire and longing coursing through my veins. The warmth of his presence, the intensity in his gaze, the promise in his words—it was all intoxicating.

"Cade," I whispered, my voice barely audible. "I feel the same way. But we're from different worlds, different elements. Our very blood prevents us from being together without suffering."

His hand reached out, gently brushing against my cheek. The touch was electrifying, sending sparks of pleasure through my body. "I don't care about the consequences, Ash. I care about you. About us. We'll find a way to make this work, no matter what it takes."

The roughness of his fingertips traced a path down my neck, eliciting a soft moan from deep within me. The sensation was overwhelming—a mix of pleasure and anticipation that made me yearn for more. He leaned in, his lips brushing against my neck, leaving a trail of hot, wet kisses that sent goose pimples erupting on my skin.

I melted into his touch, my body responding to his every

movement. His hands slid down my arms, caressing my bare skin, making me acutely aware of every nerve ending. He slowly slid the sleeves of my shirt down, revealing my shoulders, my breath catching in my throat as the fabric fell away.

"You're so beautiful, Ash," he murmured, his voice thick with desire. "I want you more than anything else in this world."

His words inflamed my desire, making me yearn for him with every fiber of my being. I knew that what we were doing would lead to pain, to suffering, but the pleasure was too intense, too consuming to resist.

He leaned his staff against the cave wall, the red glow casting long shadows that seemed to dance with our movements. His hands slid underneath my belt, his fingers finding their way to my most sensitive spot. I let out a soft gasp as he rubbed my clit, the sensation sending waves of pleasure coursing through me.

"Cade," I moaned. "I want you too. I don't care what happens. I just want to be with you."

His mouth found my nipples, sucking and teasing them gently as he continued to rub my clit. The combination of sensations was overwhelming, driving me to the brink of ecstasy. I could feel the heat building within me, the tension coiling deep in my core, ready to explode.

But as his fingers worked their magic, I felt a growing discomfort, a familiar pain that always accompanied our elemental union. He was Cinderyn, and I was Aqualorian; our cursed bond. My body tightened, to dry out as the steam rose from between us. Sweat dripped from my brow, but I refused to let the pain overshadow the pleasure.

Cade's mouth moved higher, kissing and sucking my neck as he continued to rub my clit. The sensation was exquisite, a mix of pleasure and pain that was both intoxicating and dangerous. I knew that if we continued, the pleasure would eventually be eclipsed by the pain, but I couldn't stop. I didn't want to stop.

He unbuckled my pants, his fingers moving deftly as he undid

ZANDER WOLFE

the clasp. But just before he could slide my pants down, I stopped him, placing my hand on top of his. His eyes met mine, a mix of confusion and desire swirling within them.

"Wait," I whispered, my breath coming in ragged gasps. "Let's try something else. To see if it works better."

I pushed him gently back against the cave wall, my hands sliding down his chest to his belt. I knelt down before him, my heart pounding with lust and desire. Slowly, I undid his belt, my fingers trembling slightly as I unbuttoned his pants. His cock hinged out from his pant leg, swinging toward me, stiffening with excitement. A silvery pearl of his cum beaded at its crest.

He let out a deep moan as I kissed the head of his cock, the taste of him sending shivers of pleasure through my body. I licked the tip, savoring the feel of him, the taste of him. I wrapped my hand around his huge, veiny shaft, dwarfing my hand. His raw power throbbed for me, and I ached for him—all of him. When he moaned again, deeper and more intense, I took him fully into my mouth, wrapping the head of his cock with my mouth and tongue.

The sensation of him throbbing in my mouth was exhilarating, a mix of pleasure and power that was both intoxicating and addictive. I moved slowly at first, getting accustomed to the feel of him, the taste of him. But as his moans grew louder, more insistent, I increased my pace, taking him deeper, driving him to the brink of ecstasy.

I could feel the tension building within him, his body tensing as he approached the edge. But even as I felt his cock throbbing in my mouth, I felt the familiar pain returning, my body tightening up, drying out. The steam billowed up from between us, sweat trickling down my brow.

I pushed past the pain, determined to give him the pleasure he deserved. The taste of him was too much for me to resist, too much for me to stop. I took him deeper, my lips and tongue working in unison, driving him to the edge. With my other hand,

I took his massive manhood and squeezed gently. He moaned my name, and I quickened my pace, letting his huge head slide on top of my tongue.

Finally, he came, his body convulsing as he released into my mouth. The taste of him was spicy, like peppercorns on my tongue. It burned at first, but then I craved the taste of him, the essence of him. It was addictive, a sensation that I couldn't get enough of.

I released him, falling back weakly, my body drained and exhausted. The pain was intense, but the pleasure lingered, a memory that was etched deep within me. He caught me, his arms wrapping around me as he pulled me to him. We sat there, our breaths coming in heavy gasps, our bodies slick with sweat and steam.

"Ash," he murmured, his voice filled with concern. "Are you okay?"

I nodded weakly, my body trembling from the intensity of what we had just shared. "I'm okay," I said, my voice barely audible. "I just... I just need a moment to recover. I need water. I need water badly..." My mouth and throat burned as if I'd swallowed molten iron. Sweat poured down my brow, and a deep weakness felt as if my bones might snap.

He held me close, his arms wrapped around me, his heartbeat pounding and heat emanating from his chest like a fiery furnace. I pushed myself away as I was about to collapse into exhaustion and unconsciousness. "I'm sorry if I hurt you," he said, his voice filled with regret. "I don't want to cause you pain. I want to find a way to lift this curse, to make this right."

I looked into his eyes, seeing the sincerity, the determination within them. "I know you will, Cade. I trust you. I believe in you."

"Even if it means traveling to the distant stars, I'll find a way to fix this. To fix us. I promise you, Ash. I will find a way. No matter what it takes, I will lift this curse."

We sat there in silence, our breaths slowly returning to

normal, our bodies pressed close together. The red glow of his staff cast a warm, comforting light on the cave walls, a cocoon of warmth amidst the darkness.

I didn't know how we'd ever be able to be together. But he gave me hope. The way it felt being with him, tasting him, swallowing him, it was driving me insane. The thing I wanted most in this world, and it was literally killing me...

How could he lift the curse, though? That was impossible. It was in our blood. It was a curse as old as time. Fire versus water. Cinderyn against Aqualorian. How could that ever be overcome? Deep in my heart, I want to believe him. But I feel it's impossible. A dream. A fleeting dream with no happy ending... my heart hurt... like a hot needle poked into its center, causing my whole chest to heat.

As the minutes passed, the pain in my body eased, replaced by a sense of contentment and satisfaction. I knew that what we had just shared was dangerous, that it would lead to pain and suffering, but I also knew that it was worth it. Our bond, our connection, was worth the risk.

I leaned into him, my head resting on his chest, feeling the steady beat of his heart. The storm outside had subsided, the rain now a gentle whisper against the cave entrance. The soft crackle of the distant fire was soothing, a reminder of the warmth and comfort that awaited us outside. I staggered with trembling legs back up the cave to the fire and to our friends. When I got there, I guzzled down water from my watersack, all the while Bella glared at me with a snarky gaze and an upturned eyebrow. Cade cleared his throat as he sat, sending a soothing smile my way.

CHAPTER 33

*W*ith a thunderous roar, Errax launched into the sky, her immense wings flapping powerfully. The force of her ascent sent shivers down my spine, a thrill that filled me with awe and wonder. The morning air was cool, and the wind rushed past us, carrying with it the sounds of the forest below. The trees were a distant blur of green and brown, a sea of vibrant colors that seemed to stretch endlessly.

As we climbed higher, I marveled at the view. The forest was a breathtaking landscape, with the sunrise casting a golden glow over the treetops. The river sparkled in the sunlight, its meandering path a reminder of our journey ahead. The terrain was rugged and ancient, a testament to the eons that had passed before us.

Errax soared through the air with a steady rhythm, her powerful wings beating the wind with a mighty force. The sensation was exhilarating, a thrill that filled me with a sense of freedom and empowerment I had never known before. With each stroke of her wings, I felt more alive, more determined than ever.

Cade flew beside us, his expression steady and focused.

Krakos' dark scales shimmered in the sunlight, his powerful form a sight that would have filled me with dread only weeks ago. The dragon's eyes were deep red, almost glowing with a burning intensity. The fire within him was palpable, a raw power that could easily consume almost any form of life in Allovan.

Hunter and Bella flew behind us, their forms silhouetted against the brightening sky. The sun ascended higher, casting a warm glow over the landscape below. The day was clear, and the air was fresh—a perfect morning for our journey.

As we continued deeper into the Faewood toward the spot they'd found the mystic, the terrain changed. The trees grew taller and denser, their ancient trunks thickening with age. The river narrowed, its path becoming a winding snake through the dense underbrush. The rocks became more pronounced, their jagged edges sharp and imposing.

"Ash!" Bella called out, her voice filled with excitement. "Look over there!"

I looked in the direction she was pointing, and my heart leaped into my throat. In the distance, a massive structure loomed, its stone walls towering above the treetops. It was a building unlike any I had ever seen, its ancient stones etched with intricate carvings and adornments. The structure was immense, its decrepit, time-worn towers reaching high like jagged fingers pointing toward the heavens.

Cade nodded, his voice steady despite the awe of the sight. "That's the mystic's sanctuary," he said. "The old world ruins, hidden deep within the Faewood. We need to be wary. This place is ancient and unprotected."

Hunter and Bella nodded in agreement, their expressions serious and focused. Errax let out a low rumble, her emerald eyes reflecting the sunlight that filtered through the dense canopy. I could feel her unease, but pressed her forward. I focused my thoughts on her, reaching out with my mind. This is the place,

Errax. Take me down there, and remain vigilant. I thought, my mind reaching out to her.

Errax responded with a surge of speed, her wings slicing through the air with a force that sent my hair whipping behind me. She dove lower, scanning the forest below with a keen intensity. I clung to her scales tightly, my heart pounding as I scanned the landscape for any sign of shelter.

As we approached the sanctuary, I marveled at the intricate details that covered its walls. The stone was ancient, worn with age and weather, yet it held an aura of power and majesty. The building was a relic of a past long forgotten, a testament to the skill and craftsmanship of those who had come before.

Cade led the way as we descended, his expression serious and focused. Hunter and Bella followed closely behind, while Errax's powerful wings flapped with a steady rhythm that seemed to echo the beat of my own heart. The sensation was exhilarating, a reminder of the incredible creatures that carried us through the sky.

As we landed, the ground beneath us trembled slightly, the earth compressed under the weight of the dragons. The air was still, wet with morning dew, a stark contrast to the wind that had accompanied our flight. The sanctuary loomed before us, its massive stone walls casting a long shadow over the forest floor. The ancient structure seemed to hold a deep, hidden history, a story of power and knowledge that had been lost to time.

"Stay alert," Cade warned, his voice low but firm. "We don't know what lurks in this old part of the forest."

Hunter and Bella nodded in agreement, their expressions steady and focused. Errax let out a low rumble, her emerald eyes scanning the surrounding forest with a keen intensity. I could feel her unease, her instincts urging her to find shelter. I focused my thoughts on her, reaching out with my mind. Stay alert, Errax. I thought, my mind reaching out to her.

Errax responded with a powerful surge, her wings flapping

with a force that sent my hair whipping behind me and my clothes billowing against my body. Hunter and Bella gasped, their expressions filled with a mix of awe and concern. Cade's voice was steady but alert, his eyes never leaving mine.

"This is it. This is the place we found the mystic..."

We approached the sanctuary cautiously, the massive stone walls towering above us. Errax's wings brushed against the ground, leaving a trail of disturbed earth in her wake. As we neared the entrance, I marveled at the intricate carvings that adorned the door. They were ancient symbols, their meaning lost to time, yet they held a power that seemed to resonate deep within me. As we walked further inside, the darkness loomed like ancient fog.

Cade walked at my side as we walked straight through the moss-covered sanctuary. At the center of the wide room was a single chair. A throne of sorts, with vines that crept all the way along the floors to tie in knots all around, creating a sort of nest of thorns and red flowers decorating the throne. But besides the eerie feeling that crept down my skin, was the nervousness I felt in Cade as he stood beside me, itching his cheek.

"Where is he?" Hunter asked from behind.

"He's supposed to be here?" I muttered, Cade taking staggering strides forward, his fingers spread wide and his gaze searching the room anxiously.

"Where is he?" Cade scanned the room feverishly. "He was here. He was right here."

"He's got to be near." Hunter aided in the search around the dark room with no ceiling, only the branches above that scratched in the wind. The air hung heavy with silence as Cade's hand slammed against a thick wall of thorny vines, shaking the structure to its core. "He's gone," he muttered, his voice thick with disbelief and frustration. "Vanished."

The room we stood in was dark and cavernous, the only source of light the faint rays of sunlight filtering through the leaves of the ancient trees that surrounded the mystic's sanctuary. A heavy sense of unease settled over me as I looked around, my senses heightened. The only light that illuminated this place was that of a thousand fireflies that had made their home in the thorny vines. The air grew thick with an unnerving stillness, amplifying the sense of abandonment. The stones beneath our feet seemed to hum with a forgotten energy, the remnants of a civilization lost to time. I couldn't shake the feeling that this place held a deep, sorrowful memory, as if it had witnessed an ancient tragedy and was now whispering its secrets to the wind. It pressed on me—the feeling that something wasn't right. I felt my stomach drop to my toes.

This isn't good, I thought, my gaze shifting to Cade. His face was pale, his jaw clenched tightly as he paced back and forth, his frustration palpable. I'd never seen him like this, so consumed by anxiety, and it sparked a new fear in me. He was so confident, so in control, so prepared for what lay ahead. But now, his carefully laid plans had crumbled, and the uncertainty in his eyes mirrored my own growing dread.

Hunter placed a reassuring hand on Cade's shoulder, his voice calm and steady. "He can't be far, Cade. He's probably just meditating somewhere nearby. We'll find him."

Cade shook his head, running a frustrated hand through his long, dark hair. "This was my last hope, Hunter. My father told me... he said the mystic would have the answers. He said Myrathyn would know what to do." His voice cracked with a vulnerability I'd never witnessed before, and it made my heart ache for him. He looked so lost, so utterly defeated. It was a side of him I hadn't seen before, and it sparked a protectiveness within me—a fierce determination to help him, to find a way forward, even if I didn't have a clue what I was supposed to do. This wasn't Bramblebash anymore. I had magic, I had a dragon, and I had him.

"We'll figure something out, Cade. We always do." Hunter's words were laced with perseverance, but with a tinge of worry.

His words, though meant to comfort, hung heavy in the air. We always do. But did we? This wasn't like escaping Garris or outsmarting a drunken forge worker. This was the Blaze Queen we were up against—a woman who commanded armies, wielded fire magic, and sought ultimate power. What chance did we really have?

I looked around the crumbling ruins, the ancient stones whispering old tales as I let out a deep breath, knowing that the only way forward was to face the uncertainty, to take each step as it came. But the worry gnawed at me, a sense of disquiet that whispered doubts through my mind. The only sound in the room was the low crackle of Errax shifting her weight behind me, feeling my unease as she grunted.

"The forest. We need to search the forest. He can't have gotten far. Maybe he left a clue... or something." My voice cracked, but I forced myself to press forward, fighting off the despair that threatened to consume me.

Cade nodded, but his gaze was distant, his thoughts elsewhere. "We should split up," he said, his voice barely audible. "We need to cover more ground. If Myrathyn is out there, we need to find him quickly. Before the queen finds us."

Hunter glanced at Bella, his expression hardening. "Come on, Bella. Get on Talonor. We need to find your mystic and get the answers we need."

Bella nodded, her face pale but determined. She followed Hunter out the door, leaving Cade and me alone in the sanctuary.

As the sounds of their footsteps faded away, I looked up at Cade, my heart aching for him in a way I hadn't expected. He looked so utterly orphaned, like a child lost in the woods, and it sparked a fierce need in me to protect him, to save him from the pain that seemed to consume him.

"Cade..." I breathed, my voice barely audible.

He looked at me, his eyes filled with a sorrow that mirrored my own despair. "I'm sorry, Ash. I thought... I thought the mystic would be here. I thought..." His words trailed off, and he looked away, running a hand through his hair with a heavy sigh.

I stepped closer to him, my heart pounding with a mix of fear and longing. I reached out, my hand hesitating slightly before it landed gently on his shoulder. "You need to hold on to hope, Cade. We're going to find Myrathyn, and he's going to help us. We have to hold on to hope, Cade," I whispered, my voice filled with determination.

He looked at me, his eyes filled with a sorrowful gratitude that made my heart ache for him. His hand found mine, covering it gently as he squeezed. "Thank you, Ash. You have no idea how much that means to me..." His words were barely audible, but they filled me with a warmth that seemed to burn away the despair that threatened to consume me.

"We're going to find Myrathyn, Cade. I promise." I whispered.

His eyes met mine, filled with a mix of pain and hope. "I hope so," he said. "But if we don't... if I can't save you from the queen..." He squeezed my hand again, his gaze never leaving mine. "I need you to promise me you'll keep running, Ash. I can't lose you..."

My heart pounded with a mix of emotions, the weight of his words threatening to crush me beneath their weight. "I promise," I whispered, my eyes filled with tears. "But you can't lose hope either, Cade. Promise me that you'll keep fighting, that you won't give up on me..."

He nodded, his eyes filled with determination. "I promise, Ash. I'll fight for you, and for Allovan. I'll find a way to defeat the queen and bring an end to her tyranny," he said, his voice filled with resolve.

"Then let's go find Myrathyn. Whatever we need to defeat the queen, he'll have the answers."

Cade nodded, his gaze shifting to the door. "We need to get moving. Every moment we waste here..."

"I know. Let's go."

Without another word, we turned and made our way out of the sanctuary, our determination to find the mystic fueling every step. As we left the ancient structure behind, the forest swallowed us, its dense underbrush thickening the air with an ominous hum. The shadows of the trees seemed to darken the morning light, casting a threatening veil over everything. But our resolve never wavered, our determination to find the mystic and defeat the queen fueling every step. We needed answers, and we were going to get them... no matter what it took, no matter what we had to face.

The winds halted, and I stopped mid-stride. The others continued on as I paused. Looking around, I noticed the eerie forest had gone deathly silent. No chirping insects, no hooting owls, no pecking woodpeckers. Nothing.

"Ash?" Bella noticed me falling behind.

"Listen," I breathed.

Cade and Hunter glanced around with deep worry, quickly noticing the lack of life.

Like the beat of a heavy drum, or the blowing of a silver, royal horn, the thunderous explosion of wildlife lifted from the trees. Thousands of birds of all varieties took to the sky, accompanied by every winged creature I could imagine. Everything from locusts to bats scuttled off into the sky, heading south. I gasped, sweat wetting my palms.

"Cade?" I muttered.

Then we got our answer in the form of the most terrifying sound I could have imagined. It was monstrous, like nothing I've heard before. Deep and brimming with a thirst for violence. Distant enough to be drowned out by the forest, but near enough to know exactly that nothing else in the world could make that sound. It was a roar from the north that caused every beast in the forest to flee for their lives. It quickly hit me that the animals didn't flee at the appearance of Krakos, but they fled from this new monstrosity.

"It's her..." Cade put his hand quickly on the hilt of his huge sword.

"Brigodon," Hunter uttered with deep concern.

She's finally come for me... No more Sythers, no more ogres or hunters... The queen has finally come for me... I clenched my wet fists, but deep down I knew... I knew I wasn't ready to fight the most powerful being in existence.

"Ash," I heard the wise, old tortoise's voice beside me. Looking down, I saw his half-translucent head beside my thigh, the rest of his body still invisible. "Run! Fly! You're not ready! She can't capture you. Not yet! Run!"

I didn't hesitate, as we all ran with all our strength to the dragons as the sky darkened from the mass amount of life fleeing the forest, as another ghastly roar sounded from the queen's dragon, and a deep, deep fear gripped me.

I wasn't ready to die. Not now. Now that I'd tasted freedom, I couldn't let this be the end.

Fly, Errax! Fly like you've never flown before!

CHAPTER 34

*T*he sky was alive with fear as Errax soared through the air, her powerful wings cutting through the wind with precision. Beside me, Krakos and Talonor kept pace, their forms echoing the same tension that coursed through my veins. We were fleeing from the impending force of the Blaze Queen and her monstrous dragon, Brigodon. The horizon ahead seemed like an unattainable refuge, a promise of safety that felt impossibly far away.

"Faster, Errax!" I commanded in my mind, feeling the urgency pumping through every beat of my heart. Errax responded instantly, her wings flapping with renewed vigor, propelling us further into the sky. The sound of dragonfire behind us was like the roar of a distant thunderstorm, a menacing reminder of the force that pursued us with unrelenting ferocity.

Cade's voice boomed over the wind. "Ash, keep flying south! We need to find cover before they catch up to us!" His eyes were fixed ahead, but the strain was evident in his jawline. Hunter and Bella, on Talonor, were equally focused, their dragon syncing with the others as their wings cut through the sky.

Suddenly, a harsh, ominous voice filled my mind. It was the

same voice from the first time I felt the awakening of my magic. My fingers lifted from Errax's scales, unintentionally covering my mouth at the sound of the archaic voice in my head. "The time to fight is now. You can't hide forever from the queen. You're strong, even if you haven't reached the pinnacle of your magic. Trust Cade. He's young, but he's a true warrior. The queen wants your power to unlock her divinity, but you can't allow that to happen. You need to fight, Ashlyn Moonriver! It's your time to let your spark shine in this dark world. Fight! Fight like the world depends on it!"

The words reverberated in my mind, igniting a spark within me that refused to be extinguished. "Who are you? Why are you calling me Ashlyn Moonriver?" I thought, grappling with the implications of this hidden part of my identity. I had grown up knowing only the slave name of Mist, and even Ash had been a name of convenience. Ashlyn Moonriver felt like a fragment of a forgotten identity, a part of me that had been locked away, waiting to be unveiled. The name Moonriver caused my throat to nearly squeeze shut, and a deep pit lurched in my stomach, causing a pain that only a lost orphan like me could know.

Moonriver. That name erupted something dormant in me. Like a birth glowing brightly inside me. There was a power behind that name. And all at once, it felt right. Now that I knew my name... I might be able to figure out who I really am... if I survive.

Despite the pain throbbing in my side from the Sythers' attack, an unyielding resolve filled me. The monster that was Brigodon had been a symbol of fear and tyranny for too long. I couldn't allow it to continue, not while I had the power to potentially make a difference.

"Errax, turn!" I commanded in my mind, feeling the tense muscles beneath my fingers shift as the dragon obeyed. The sudden change in direction caused Cade to yell out in alarm, but I wouldn't be deterred. My heart pounded with a mix of fear and determination as Errax wheeled around to face the oncoming threat.

"Ash, what are you doing? Turn back!" Cade's voice was laced with panic as he made Krakos swing around to follow me. Hunter followed suit with Talonor, the dragons forming a protective wedge around me.

Brigodon and the Blaze Queen loomed closer, an imposing sight of dark scales and the cold gleam of black armor. The queen's whip of fire crackled in the air, a deadly lash that seemed to cut through the very winds. Her eyes glistened with unrestrained and hungry malice, her intentions clear—she wanted my power.

The queen's royal armor was slender, and glossy black with weaving reds, oranges and golds throughout in intricate patterns like thorns spiking around lavish flowers. Her long silver hair flapped madly out behind her dragon-head helm, fierce with rubies for eyes and ivory for teeth, from out which her pale, angular face crept. Her gaze was an infinite abyss of a deep black, unlike anything I'd ever seen, and a hint of a smirk crept onto her thin red lips at the sight of me.

Brigodon was the embodiment of terror. His enormous size dwarfed Krakos, and its immense body was covered in thick black scales weathered with deep age. It was rumored the dragon was over a thousand years old, rivaling in age only the king's lost dragon. The crimson webbing of its wings gave the dire warning a black widow would to the world. Beware my venom! Beware my wrath! The huge ivory horns on its head curled to sharp points, and the rest of the horns down the center of its back were a bleak gray like stone piercing its thick hide. Its eyes were a devilish violet, unnatural in all aspects, like violets that would only bloom in the Infernal Depths.

"Now, let's see what you are made of, Gold-Marked," the Blaze Queen called out, her voice echoing over the stretch between our dragons. Her gaze was as dark as pitch, locked onto me with unwavering intensity. "I've been searching a very, very long time for you..."

Dread washed through me like acid in my blood, but I pushed it away, focusing on the golden light within me. Eden, the magic that had become a part of me, swelled and pulsed in response to the threat, ready to fight as I commanded. The pain in my side was a distant ebb, overshadowed by the adrenaline and resolve pumping through my veins.

Krakos' roar filled the air as he lunged forward, his claws and teeth aimed at Brigodon with feral ferocity. Talonor followed, his crimson horns gleaming with deadly intent. Errax, attuned to my command, dove straight toward Brigodon, the three dragons forming a united front against our adversary.

The Blaze Queen was ready, her whip snaking through the air with punishing speed. She aimed it at Krakos, and the fire licked against his scales, eliciting a pained roar from the mighty dragon. Cade responded with a burst of fire from his staff, the flames erupting in a blazing arc that the queen narrowly avoided with a swift swing of Brigodon.

Errax and I dove beneath Brigodon's massive form, using our smaller size to our advantage. I focused my magic, feeling the golden light surge through my arms and legs. Now, Errax! I thought, and the dragon responded with a sharp twist, her jaws snapping at Brigodon's underbelly.

Brigodon recoiled, its massive wings flapping with brutal force as it swung around to counter our attack. The Blaze Queen snarled, her black eyes narrowing into slits as she pivoted, her serpent's head scepter glinting ominously in the sunlight. A wave of flames erupted from the tip of her staff, scorching the air around us. I'd never felt anything like her fire. It was far hotter than anything I'd ever felt, as hot as dragonfire, and as hot as I'd imagine burning in the sun's center.

Her magic was too powerful. Even Cade and I together couldn't match that sort of raw power.

Hunter and Bella joined the fray, Talonor's horns clashing against Brigodon's scales with a resounding crack. The queen let out a frustrated growl, her whip lashing through the air, snapping ferociously around Cade's sword arm. He grunted in pain, but he remained resilient, slicing at the fiery tendril with a swift strike of his blade.

Errax maneuvered deftly, avoiding a swooping attack from Brigodon. The air was filled with the rumble of dragonfire and the clash of steel against scales. I could feel the heat, smell the smoldering brimstone stinging my nostrils. The battle raged on, each attack met with swift and brutal counter-movements. We weaved through the skies, our dragons dancing in a deadly ballet with the Blaze Queen's terrible dragon.

I clung tightly to Errax's scales, my focus never wavering. The golden magic within me surged through my veins, pulsating with my heartbeat. Again, Errax! I thought, commanding the dragon to dip and twist, evading another assault from Brigodon.

The Blaze Queen's eyes locked onto me, her malicious gaze burning with hatred and greed. "You cannot escape me, Gold-Marked," she hissed, her voice echoing through the cacophony of battle. "Your Gilded Radiance will be mine. I hunger for it. I need it!"

I felt a fresh surge of determination, refusing to be intimidated. Eden stirred within me, and a wave of golden light emanated from my hands. I focused the magic, directing it toward the queen. The golden energy collided with the queen's fire whip, momentarily halting its deadly dance.

Cade, seeing the opening, commanded Krakos to strike. The black dragon's jaws clamped down on Brigodon's neck, drawing a pained roar from the larger beast. The Blaze Queen's scepter blazed with renewed intensity, sending a torrent of fire toward Cade, driving Krakos back.

Hunter and Bella swooped in on Talonor, their combined might lending crucial support. Talonor's horns grazed Brigodon's flank, leaving long scrapes on the monster's armored scales. The Blaze Queen's reaction was immediate and fierce, her whip crackling with a renewed burst of flames.

I felt the pain in my side intensify, but I pushed it aside, focusing all my energy on the fight. "Eden, help me," I muttered under my breath, drawing on the deep well of power within me. The golden light intensified, enveloping me and Errax in a protective aura.

The queen, seeing the glimmering barrier, sneered. "Your tricks won't save you, girl. You're a mere insect compared to my power." She hurled another bolt of fire, the torrent colliding with my protective shield. The impact sent shockwaves through the air, the force threatening to shatter the magical barrier. Errax pulled back, sending us diving down.

I gritted my teeth, my hands trembling from the strain. "We can't keep this up," I shouted to Cade and Hunter, who were engaged in their own battles against Brigodon's relentless assault. "We need another plan." Cade dodged a sweeping strike from the queen's whip, his staff flaring with fire. "We need to outmaneuver her, use our agility to our advantage."

Hunter nodded, Talonor veering sharply as another flame whip sang through the air. "But she's too powerful. We need to find her weakness."

I thought quickly, my mind racing. "Her battle armor—it might have weak points." I focused on the queen, studying the intricate patterns on the black and orange armor. "The scepter and whip are her main weapons. If we can disable them…"

Cade's expression hardened with resolve. "It's risky, but it might be our only chance." He turned to Hunter. "Hunter, flank her from the left. Ash, use your magic to draw her attention. I'll make my move from behind."

Hunter nodded, his eyes determined. "Let's give it everything we've got!"

I took a deep breath, feeling the weight of our plan settle on my shoulders. "All right, Eden, let's make this count." I focused my magic, drawing on the deep reserves of power within me. The golden light intensified, swirling around my hands.

I directed Errax to rise higher, positioning us in full view of the queen. The Blaze Queen's gaze locked onto her immediately, her eyes narrowing with malice. "Your pitiful magic won't save you, Gold-Marked. Not against me. I've defeated all Gold-Marked that rose before you, and they all fell... Every... Single... One..."

I ignored the taunt, my focus unwavering. I thrust my hands forward, sending a surge of golden energy toward the queen. The magic collided with the fire whip, momentarily disrupting its deadly dance. The queen snarled, her serpent's head scepter blazing with renewed intensity.

At the same moment, Hunter and Talonor shot forward, their movements after the plan I'd devised with Cade were already synced up perfectly. But fate, unfortunately, rarely aligns with the best laid plans, and the day quickly turned to chaos.

Brigodon, sensing the synchronized attack, roared and twisted. His massive body slid through the sky, the momentum taking him and the queen clear out of range for my magic to reach.

I knew Bella had seldom seen battle, let alone the horror of the Blaze Queen. When Brigodon swiveled, swinging his tail, he clipped Talonor with such overpowering force that they were knocked back. Hunter tried to manipulate the stumble with flares of slope-gliding, but the impact was too massive. Talonor, taking the hit, chipped a horn so fiercely it broke right off his head. Hunter did his best to stay in flight, despite the pain and shock from Talonor's injury that was palpable in the air.

"Hunter! Bella!" I screamed, trying to guide Errax toward them, but the battle had us separated, and we all needed to constantly evade Brigodon's assaults.

Riding on Errax, I tried to get closer, but the air was heavy with hazard and flames, creating a thick barrier. Krakos, with Cade on his back, banked hard around Brigodon, trying to locate an opening. The Blaze Queen laughed sadistically, her voice slicing through the chaos like a wicked blade. "Pathetic puppets," she hissed, "playing at being warriors. Your end is near. You cannot defeat me. I enjoy this game. I love the hunt!"

Cade and Krakos raged on in the battle with the queen as I sent Errax diving after Bella, Talonor still tumbling down from the shock of the queen's attack.

"Bella! Hold on! I'm coming!"

CHAPTER 35

*E*rrax dove sharply, her massive wings slicing through the air with a ferocious intensity. The sky was a chaotic blend of fire and smoke, the air thick with the scent of brimstone and the crackling energy of the Blaze Queen's dark magic. Below, Hunter's dragon, Talonor, was tumbling through the air, Bella holding onto Hunter for dear life as they plummeted toward the ground.

"Bella! Hold on!" I shouted, feeling the desperation rise in my throat. I could see the terror in her eyes, her glacier-blue irises wide with fear. I reached deep within myself, drawing upon the golden energy that was the essence of my magic, Eden. The power surged through my veins, crackling with an intensity that sent the electricity surging through every nerve in my body.

"Errax, faster!" I commanded, my voice steady despite the surrounding chaos. The dragon responded instantly, her speed increasing as she swooped down toward Talonor. I extended my hands, the golden light of Eden radiating from my fingers like a beacon of hope in the midst of the inferno.

"Bella, I've got you!" I called out, focusing the energy into a spell that I hoped would save them. The golden light wrapped around Talonor, a shimmering halo of power that pulsed with life. The dragon's wings snapped back into consciousness, the golden magic waking the beast and restoring some of the dragon's strength.

Talonor roared, a sound of renewed vigor that sent a surge of relief through me. Hunter and Bella's dragon stabilized, its wings flapping powerfully as it regained control of its flight. Bella looked back at me, her eyes filled with gratitude and awe.

"Ash, you saved us!" she shouted, her voice filled with relief.

"We're not out of danger yet!" I called back, turning my attention to the sky above. Cade and Krakos were engaged in a brutal fight with the Blaze Queen and Brigodon, their forms silhouetted against the darkening sky. The air was filled with the crackle of fire and the screams of dragons, the battle raging with an intensity that was almost overwhelming. Their dragons clashed in the air, fire and claws tearing at each other with a savage hunger. Cade's staff glowed with a fierce intensity, the phoenix head at its top now ablaze with fire, while the Blaze Queen's scepter crackled with dark energy, the serpent's head spitting venomous flames.

The queen's laughter echoed through the sky, a chilling sound that sent shivers up my back and deep into my head. "You are pathetic, Cade," she sneered, her voice filled with disdain. "You cannot hope to defeat me. I am the embodiment of fire itself!"

Cade growled, his eyes filled with determination. "You underestimate me, Mortriana," he retorted, his voice steady despite the chaos around them. "I am not the child you once knew. I have grown, and I will not let you destroy my kingdom!"

The Blaze Queen's eyes narrowed, a cruel smirk playing on her lips. "You are still a naïve fool, Cade. You cannot hope to defeat me. I have the knowledge of the old world and its secrets. I've been honing my powers, preparing for the day when I would ascend to godliness. And you, a mere mortal, think you can stand in my way?"

Cade's response was a fierce burst of flame from his staff, the fire arcing through the air like a comet. The Blaze Queen raised her scepter, the serpent's head flaring with dark energy as she deflected the attack. The surrounding sky darkened, the clouds churning and roiling as if in response to the queen's malice.

As Errax ascended, carrying me back into the fray, I could see the battle more clearly. To my amazement and dismay, I saw black clouds billowing out from the sky behind her, and the blue sky deepened into an unworldly, deep black. The Blaze Queen's dark clouds billowed and swirled, rich with an ominous power. Red lightning streaked through the sky, a web of deadly energy that made the air crackle and hum. The changes in the sky made it dangerous for me and Hunter's dragon to get close, the lightning striking out with wild abandon.

Cade and the queen continued their brutal dance in the storm, their dragons twisting and turning in a deadly ballet. Krakos' scales glistened with sweat and blood, his eyes wild with battle lust. Brigodon, on the other hand, seemed almost untouched, his massive form a testament to his ancient power.

As we neared the heart of the storm, I could feel the tension in the air, the crackling energy that threatened to consume us all. Errax growled low in her throat, her wings flapping powerfully as she maneuvered through the chaotic sky.

As we raced toward the battle above, my heart yearned to help Cade. Now that we had each other, I couldn't let her take him from me. Not now. Not ever!

Cade landed a powerful blow, his staff striking the queen with a burst of flame that sent her reeling. She screamed in pain, her scepter momentarily faltering. The dark clouds around us seemed to shiver, the red lightning flickering as if in response to her pain. A guttural roar left my throat, and I felt the scratch from the shrill excitement deep in my core.

The Blaze Queen's eyes flashed with rage, her anger palpable in the air. "You dare to strike me, Cade?" she hissed, her voice filled with venom. "You will pay for your insolence!"

With a wave of her scepter, the queen summoned a storm of fire, the air around us filling with a whirlwind of flames. The tornado of fire spun with a savage intensity, the heat scorching the air and making it hard to breathe. Cade and Krakos were momentarily engulfed in the inferno, their forms barely visible through the wall of flame.

"Cade!" I screamed, fear gripping my heart. Errax roared, her wings beating against the wall of fire as we tried to reach him. The heat was immense, with the flames licking at our skin and threatening to consume us.

As we fought through the inferno, the Blaze Queen's laughter echoed around us, a chilling sound that sent shivers down my spine. "You cannot hope to save him, Gold-Marked," she sneered. "He is mine to destroy, just as you will be!"

Anger surged within me, a fierce determination that refused to be quelled. I drew upon the power of Eden, the golden light flaring to life within me. The magic pulsed through my veins, a force that seemed to resonate with the very heart of the world. I focused the energy, directing it toward the whirlwind of flames that threatened to consume Cade and Krakos.

"Eden, help me!" I shouted, my voice filled with desperation and hope. The golden light flared out from my hands, pushing against the wall of fire with a force that made the air shimmer. The flames parted, revealing Cade and Krakos, their forms battered but unbroken. I thought of Cornelius, and let his strength fuel me.

Cade looked at me, his eyes filled with a mix of gratitude and determination. "Ash, we can't let her win," he said, his voice steady despite the surrounding chaos. "She's been keeping the war going intentionally. It's called the Rite of War—a law that allows the spouse of the king to take over during wartime if the firstborn isn't ready. She's been using it to maintain her grip on power, waiting for the chance to ascend to godliness by consuming your Gilded Radiance."

The Blaze Queen laughed, her voice echoing through the storm. "It matters not what you say, boy. But I will ascend! It is my destiny! I will become what I was meant to be! And once I consume the Gold-Marked's power, I will ascend to divinity, and this world will know eternal peace—under my rule!"

Anger boiled within me, a rage that was fueled by the injustice of it all. I couldn't let her continue to cause so much suffering, to keep dividing the continent and letting people die in this meaningless civil war. I turned to face the queen, my eyes filled with a burning determination.

"You won't win, Mortriana," I shouted, my voice filled with defiance. "I won't let you continue to cause so much pain and suffering. I've endured more suffering than you can imagine, and I won't let you inflict it upon anyone else! No one deserves the life of a slave, and no one deserves to grow up in your pointless war! This war ends now!"

Cade nodded, his gaze locked onto the queen with a fierce intensity. "Together, we will end this, Ash. We will bring peace to Allovan, no matter the cost."

With a roar, Cade and Krakos launched themselves at the queen, their forms silhouetted against the dark sky. The Blaze Queen laughed, her scepter crackling with dark energy as she prepared to meet their assault. I drew upon the power of Eden, the golden light flaring to life within me as I prepared to join the fight.

The battle raged on, the sky filled with the crackle of fire and the roar of dragons. Cade and Krakos fought with a ferocious intensity, their attacks coordinated and precise. The Blaze Queen met their assault with a savage grace, her scepter lashing out with bolts of dark fire that tore through the air.

I joined the fray, Errax's powerful wings carrying us through the storm. The golden light of Eden pulsed through my veins, a force that seemed to resonate with the very heart of the world. I focused the energy, directing it toward the queen with a series of powerful blasts. The golden magic collided with her dark fire, the air around us crackling with energy as the forces clashed.

The Blaze Queen snarled, her eyes filled with rage and frustration. "You cannot hope to defeat me, Gold-Marked!" she hissed, her voice filled with venom. "I am the embodiment of fire itself! I will consume your power and ascend to divinity, and there is nothing you can do to stop me! You are the last. And you certainly aren't the strongest I've killed..."

Cade and I exchanged a glance, our determination unwavering. We knew we couldn't let her win, that we had to fight with everything we had to bring an end to her tyranny. With a roar, we launched ourselves at the queen, our attacks coordinated and precise.

But the Blaze Queen was not so easily defeated. With a wave of her scepter, she summoned another massive tornado of fire, the whirlwind of flames spinning with a savage intensity. The heat was immense, the flames licking at our skin, and I felt my eyelashes and hairs in my ear sizzle. Cade and Krakos were engulfed in the inferno, their forms barely visible through the wall of flame.

"Cade!" I screamed, fear gripping my heart. Errax roared, her wings beating against the wall of fire as we tried to reach him. The heat was intense, with the flames scorching the air and making it hard to breathe.

As we fought through the inferno, the Blaze Queen's laughter echoed around us, a chilling sound that made my skin crawl and my stomach sink into Errax. "You cannot hope to save him, Gold-Marked," she sneered. "He is mine to destroy, just as you will be!"

"You won't hurt him!" I shouted in the blinding inferno. "He's mine now!"

The queen wasn't visible, but I saw the dark form of Brigodon darkening the tornado as the great dragon swooped through the sky.

"Oh," the queen's words echoed in the storm. "That was something I didn't expect, and yet, now that I think about it, it's wildly predictable... You love him. A slave girl from nowhere loves the prince of Allovan. How absolutely delicious... I'm going to enjoy snuffing out his life all the more now..."

My gaze darted through the storm, trying to fix a spell on the queen, but her dragon was too swift, too vicious, and too strong.

"You don't know what you're talking about..." I said through gritted teeth. She's right, but I can't let her know that... I've got to distract her from Cade, get her attention on me... "Come fight me, you witch!"

"I should've killed him when he was just a weak, insolent, mopey brat. But he served his purpose. He led his father's armies well, as he led mine." The Blaze Queen's voice turned dark, sounding like an extension of the fiery storm swirling and growing all around. "But his time has come. It's time to wipe the line of Phoenixfires from this world. And so, will my true, unencumbered reign begin... and a beautiful, glorious reign it will be..."

CHAPTER 36

The storm of flames raged around us, the heat intense and the air thick with the acrid smell of brimstone. The Blaze Queen's laughter echoed through the inferno, a chilling sound that seemed to shatter the very air around us, and I felt the world may be breaking apart. If I didn't find a way to stop her, then there would be no tomorrow for any of us. Everything I loved was in her devilish gaze, and I'd do anything to protect them. Errax roared defiantly, her wings beating against the wall of fire as we fought to break through to Cade and Krakos.

A dark form swept through the flames, the enormous body of Brigodon materializing like a nightmare. The Blaze Queen sat atop her monstrous dragon, her obsidian eyes gleaming with malevolence and her laughter reverberating through the chaos.

"You cannot hide forever, Gold-Marked," she hissed, her voice cutting through the roar of the flames. "I will have your power!"

Brigodon flew at terrifying speed above me, the enormous body of the dragon hiding the crackling red streaks of lightning above, darkening the sky like a mountain floating above us.

With a swift and agile movement, the queen leaped from

Brigodon's back onto Errax. Bella shrieked somewhere in the storm, and all of my senses surged alive. It was something I didn't expect, and the queen was suddenly upon me, sending me into a sheer panic. Her grip on my arm was crushing and intense. I could smell the hate on her breath as she squeezed with vice-like strength. A smoldering black magic seeped from the pores in her skin, snaking onto my skin. I gasped in pain, feeling her dark energy begin to siphon my magic. I fought, squirming and clawing to break free of her grasp, but I was powerless against such a monster, and terror roared in me like hot needles piercing all of my soft skin. The golden light of Eden flickered, struggling to resist the queen's malicious pull.

"No!" I screamed, grappling to free myself from her iron grasp. But the queen was impossibly strong, her fingers digging into my flesh like talons. I could feel the strength draining from me, the golden magic ebbing away as the queen feasted on my power.

Cade roared in fury, Krakos diving toward us with ferocious speed. But the queen was prepared, her scepter flaring with dark energy as she lashed out with streaks of red lightning. The bolts struck Krakos, sending the dragon reeling and Cade struggling to maintain control.

Bella's screams pierced the air; her voice filled with desperation. "Ash! Hold on!"

The queen's gaze fell on the wound in my side, and a cruel smile curled her lips. "Ah, you've already been touched by battle," she sneered, pulling a dagger from her belt, and driving its sharp blade into the injury with a savage twist. The pain was excruciating, searing through my body and blurring my vision. I cried out, feeling my strength wane as the queen mercilessly sucked the life from me. The world fogged from the pain, and the storm's deafening thunder and sizzling lightning faded.

"You cannot defeat me, Gold-Marked," the queen taunted, her voice filled with sadistic glee. "You are weak, pathetic. You're like all the others. I honestly hoped you'd be more, if not only to savor your death and my final victory more. Your Gilded Radiance will be mine, and with it, I will ascend to divinity!"

I gritted my teeth, fighting against the agony that threatened to overwhelm me. I could feel the voice of the dragon in my head again, its words cutting through the haze of pain and despair. "You must survive, Ashlyn Moonriver. If you fall, a new age of torment and death will dawn. The queen will enslave all who oppose her. You must fight, for the sake of all those who cannot. Fight... fight for what you have, for what you've lost, and for what you wish your world to be! For if you lose, there will be no tomorrow for all that you hold dear, for all that you love..."

The words sparked a deep well of determination within me, a reserve of strength I hadn't known I possessed. I drew upon the power of Eden, feeling the golden light surge through my veins. The magic pulsed with renewed vigor, countering the queen's dark energy and pushing back against her siphoning grip.

The air around me crackled with energy, and I felt the moisture in the air coalesce, drawn to me by the magical force. The water swirled around me, forming a shimmering barrier that repelled the queen's dark magic. The golden light intensified, and I could feel the wound in my side beginning to heal, the pain ebbing away as the magic mended my flesh.

The queen's eyes widened in surprise, her grip on me faltering as the golden light pushed her back. I seized the opportunity, my hands moving instinctively to summon a weapon from the magical energy. A golden sword materialized in my grasp, its blade gleaming with an ethereal light. At the same time, golden armor formed around my body, the metal plates fitting perfectly and imbuing me with a renewed sense of strength and invincibility.

"You will never defeat me, Mortriana," I growled, my voice filled with conviction. "Not as long as I draw breath." I needed to believe my own words. Because if we didn't survive this, then it was the end of everything. More than Bella, more than Cade and me. I had to believe in Eden. I was given this power for a reason. It was for a purpose. And right then, my purpose was to kill that rotten bitch!

The queen snarled, her scepter flaring with dark energy as she lashed out at me. I parried her attack with my golden sword, the blades clashing with a burst of sparks. Errax roared, her head turning to spout scorching, unbearable dragonfire at the queen. The flames engulfed Mortriana, but she emerged unscathed, her dark magic shielding her from the inferno.

Cade, having regained control of Krakos, joined the fight, his staff blazing with fire as he sent a fresh plume of magical flames at the queen. The combined assault forced Mortriana to focus on defense, her scepter whirling and deflecting the attacks with precision.

I lunged at her, my golden sword clashing against her scepter as we traded blows. The queen was a formidable opponent, her movements swift and fluid, but I was fueled by a renewed sense of myself. I am strong. I am strong enough. I can change the world. I can save those who can't defend themselves. I am enough. I have to be! I fought with a ferocity I had never known, my sword striking with speed and accuracy that surprised even myself.

The battle raged on, the sky filled with the crackle of fire and the shimmering glow of golden magic. The queen's attacks were relentless, her scepter lashing out with streaks of dark energy that sought to incapacitate me. But my golden armor absorbed the impacts, the magic within it negating the queen's assaults.

With every clash of our blades, I could see the frustration mounting in the queen's eyes. Her confidence wavered as she realized I was not the weak, pathetic slave she had expected. I was a force to be reckoned with, a warrior imbued with the power of my Eden, and I would not be defeated so easily.

In a moment of fierce resolve, I summoned all my strength

and lunged at the queen, my golden sword slicing through the air with blinding speed. The blade met the resistance of her scepter, but the impact was enough to send her off balance. Seizing the opportunity, I spun around, my sword arcing in a deadly dance as it sought the queen's flesh.

The blade bit deep into the queen's side, cutting through her armor and drawing a gush of fresh, crimson blood. The queen roared in pain, her eyes wide with shock and disbelief.

"So... you do bleed," I said, my voice steady and cold. "You're no god. You're no savior. You're mortal... and all things mortal must die."

The queen's face contorted with rage, her dark eyes blazing with a fury that seemed to ignite the very air around her. "You dare to cut me?" she hissed, her voice a venomous whisper. "I am the embodiment of fire, the rightful ruler of Allovan. You cannot hope to defeat me!"

But her words lacked the conviction they once held. I could see the doubt flickering in her eyes, the fear that her reign of terror might finally be coming to an end. I pressed my advantage, my golden sword poised to strike the final blow.

Just as I was about to plunge the blade into her heart, the queen leaped off Errax, her form tumbling through the sky. I heaved breaths from the battle, desperately hoping for the queen to fall to her death, but I knew better. Brigodon, sensing his master's distress, swooped down with remarkable speed and caught the queen on his back. The monstrous dragon roared, his eyes filled with a primal rage that matched his mistress's fury.

The queen, clutching her wounded side, glared at me with a mix of hatred and disbelief. She hefted her scepter in her hand, sheathed her bloody dagger, oozing with my blood, and grabbed her whip again. Brigodon tilted his massive wings, flapping them to return back to the battle.

I steadied myself, trying to calm my erratic breathing. Adrenaline was doing what it could to kill the pain in my side, but it only did so much. I winced, dropping to a knee on Errax's back as she let out a moan. Bella screamed my name in my dizzying pain.

Focus, Ash.

You're so close. You have to finish this. You can't let her win.

But she's so strong... How is she still fighting? I... I've got to stand up. I've got to find a way to keep fighting. Remember Cornelius' lessons. Focus on his words. You are strong. You are strong enough.

You've got to keep going... Stand up. Stand up Ash!

My boot got under me, but the pain was unbearable, and I fell onto my back, my hand clutched to my wound to slow the bleeding. I... I don't know if I can...

"Ash!" Cade shouted with deep, guttural worry. "Ash, hold on! Hold on! I'm coming!"

The queen's dragon sped in, spewing dragonfire everywhere. It felt as if I'd been taken to the Infernal Depths, and this was what death felt like. A terrible mix of pain and the feeling of loss.

"You're mine, you bitch!" the queen shrieked, her words laced with disdain and bloody hatred.

As she spoke, a distant roar echoed through the sky, a sound that opened the floodgates of hope inside me. I could tell by the pitch that it was a small dragon, but as I turned to see the dragon and its rider approaching from the south, its form silhouetted against the stormy sky, I knew instantly what it was. More roars joined it, the sound growing louder and more insistent as a dozen dragon riders entered the fray, their shadowy forms dotting the red sky behind.

Hunter's voice rang out, filled with renewed vigor. "The Stormscales! They've come to aid us!"

The queen's expression darkened, her eyes narrowing as she took in the new arrivals. Hope welled within us, and a seething hate erupted in the queen. She glanced all around, overwhelmingly surrounded, knowing that she might not be victorious against such numbers. She shot me one last glance as my vision wet with tears from the pain. She said no words, but her gaze was so burned into me, it was a moment I knew I'd never forget. And as she mouthed the words, "You're all going to die," all my Gilded Radiance faded. The golden magical sword, the armor, and all of Eden evaporated in the storm. With a final, scathing glare, she turned Brigodon northward and retreated, the Stormscales in hot pursuit.

Cade, seeing the queen's retreat, moved to give chase, but his gaze fell on me, and his expression changed from one of determination to one of concern. I could feel the warmth of my blood dripping from the wound in my side, the pain and exhaustion finally catching up with me. My vision blurred, and I swayed on Errax's back, the world around me spinning out of control.

"Ash!" Cade's voice cut through the haze, filled with urgency and worry. I tried to stay conscious, to hold on to the strength that had sustained me through the battle, but the darkness was too powerful. I felt myself slipping, the world fading to black as I tumbled from Errax's back.

I fell. I fell, tumbling into the darkness. My fingers tried to grasp anything, but it was only air that slipped between my fingers. I felt I was going to die. I'd put up a good fight, I'd held my own against the queen, but this was the end. In that moment of utter helplessness, I felt strong arms catch me, cradling me with a gentleness that belied their strength. I opened my eyes to see Cade's face, his eyes filled with a mix of relief and concern. His handsome features were a beacon of hope in the chaos that surrounded us.

"You saved me," I whispered, my voice barely audible above the roar of the wind and the distant cries of the Stormscales.

Cade's gaze softened, a tender smile playing on his lips. "No, Ash," he murmured, his voice filled with a warmth that seemed to envelop me. "You've saved me."

And with those words, the world faded to black, the pain and exhaustion finally claiming me as I surrendered to the darkness, knowing that I was safe in Cade's arms.

As I drifted into unconsciousness, I knew that our battle was far from over. The Blaze Queen was still out there, her hunger for power and dominion unquenched. But for now, we had won a victory, a moment of respite in a war that had raged for too long. And with the Stormscales at our side, we had new allies, a new hope for a brighter future.

The journey ahead would be fraught with danger and uncertainty, but with Cade by my side, I knew that we could face whatever challenges lay ahead. Together, we would fight for a better world, a world free from the tyranny of the Blaze Queen, a world where love and hope could flourish.

And as I slipped into the embrace of darkness, I knew that I was not alone. I had friends, allies, and a power within me that would not be denied. I was Ashlyn Moonriver, and I would not be defeated. Not now, not ever.

Then, the darkness fully took me.

CHAPTER 37

*T*he descent to the sanctuary was filled with an eerie silence, broken only by the flap of the dragons' wings and the distant thunder that rumbled like the growling of a primordial beast. As we landed, the ground crunched under the mighty paws of the dragons, and the ancient structure of the sanctuary loomed before us, its ancient stones a somber and foreboding sight.

Cade, his face etched with deep worry, carried me in his arms as we entered the sanctuary. I could feel the warmth of his body against mine, but the pain in my side was overwhelming. Each step he took sent a fresh wave of agony coursing through me. He laid me down gently in the throne of thorns, the vines creeping around, creating a nest of knots and red flowers, their scent a faint reminder of a forgotten spring. Blood poured down my side, soaking the throne.

Bella knelt beside me, her glacier-blue eyes filled with tears as she clutched my hand tightly. "Ash, you're going to be okay," she whispered, her voice trembling with fear and uncertainty.

Cade, his heart pounding audibly, tore a strip of cloth from his own tunic, pressing it firmly against the wound in my side.

The blood soaked through almost instantly, and I could see the desperation in his eyes, the fear that he might lose me. "Come on, Ash. Stay with me," he urged, his voice thick with emotion.

I tried to offer a reassuring smile, but the pain was too much. "It's all right," I whispered, my voice barely above a breath. "If I die, at least I got to live free for a little bit. I got to ride on a dragon's back... I even got my own dragon." My voice faded as a new surge of pain washed over me. Wetness flooded my vision as I realized I was dying.

"Stop talking like that," Cade commanded, his voice firm but filled with anguish. "You're not going to die. I won't let you."

Hunter stood nearby, his brow furrowed with concern, his hand resting on Cade's shoulder in a silent show of support. The dragons moaned sadly, their low, mournful cries echoing through the sanctuary, a chorus of grief that seemed to envelop us all.

As the seconds ticked by, I felt the life ebbing from my body, the pain a constant, pulsing ache that threatened to drag me into the darkness. Cade continued to press the cloth against my wound, his hands trembling with the effort, but I could see the despair in his eyes, the realization that there was nothing he could do to stop the bleeding.

"It's all right, Cade, it's all right, Bella... at least I got the queen. I got her! She can bleed just like the rest of us!" I coughed, and blood spattered down my chin. The pain made my side feel like fire erupted, splintering hot nails into the deep muscle and bone. "You can do the rest without me. But Cade... I'll miss you. I'll miss what we could've had, but I'm grateful for what we did."

"Stop talking like that, Ash." Cade's head finally collapsed into my lap, him heaving with deep sobs. "I can't do this without you. I can't..."

"I wish Rosa was here," Bella muttered, her voice thick with desperation, wiping her own tears onto her sleeve as she crouched beside me, her hand on my thigh. "She'd know what to do..."

Just as she spoke, an eerie wind swept through the sanctuary, a gust from a distant, ethereal place. It carried a chill that seemed to seep into my very bones, making me shiver despite the heat radiating from my wound. The wind carried the scent of ancient forests and forgotten dreams, and it felt like the world itself was whispering secrets.

A figure appeared in the doorway to the throne room, its form draped in ragged clothes. The hood was pulled low over their head, and the cloak they wore was burned at the edges, as if they had walked through the fires of the Infernal Depths themselves. The face beneath the hood was gaunt, the skin etched with more wrinkles than cracks on a mountain. Scraggly gray hairs hung out from under the hood, and a long beard flowed down to their belt, a testament to the countless years they had walked the earth.

Hunter and Cade drew their swords instantly, their eyes narrowing as they prepared to defend us against this new threat. But Cade's expression changed quickly, his sword lowering as realization dawned on his face. "It's him," he whispered, his voice filled with a mix of relief and reverence. "It's Myrathyn."

Bella stood protectively between the mystic and me, her fists balled up, ready to fight if necessary. But Cade placed a gentle hand on her shoulder, urging her to step aside. "Let him approach," he said, his voice steady despite the anxiety that gripped us all.

Myrathyn walked slowly toward me, his steps measured and deliberate. He knelt down beside me, the scent of warm spring sunshine and dew filling the surrounding air. He took my hand in his, his touch gentle but firm, and kissed my fingers. His lips were dry like tree bark and scratched my skin. I opened my eyes to the feeling of bursting light and flower petals inside me, a sensation that was both breathtaking and overwhelming. It was as if the very essence of spring had exploded within me, filling me with a warmth and vitality that seemed to radiate from every pore. The pain in my side vanished, replaced by a tingling sensation that spread throughout my body, healing and rejuvenating me.

I sat up, my heart pounding as I looked around in amazement. The wound on my side was gone, sealed and healed as if it had never been there. I felt a surge of strength and energy, a renewed sense of purpose and determination.

Myrathyn stepped back, his eyes filled with a knowing wisdom that seemed to reach into the depths of my soul. I quickly realized I was sitting on his throne, the vines and thorns intertwined in a pattern that seemed to reflect the very essence of the ancient sanctuary.

I jolted out of the throne, my eyes widening as I took in the sight of the mystic. "You... you saved me! Thank you, thank you!" I stammered, my voice filled with awe and reverence.

I stepped back in awe of the mystic as he groaned, slowly taking his rightful throne. He slumped, seeming as old as time itself. His beard folded onto his legs, and his dim eyes gazed down and to the side. It almost appeared he was going to return to his long slumber. The throne itself was carved from the root system of a long-dead tree, its gnarled wood fused with stone and crystal, pulsing faintly with a green light that throbbed in time with his breath. Vines shimmered with dew despite the absence of rain, and bioluminescent fungi clung to the walls of the sanctuary, casting a soft, ghostly glow. The air hummed with something ancient—older than language, older than fire—a kind of quiet knowing. As he finally lifted his gaze to meet ours, the temperature in the room dropped, and runes hidden in the stone walls flared to life, tracing the edges of the chamber in slow-burning lines of silver. Time seemed to bend inward, folding around this moment.

The others approached the old mystic cautiously. They

muttered that they couldn't let him fall back asleep. They needed to wake him somehow. While they we all three distracted, I felt a familiar, and welcome presence behind me.

Cornelius half-appeared behind me, his voice filled with urgency. "Ash, listen to me. The mystic is a Druidaan. It's a race of men that are gifted with ancient magic. This one is in its final stage of life. Some call them prophets or sages, but they're known for their rarity and their ability to see truth—past or present. You can ask the Druidaan one question, and he will give you the truest answer. Be very specific about the question you ask, and think carefully about what you ask. You must place your hand on his, and he will cover your hand with his other. Then you ask the question in your mind, and he will answer back."

Cornelius disappeared, leaving me with a sense of urgency and importance. I turned to the others, my voice filled with a mix of excitement and trepidation. "He's called a Druidaan. Each of us can ask the mystic one question. He will give you the truest answer. But be careful and specific about what you ask."

The sanctuary fell into a hushed silence as each of us thought deeply about the questions we desired to ask.

Bella was the first to step forward, her glacier-blue eyes filled with a mix of fear and hope. "I think I know mine..."

"Go ahead," I said.

She placed her hand on the mystic's, and he covered it with his other hand, his gaze steady and unyielding. Bella closed her eyes, her lips moving silently as she asked her question. Tears welled in her eyes as she received her answer, a flood of emotions threatening to overwhelm her. She stepped back, her face pale but filled with a newfound determination.

She came beside me, and I put my hand on her back as she sobbed.

"I'm ready," Hunter said, his voice courageous. With a deep breath, he approached the mystic sitting on his old throne overtaken by time.

He went next, his expression stoic and unreadable. He placed his hand on the mystic's, his gaze locked onto the ancient figure before him. After receiving his answer, Hunter's face went white as a ghost, his eyes wide with shock and disbelief. He stepped back, his hand trembling slightly as he tried to process the revelation. He stood at Cade's side, but then dropped to his butt with his legs crossed, still stuck in shock of whatever answer he received.

Cade approached the mystic with a stern and resolute expression, his eyes never leaving the ancient figure. "There's only one question I have and need the answer to. Here it goes..." He placed his hand on the mystic's, his jaw set firmly as he asked his question. After receiving his answer, Cade looked at me with a stern and knowing glance, a nod of understanding passing between us.

The curiosity about what the others asked was brimming inside me like a soapy bubble ready to burst. But there would be time for that later. I took a deep breath, looking beside me to Bella's kind eyes. She wiped her tears away. "Go ahead, Ash."

Finally, it was my turn. I took a deep breath, my heart pounding as I approached the mystic. I placed my hand on his, feeling the warmth of his touch and the ancient power that seemed to radiate from his very being. I closed my eyes, my mind racing as I thought carefully about the question I wanted to ask. There were many answers I yearned for, but I could only pick one. I wanted to know about my parents, but now that I knew my real family name, and was no longer a Mist, I may get answers later. I wanted to know the secret of life, where we came from, and what our purpose was. But... There was only one question that I truly needed an answer to...

"How do I defeat the queen so that no one may ever be born into the life of slavery I was forced into?" I asked in my mind, my voice filled with a mix of hope and desperation.

The mystic's voice echoed through my thoughts, his words filled with a profound wisdom and truth. "You may or may not defeat the queen. That much has many variables I cannot see. But to defeat the queen, you must reach deep into yourself and your ancestry. She is Cinderyn, and you are Aqualorian. Cinderyn has always held the position of top predator in this world, so for you to defeat the queen, you must be prepared to suffer, to get close, and when the time comes, to search your soul for the one strength you have over her. In that moment, I hope you find what you need. But remember, you are far more than a mere slave girl, Ashlyn Moonriver. You are the Gold-Marked. You command the Gilded Radiance, the finest gift of Odiun. You must persevere and find a way. For if you can't defeat the queen, then I fear no one else can. Cade will die, Bella will die, and your dragons will die. Where there is courage, there is hope, and while you cannot change who you are, you can plant a seed there, and from it will grow a tree of mighty roots, roots so deep, legends will be told of it for ages. Farewell. Be true to yourself, and trust in your friends. We will not meet again."

I opened my eyes wide with a newfound energy and a warm smile as I looked at the old man. "Thank you." He nodded back. With a groan, he shifted on his throne and fell into a deep sleep. He looked as if he were a part of his throne.

I stepped back beside the others as his eyes closed as he returned to his never-ending, magic slumber.

Bella put her arms around me, and Cade's burning gaze fixed on me. Hunter stood beside us all, still pale, but looking better.

There was so much to do, so much yet to fight for.

The Stormscales had arrived. We were all determined to take the fight to the Blaze Queen's doorstep. No longer would we passively wait for her to make her next move.

A deep breath settled my heart and mind, and I looked around the room. The friends I'd made along this journey were here, together with me. The sacrifices we'd made had brought us closer than I ever imagined possible. And Cornelius... the old tortoise who had been my guide for almost as long as I could remember. I knew he still had secrets to share, and I hoped that one day, I'd have the time to learn them all.

As we walked out of the sanctuary, I could feel the power within me growing stronger. The magic that had once seemed so foreign and frightening now felt like a part of me. Like an extension of my soul.

Errax was waiting outside, her emerald eyes shimmering in the sunlight. As I approached her, she lowered her head to my hand, allowing me to stroke the scales behind her horns. Her presence was comforting, a reminder of the bond we shared and the battles we'd fought together.

"We did it, girl," I whispered to her, a smile creeping onto my lips. "We fought the Blaze Queen, and we're still alive."

Errax growled in response, her wings rustling in the breeze. She knew the war was far from over, but she also knew that we were ready to face whatever lay ahead.

Cade, Bella, Hunter, and I looked out over the vast forest that stretched out before us. The sun was beginning to set, casting a golden glow over the treetops. The forest was alive with the sounds of nature, the chirping of birds and the rustling of leaves filling the air.

"We'll need to rest before we set out again," Cade said, his voice filled with determination. "But we can't stay in one place for too long. The queen won't give up so easily. She'll be back, and she'll be coming for us with all she has."

"Let's gather the Stormscales that have come to aid us," I added, scanning the horizon. "We're on the same side now, against the queen. The queen is wounded, but she's far from defeated."

Bella nodded, her blue eyes filled with conviction. "We need to find the others who share our cause. The ones who have been hidden and forgotten, the ones who have been waiting for a chance to rise up against the queen. We need to gather our allies and prepare for the final battle."

I turned to face them, my heart filled with a renewed sense of purpose. "We can't give up now. Not when we've come so far. We've fought the queen, we've learned the truth about who we are, and we've found hope in the midst of darkness. We can do this. We can defeat the queen and bring an end to this war."

Cade met my gaze, a smile playing on his lips. "Together, we can. Together, we will."

The future was uncertain; the road ahead was filled with challenges and dangers we had yet to face. But with the help of my friends, the strength of our bond, and the wisdom of the mystic, I knew that we had a chance to change the world. A chance to create a future where love and hope could flourish, where the bonds of slavery could be broken, and where the tyranny of the Blaze Queen could be brought to an end.

"This time though..." the words seethed in anger and determination as they left my lips, "... we take the fight to her."

The End

CONTINUE READING

Emberveil Empire concludes in Book 2
Queen of Chaos and Ruin
Read it Now

AUTHOR'S NOTES

Welcome to the world of Allovan.

This book marks a very special turning point in my writing career. For many years now, I've poured my heart into creating fantastical worlds filled with magic, dragons, swords, and epic battles. I've written many tales of heroes and heroines facing impossible odds, and I've always loved the adventure, the stakes, the danger, and the triumph that come with fantasy fiction. But with this story, I wanted to explore something new. Romance.

I've been a fan of romantacy novels for years now. Yes, you heard that right—romance. And let me tell you, there's something profoundly moving about the dance between two characters who are drawn to each other, who can't quite figure out how to navigate the deep, turbulent waters of love and desire. Even though I'm a guy, I've always believed that love stories—true, complicated, fiery, and at times frustrating—are at the core of what makes us human. And while this may be my first foray into romance, it's something I've long been eager to explore in my own unique way.

With Ash and Cade, I wanted to create a deep, hard connection. Ash, the heroine, is someone I absolutely adore. In many

ways, I'm probably her biggest fan. She's fierce, strong, independent, and adventurous in ways that will keep you on the edge of
your seat, but she's also vulnerable and questioning of her own
worth. She's breathtaking and sexy as hell, but she doesn't believe
me when I tell her that lol. And don't even get me started on
Cade. Brooding, mysterious, and raw in his masculinity, he is the
kind of hero you can't look away from. I love their chemistry. It's
messy, it's complicated, it's passionate.

Writing Prince of Blaze and Embers has been one of the most
enjoyable challenges of my career. Their journey is one of self-
discovery, growth, and learning how to trust not just each other,
but themselves. And with every page, I found myself more and
more invested in their relationship, in their story. It's complex in
all the best ways, pulling you through every emotion imaginable.
There's a rawness to their bond that kept me awake at night,
eager to explore where they would go next. This is not a simple
love story; it's a battle—both internal and external. I can't wait
for you to see what's in store in book 2!

But beyond Ash and Cade, this book is, as all my work is,
about the world. And let me tell you, the world I've created here
is a place I'm thrilled to share with you. Dragons are my thing.
I've always loved them—majestic, terrifying, awe-inspiring—and
Krakos is the culmination of that love. The vision of Krakos in
my mind is something spectacular. I can see it so vividly, from
the ferocity of its flight to the crashing waves beneath it as it
lands, to the sheer power of its scorching fire. Writing those
dragon scenes was such a joy, and I can only hope that I've
managed to capture even a fraction of the awe that I feel when I
think of them.

There's a certain magic to the way this story came together.
While writing, I listened to a lot of soundtrack music—scores
from American Beauty, The Hours, The Shawshank Redemption,
and The Crown—and I can't tell you how deeply they resonated
with the tone I wanted for this book. It's haunting, beautiful, and

full of tension. Each chapter, each turn of the page, is laced with the kind of drama you can't help but get caught up in.

But here's the thing—this is just the beginning. Ash and Cade is the first part of a two-book series, and I can't tell you how excited I am for what's to come. The second book? It's going to be epic. It's going to take everything we've set up and push it to the limit, and I promise you, it will be worth the wait.

So, thank you for joining me on this adventure. Writing this book has been an incredible journey, and I'm beyond excited to share it with you. I hope you find as much joy in these pages as I did in writing them. Here's to love, dragons, magic, and the thrilling, complicated, beautiful ride of life.

Enjoy the journey with me.

With love,

Zander Wolfe

ABOUT THE AUTHOR

Zander Wolfe writes the kind of fantasy he always wanted to read—filled with dangerous magic, forbidden love, and women who refuse to be tamed.

He's a firm believer that the best stories are the ones that make you *feel* something long after the last page.

He's from the Midwest, which means he grew up with a love for bonfires, thunderstorms, and people who wave at each other while driving for no good reason. When he's not writing, he's probably at the gym, hiking some quiet trail, painting late into the night, or getting lost in a romance novel he told himself he bought "for research."

Zander drinks too much coffee, listens to fantasy soundtracks like they're gospel, and has a soft spot for sad movies and complicated characters. He writes because he believes fantasy should be just as raw and emotional as it is epic—and because sometimes, the heroine deserves everything she wants.

SIGN UP AND REVIEW

Sign up here to join the Reader's Group.
www.ZanderWolfe.com

If you enjoyed this book and you want to help me the author out,
please leave a review on Amazon and/or Goodreads. The number
of reviews a book has, has a huge impact on an independent
author's success.

.

www.ingramcontent.com/pod-product-compliance
Lightning Source LLC
Chambersburg PA
CBHW031948130726
47904CB00012B/438